Also by Scott Archer Jones

Jupiter and Gilgamesh, a Novel of Sumeria and Texas

The Big Wheel

a rising tide of people swept away

And Throw Away The Skins

The Moth

Scott Archer Jones

Fomite
Burlington, VT

The Moth is set in Palatino font. First designed by Adolf Zapf in 1949 and popularized by the Stempel Foundary, Palantino is based on Rennaisance calligraphy and named for Giambattista Palantino.

Copyright © 2025 Scott Archer Jones

All rights reserved. No part of this book may be reproduced in any form or by any means without the prior written consent of the publisher, except in the case of brief quotations used in reviews and certain other noncommercial uses permitted by copyright law. This is a work of fiction. Any resemblance between the characters of this novel and real people, living or dead, is merely coincidental.

ISBN-13: 978-1-959984-68-9
Library of Congress Control Number: 2018959645
Fomite
58 Peru Street
Burlington, VT 05401
www.fomitepress.com
01/29/2025

This book is dedicated to all the Noir books and films that have infected the author's imagination.

And as always, to Sandy.

Acknowledgements

As usual with my work, this book has a debt to other stories, including Cervantes' *Don Quixote* and Raymond Chandler's *The Big Sleep*. Most of all, think of this book as a tour of an imaginary East L.A., a tour of a neighborhood too ironic to actually exist.

Chapter One of this book has appeared in *Literary Orphans*.

There is a wilderness we walk alone /
However well-companioned"
—Stephen Vincent Benét, *Western Star*

"Sometimes we want what we want even
if we know it's going to kill us."
—Donna Tartt, *The Goldfinch*

Contents

2010 — The Moth's Sorrow	1
1995 — Liar	10
1964 — House of Venial Sin	14
1967 — The Sainted Aunt	17
1969 — Lust	27
1969 — Up and Out	31
1972 — Decency	38
1974 — Ripping off Ralphs	41
1978 — Molly Legs	58
1978 — Hustling The Finance Company	67
1979 — Molly Redux	71
1980 — You Bet	76
1981 — Mortgage on the Bungalow	84
1981 — Molly Comes To Stay	89
1983 — Bong, Bong	101
1983 — The Church Deals a Hand	106
1983 — The Hammering	112
1984 — Apprenticeship	122
1985 — Sweet But Empty	125
1992 — Famine Beats The Moth	128
1997 — Detective Chelsea with the Squeeze	139
1999 — Lock Up Your Daughters	147
2002 — The Ax	157
2010 — Mickey Barat's Price	171
2012 — Starting with Reckless Tommy at the Taco Stand	178
2013 — Mickey Barat Orders Up A Death	195
2014 — The Prostitute's Babysitter	204
2015 — Binary Stars	215
2015 — Best Laid Plans	228

2010 — The Moth's Sorrow

Thick glasses glazed over the Moth's large eyes. His goatee, mustache, sideburns, and receding hairline conspired to fuzz out around his head in a halo of fine hair. The Moth's color code ran to gray: gray skin, gray hair, gray teeth. He did indeed resemble a pine moth — adorned in a brown unraveling sweater and a ragged tweed sports coat, purchased in a flea market in 2000 and now ten years ruined. The Moth was 48 years ruined.

The appearance of his L.A. pawnshop mattered more than his own — immaculate, clean to obsession. The plate glass in front had been shined to transparency, the steel bars painted a tasteful brass. The place reeked of Febreze. He had laid new unstained carpet only last month, and full-spectrum fluorescents above rained down a warm light that rendered skin beautiful. Not his skin, of course.

On Monday, the sleigh bells on the pawnshop door rang as if someone had hocked Christmas. The Moth glanced up to catch the Widow Lenora as she slipped her head around the door edge. He had a thing for the Widow. His deep and abiding thirst had become this year's central torment. When she swayed into his shop, past the jangling bell, he stared at her with such lingering hunger, he felt sick. She visited the pawnshop at the end of the month, because by then her money had dried up. He lived for this moment.

She glided to the counter, and he held his breath. She tipped her oval face, framed in black hair with a jarring streak of white. Her woeful eyes, large and rimmed in pink, blinked at him, shining like jewels. She opened her purse and rested a tissue on the counter, unfolded it, and revealed a silver bracelet with some semiprecious stones.

He stared at her bracelet and drank in her cheap perfume. *Why me, of all the pawns?*

The Moth didn't own one of those glittering pawn shops that resemble big box stores and cluster on four-lane streets near super liquor stores and hospitals. *Those* pawns had sprung up during the recession of 2001 and the global financial collapse of 2008, with a business model based on the harvest of body parts from the newly poor.

He'd based his pawnshop on hundreds of years of tradition, the unfailingly poor. From St. Petersburg to Constantinople to London to Tijuana, for centuries, the always-poor had pawned the same items many times each year and redeemed them when a bit of money trickled in. Here in East L.A., the women, most of them sad and exhausted by childbirth or husband, dragged in small cherished possessions and let him store them for a month or two, for a margin that ranged from thirty to eighty percent. He also wrote pawn on flat screen TVs, guns, aluminum wheels, and tools. Gold chains, watches. The men should likewise have to bleed.

Of course, to own a shop stuck up a nothing-street in a nothing lineup of businesses wasn't owning a money machine. It didn't even cover the mortgage. Pawn slid to second place, only a sideline.

He considered himself a purveyor of criminal implements, information, and arcane paraphernalia. The shop acted as his crime-tool outlet. He sold slim-jims, lock picks, bump keys, alarm bypasses, license plates, various forms of bugs, autonomous surveillance cameras, and firearms without serial numbers. He sold social security numbers, drivers licenses, and even voter registrations. He could supply uniforms from security companies and factory manuals for safes. But he never fenced. He had learned that to procure and sell stolen property held a lot more risk than selling I.D's.

And he had his personal code. No drugs. No guns or knives to minors. No home invasions.

He called his shop Pachuco's, because he was crafty, stealthy. Because he didn't want people to realize an Irish-Lithuanian ran their pawnshop. Which they all did. The 'hood thought it comic he tried to pass as Mexican.

When he gazed back, the first week of August didn't turn out so splendidly, starting with the Widow.

The Moth blinked at Lenora. He could sense his eyebrows brush the top frame of his glasses. She'd never redeem the bracelet and it'd only bring him fifty bucks. "Two hundred," he said. Even to him, his voice sounded out as a raspy croak.

"Thank you. Thank you!" Only she said it in her native language. A melody of liquid Spanish. She batted her eyes and peeked up at him sideways through those long black lashes.

He knew how she manipulated him. His heart fell to pieces anyway. He loved her plump body, her sleek, stockinged legs, the red high heels. So much like the legs from his first crush.

She reached forward and touched his hand. "Could I trade you the money for that gun over there?" She pointed into the glass case, where a snub-nosed .32 nestled on a washcloth, priced at two-fifty. "I need it for Alan. He's released next Wednesday and he comes back to us, to me and the children. He has many friends. But some enemies too."

"And Alan is?"

"Mi esposo."

She transfigured from a widow into a wife. His chest caved in from the pain in its core, his shoulders hunched over. His breath wheezed out. "You're married?"

"O, sí."

"Why are you called the Widow Lenora?"

"Because Alan, he's away so much in la pinta. The jail."

She had married a con. And she had milked the Moth for months. Unbearable. But he said, "Can you fill out the paperwork? For the Feds' background check?"

"Oh no no!"

He opened the case and fumbled out the revolver, wrapped it in a paper towel and handed the bundle to her. She plunged it deep within her capacious bag, and on leaving, clanged the door shut on his sorrow.

East L.A. had always been a tough, chewy steak of a neighborhood. Dating back to World War II, Latino gangs had shoved territorial boundaries back and forth, fought for precious little with precious blood. Now in 2010, the unincorporated community narrowly held on to control, scarcely protected the dense-lined blocks of casitas filled with padres and madres. Still running the old trades of illegal liquor, protection, and prostitution, the gangs now worked guns and drugs, political favors, illegals smuggling, and child trafficking. The County Sheriff's Department could barely mop up the drive-bys, much less

2010 – The Moth's Sorrow

prevent them. Four brown gangs shook the 'hood, and the new kids on the block, Mara Salvatrucha, were determined to chase those four back into the dark. Overprinted on this was the Russian Mafia settling in from the north, and guest appearances of the Bloods and the Crips out of South L.A. A young, merciless man could take a bite out of this neighborhood, but he was liable to choke on it. A middle-aged shopkeeper had to gnaw away at it.

On Tuesday, Mickey Barat's twenty-something son crossed the pawnshop threshold, and not to hock a guitar for weed money either. Mikhael Barat, with backing from the Brighton Beach Russians, owned enough of the neighborhood, both legally and feloniously, to be the de facto mayor. His kid Alexander, known as Butch, opened the door enough to materialize through the crack and sidled in. He edged around the shop, fingered the pawn and stared at the price tags the Moth had strung on each piece. Stalling. He worked around to the cash register where he mumbled something to the Moth.

The Moth surveyed the whey face with its sprinkling of acne, sought out a clue. "What?"

"I was wondering, maybe you got some guns for sale."

Butch's age slid over the Moth's line; he wasn't a minor. But word percolated around that Butch didn't connect the dots. "You walked right by the case. Three revolvers, a deer rifle, and a crossbow. That's all I have."

"I meant... special guns. Semi-autos for instance."

"Aren't you Mickey Barat's son?"

"So what?"

"Does your dad know you're in here?"

Butch's face screwed up in a scowl. "Sure. He sent me."

The Moth locked his eyes on Butch, bored into him. "You wouldn't mind if I called him?"

The kid gave him the most steely-eyed glare he could. "Sure, go ahead. I hope you piss him off." He ruined the effect when his voice cracked into a soprano on the last word.

"Look, Mr. Barat. What's this all about?"

"Some guys, see...."

The Moth waited.

"These guys over on Escuela cheated me out of my pink slip in a card game, took my ride. I got to get it back. I can't let something like that happen, not close to my own neighborhood. And I can't ask my Dad. So I need a gun that will scare the crap out of them."

"What did you have in mind?"

"A 9 mil. Big and shiny. Lots of rounds."

The Moth knew patience. He knew how to linger, hold back for the revelation.

"Come on, man. Just this once. I'll owe you. The Barats always pay back favors."

The Moth knew a lie when he heard it, but he didn't mind. All part of business. "I'll rent you a gun, one that can be used for intimidation. Step back to the door. Check out the street." *Make the money now, feel bad later.*

"Why? You think someone would tail me here?"

"Do what I ask."

Slope-shouldered Butch stumped over to the door. "Ain't nothing out there."

"Lock the door and keep your back to me." The Moth dropped to his knees onto his rubber mat, twitched back one of the mat's black rectangles and jerked open a hatch. With his other hand, he grabbed a long object wrapped in cloth. The Moth rose like the ceiling jerked him up and glided it onto the counter. "Okay, you can come back."

With a face full of doubt, Butch shuffled back to the counter. The

Moth unwrapped his treasure and exposed a shotgun with a folding stock and ten-inch barrel. He clunked a half-box of shells beside the gun. "Here's my suggestion. The shotgun priced out as a thousand even before modification. I rent it to you for four hundred. You go talk with your associates and collect your car and title, then return the shotgun. I suggest you obtain an additional four hundred from them for your own trouble. If something goes wrong, just squeeze and pump. You don't have to be any good with this weapon — and you leave minimum forensic evidence."

Butch's eyes glowed like saucers under the fluorescents. His hand reached up, stroked the plastic stock. "Deal." He dug into his pockets and paid with a mixed collection of hundreds, twenties, and fives — greasy, wadded-up bills.

The Moth stuffed the money in a bank bag, watched Butch slink out, and spurted a glob of hand disinfectant onto his fingers.

The next night, as he hunkered down in the apartment back of the pawnshop, the Moth listened to a police scanner and heard the call. A homicide and a fire — shots at a house on Escuela. The caller indicated a loud booming and several small pops. And someone torched the place. Couldn't be sure, but he didn't think he'd ever get a glimpse of his shotgun again. *I should have asked for a deposit.*

Bright and early the next day, he called a contact who worked in the County Morgue. Alexander Barat was on the cold slab. Butch hadn't known one end of the gun from the other. Pity. But it didn't hurt the Moth's feelings the Barats picked up some serious trouble.

Thursday, and the door banged full back. An angry black man pounded his way to the counter. Reaching across, he seized the Moth by the lapels and dragged him forward over the glass. Spraying spittle, he barked into the Moth's face. At this range, the Moth cataloged a cratered face, a scar that ran out of one eye, cream-colored teeth like an old piano keyboard. The face, too close and personal, belonged to Eloy-the-Rent Poulter.

"Goddamn you, you gray pocket shit. Where's my money?"

The Moth's luck — under the thumb of one of the few black men in a Mexican town. He dropped his jaw as far as it could hang, opened his eyes to their limits; he knew the reaction Eloy wanted. "Here! Got it here!" He fumbled in his pants pocket, handed over four hundred. The same four hundred he had charged Butch, held ready for Eloy-the-Rent's visit.

Eloy threw him back behind the counter. The Moth sprawled against the cabinets, recovered his balance.

Eloy leaned across the glass. "You puking mini-turd. That's this week's insurance. You don't want your shithole shop burned down, you cough up next week's too. I got immediate expenses."

"Okay, I understand your problem," said the Moth. "Can I swap you something in trade? How about a stereo? A TV? Maybe a gun?"

Eloy grinned into his face, a glob of manic saliva gathered in the corner of his mouth. "You gotta Smith and Wesson? Maybe a clean new Beretta?"

The Moth swallowed hard. "How about a barely used Ruger .45. In great shape. Stainless." The Moth brought it out from a drawer in the cabinet, slid it across the glass to Eloy. "Retails for six hundred. Clip's full."

Cracking open his mouth and showing his teeth like gravestone slabs, Eloy grinned. Eloy grabbed the .45, worked the action to slot a bullet up the spout, flipped the safety on and off. He cradled the gun in his hands. The gun swung up, eased its cold muzzle onto the Moth's forehead. "Deal."

I hate the word "deal." The whole neighborhood used it and it didn't mean a thing.

Eloy shoved the gun into his waistband at the small of his back. "I'll see you in two weeks, midget man." He punched the Moth in the shoulder, hard, and stomped out whistling.

The Moth leaned on the counter, both hands on the glass. A tremor ran through his entire frame. He shrugged his coat back into place, smoothed Eloy's crumples out of the lapels. He sucked in a deep breath. He sprayed his hands and his counter with an ammonia cleaner. That helped, some. The sun crept down the aisle towards him.

He rooted a cheap mobile out of his sports coat pocket and pressed the buttons. "Hey, Detective Chelsea.... Yeah, it's me. I have a tip for you. Eloy Poulter is walking around with a handgun used in the Walgreens pharmacy job last month.... Of *course* I mean Eloy-the-Rent.... Sure I know the clerk died. So you'll have your guys pick him up? Soon?"

On Friday, Detective Chelsea Granovich called to say they hadn't made charges stick on Eloy-the-Rent Poulter. His mother and sister vouched for his alibi, *and* Eloy fingered a sick, half-dead tweaker for the gun. On Saturday, Mickey Barat called. His voice pitched down into baritone range, well-modulated, quiet. He said, "I understand you gave my son Alexander a shotgun. I think we need to talk."

1955 — Liar

The Moth was born as Frank. His name would change several times during his life, but he stayed the same and he knew it. Frank knew who he was from the start, from the womb.

Frankie remembered the rug. He piled blocks between his legs, where he could keep an eye on them. His bare knees stuck up and his shins ran down to finish in huge shoes, his favorite and only sneakers. He hated the blocks, scattered, without shape or meaning. Blocks hid his image of the rug, braided and circling round from the center out to the room edge. The rug lay out as perfect in its shape and sweep. One block carried a sharp edge that gouged his hand — the rug would never do that.

Light changed, shadow fell across him. That meant She had slipped into the room, and she stood on the perfect rug. Her voice, far away, said, "You're playing with blocks. Such pretty toys. She dropped to her knees, reached out for a block. "Would you like to build a castle, little man? Shall Mommy show you how to stack up castle walls, a tower, a gate?"

The giant stumped across the room, from the hall to the front door. His head bumped the ceiling. Da. He stared down at Frankie as he passed, touched the mommy on her shoulder. "Going out. Back by dinner." Da slammed the door. Frankie shuddered.

She knelt so close, right in front of Frankie, where he could touch her hand. Her face lit up, ready to be happy with him. He beamed, pumped his head up and down. A yes meant she'd stay, for awhile. Yes meant Mommy, as she worked the blocks.

Frank remembered school, and how its drone turned him into a self-taught thinker. And less bruised.

In the fourth grade, school was a war zone. The playground sprawled over a half acre of scrubby grass and the teachers all slouched around the door. Frank wandered along the fence that shielded the school from outside. And locked them in. He kicked a rock along, and it bounced for its own reasons behind the incinerator. He didn't like that block of cement and the boys who hid behind it. They sneaked around and behaved however they wanted. Mostly they wanted to hurt small kids.

The big one, Brad, shouted at him, "Hey, don't chunk no rock at us!" He bounded out and seized Frank by the shirt collar. He dragged Frank behind the incinerator.

Four of them pinned Frank in. He stared up into their faces, searched for some kindness, some way out from behind that pile of masonry. No smiles.

They jostled him. He bounced around between them. Shove. Poke. A fist. "Throw a rock at us, huh. Are you crazy, or do you just want to be dead?"

"It wasn't me, it wasn't me!"

Someone hit his nose hard, stinging. "You're dead, Frank."

"No no, it was Paul. Paul threw the rock. At me. He threw it and missed."

Brad stuck his face into Frank's. His incisors showed. *He enjoys it. He won't quit.*

A shoe crashed into Frank's crotch. Even though he still waited on his testicles, Frank flashed through a display of lightning behind his clenched eyelids.

They struck him in the temple, square in the mouth, in the throat. Shoved hard, he rebounded off the cinderblocks.

Frank's eyes flew open; Brad's face hung there. Between clenched teeth Brad said, "You threw that rock at us." Brad's eyes flittered.

Insane? The blood crept down his lip, dripped off his chin."No, it was Paul."

"Are you sure?"

"Yes." Paul *had* thrown a rock at him. Last year.

Frank remembered the Church. Large vistas of boredom, sometimes spiked with terror and guilt.

Frank slouched in the chair while the round bones of his spine kneaded the metal back. He read it as a sign from God. God didn't want him here; God compelled his back to hurt. If Frank lurched in the seat a bit, each knob tolled on the chair like he counted a rosary.

There were two priests, one a dreamer and one a beast. The beast Father intoned. Frank had learned that word recently. It meant to moan in a musical way. He said, "What are the four pillars of the Church and Faith?"

Frank and the rest of the fifth graders said, "The profession of faith, the celebration of the Mystery, the life in Christ, and Christian prayer." Their answers formed a wave of chants, smoothed into an overlapping murmur by their lack of rhythm.

Frank could smell stale flowers, scent carried down into the basement from the altar. And sweat, the sweat of his fellow prisoners.

The priest asked, "What else do we believe?"

"I believe in Jesus Christ His Son our only Lord... " The temperature in the room climbed, the air hung dead. Frank could sense a frayed blur close in, all around him. On the table in front of him, the words in the book bled into black smears on white.

"How was Christ begat?"

"He was conceived by the power of the-Holy-Spirit-and-born-of-the-Virgin-Mary... "

"How-did-he-die... "

The priest's hand seized Frank from sleep and hurled him back into his chair. The Father grasped his shoulder in a clerical fist, shook him like a rag. "Boy. Boy. How dare you sleep in catechism class! Do you want to suffer Hell itself?"

Calamity Class "Not hell!"

"I'll teach you to sleep!" Father's face, pockmarked, a forehead two inches high. His hand swung back, sang down.

Frank's ear burned like lightning had crashed into his head. From that ear he could catch only a dull roar.

The Father loomed above him, a tower of black. "Do you believe in Jesus Christ Your Savior?"

No, he didn't. All stories, stories from long ago. *They read all this crap out and beat you into saying you believed.*

"Do you believe?"

Frank could smell the corned beef on the priest's breath. He spotted a clot of bread stuck between canine and gum. "Yes, I believe in God who gave his only begotten Son. Forgive me, Father."

Am I such a worm?

1964 — House of Venial Sin

That year ran Frank into the meat grinder of his peers and clarified how he measured the world's right and wrong. The year lapped up at the Church steps as starters, of course. He attended all the time. His mother — beloved but a little less beloved each week — bullied, harassed, and hauled him to Mass. She revived herself at Mass. She rubbed it over her like salve. She bathed in the Mass. Frank blamed Mass on the eruption of his new zits. As bad as being seen with his mom, even though he was in the sixth grade.

He discovered the good thing about Church five times a week — the vista of young girls, arrayed in pretty dresses. They peeked out from scarves they circled over their heads and around their throats. But that couldn't go anywhere, could it? The hideous thing about Catholicism turned out to be the bow tie. Mother loved the white short-sleeved shirt and the clip-on. Frank's schoolmates rated the tie the pinnacle of comic offense, and the reason to shove him, pummel his bicep, shout at him down the street. "Sissy. Sissy. Sissy." He preferred death.

Mother explained that children, boy-children, needed to work out their feelings, find out what type of men they would be. "They will grow out of their cruelty, you will see. Turn the cheek, little man. Jesus will reward you."

His cheek had already been scraped against the Church bricks by his peers. "Can't I just stay home? Or not wear the tie?"

"Tavo siela, a soul — your soul — is at risk. Young men; you know what the priest said."

Always with the Lithuanian gibberish.

In Frank's house, the kitchen stood in for warmth and generosity. The kitchen contained four doorways that led to the back, the hall, the living room, and the dining room, four valves of a single heart. It was in this nexus that he caught up with his father eating pigs feet out of a glass jar.

He asked his Da. "Do I have to go to Mass?"

His Da, Irish himself, made it clear. "Look, you love your ma, don't you?"

Frank scuffed his toe on the kitchen linoleum. "Uh-huh." Much more than his Da.

"If you go, I don't have to. I'm bigger than you and so it's your turn to kiss the rosy ring. Enjoy yourself, and don't let her catch you in a sin."

"What is a sin anyway? The rules seem to change so no matter what I do, it's a sin."

His Da glanced over at him, threw his big paw on his shoulder. "Tell you what, I can show you what a sin is, and what isn't." He leaned over Frank, in tight. His breath smelled like beer. "You run to the corner shop, pick me up a pack of Camels."

"Okay, sure." Frank knew that shop inside out. The change left from the cigarettes went to candy. Mounds Bars. "Gimme the money."

"No." His father winked, one awful eye closing as he stuck his finger into Frank's collarbone. "This time you filch the wee pack for me, slip it down your cranny."

Frank bungled it. When his father reached the store, the shopkeeper still had his claw curled in Frank's collar, seized him tight as

Frank kept twisting and scrambling. Da jerked him from behind the counter into the aisle, unbuckled his belt, and wailed away at Frank's paltry buttocks.

He ripped out sob after sob.

Da leaned down to his ear. "Hush your mewling. Now you know. The sin isn't in the doing. It's in the getting caught."

1967 — The Sainted Aunt

The year 1967 launched Frank's nocturnal emissions and by Thanksgiving, they plagued him most every night. Aunt Audrey must have influenced some of that, especially as her visit grew near. He'd waited out on the windswept porch for a half hour to be the first to greet her, the first to spot the scintillation-red car. When he sprang to his feet, his erection bent him forward by a good fifteen degrees.

Aunt Audrey's perfume smelled floral and sweet — his head swam from the fumes. When he hugged her the vaporous cloud prompted a messy sneeze. Her voice crooned out Southern, all honey and swamp, as she dabbed at his face with a scented handkerchief. "Frankie, you'll catch your death out here." She scrubbed his noggin like she'd fondle a puppy, swept past, and left him in the cold. He ducked his head, shook it to sort his thin brown-curled frizzle back in shape. He retrieved her suitcase.

Aunt Audrey occupied a place in the universe that ranged as far from Frank's mother as the laws of gravity could allow. His mom, a Lithuanian under the thumb of a Chicago Irishman, lived in the confines of tradition and the Catholic Rule. She drew her boundaries not much further than the family, just far enough to include a few comfortable women. Women who hadn't changed since they'd clumped down the boat ramp. She had a single neighborhood. A Lithuanian church and a cat that loved only her.

Aunt Audrey, on the other hand, lived out of a suitcase and on an edge that frightened the family — she migrated with wild shifts across the country and mailed photos of nightclubs and parties. When she visited, her car parked in the garage and she appropriated Frank's room, downgrading him to the sofa.

He perched on the pillow at the headboard in what had been his bedroom and watched her unpack, his head resting against the rose-strewn wallpaper.

"I can't believe how big you've grown! Why, you're big enough to be Aunt Audrey's special boy." She planted a kiss on his forehead. Audrey's real name, her Lithuanian name, was Audra. It meant "Storm," his Ma said.

Her lips, red, waxy. She drew small lipstick points on her upper lip. Her mouth gave the impression of a pout all the time, with a painted-on kiss. Her eyes — huge, lustrously dark, and drowned in dark eyeshadow. "You're what? Fourteen? Fifteen?"

"Nearly fifteen."

"That's a special time. I remember that year — that's when my breasts blossomed and my legs stretched out. They're still quite nice legs, aren't they?"

She twirled and the hem of her dress flared out. Her tapered ankles and calves above the red heels, elegant V's. Frank stared. *Yes, nice legs*.

"Of course, I had spots for a year or two. You don't have that problem. Such beautiful skin you have, Frank." Her jumbo breasts, soft as clouds, swayed underneath her V-collared blouse. She stroked his shoulder and turned back to the suitcase.

1967 – The Sainted Aunt

She fished out a slip, ivory with lace at the bottom, and held it across her waist. It sheltered her ample hips, transformed her into a Hollywood dream. "I seldom have a man in my room, you know. It makes your Aunt Audrey all giddy."

Frank was conscious of his own swimming head as she unpacked large silken panties and flashed them at him before she settled each pair into the dresser drawer.

She slid out a Pall Mall and lit it with a delicate silver lighter. "Frank, honey, could you bring your aunt a cup of tea? Please?"

He leapt off the bed, glad to serve, if reluctant to leave. In the kitchen, his ma leaned over the table. She peeled potatoes as she watched him pop the kettle on and root a Lipton teabag out of the tin box. Her Lithuanian accent, never abandoned like her sister's, reached across to him. "Ah, she has you fetching for her, so? I am sure she flirts with you. My sister the big flirt." Ma shook her head; Frank didn't know if Ma admired or disapproved.

As he waited for the water to boil, he sneaked glances at his ma. She had tucked her iron gray hair back into a severe bun. Long pale hairs lay coarse upon her arms. The first trenches of old age marked her upper lip. Frank wondered how many years separated Ma and Aunt Audrey: maybe ten? "She's okay. Talks a lot, but I don't mind."

"So long she talks on, and all about herself. Wait until your father comes home. She will be hanging on him, kaboti, you know? He loves it."

Frank wondered if his ma resented the hanging-on.

Da thumped his way in the back door about the time the potato dumplings appeared off the stove, and the bread out of the oven. His face showed brutal marks of the working Irish and the happy grin of a man who had stopped off at the tavern. He wrapped the kitchen around his big frame, diminished the place with his clumping boots and his virility. Ma, ladle in hand, bobbed her head to him and turned back to the pot.

Aunt Audrey crashed into him like a wave hurls itself on the shore. "Michael Ignatius Mahoney! Look at you!" She stared at him, flickered her eyes in admiration, and threw herself around his neck again.

Frank watched his father's hand, a beefy brown paw, pinch Aunt Audrey's silk-clad behind. She squealed and swished her backside so the dress flipped. Frank's breath caught. She said, "Frankie, one day you'll be a giant like your daddy, a mountain. I'll have two Mahoneys to swoon over."

After dinner, Da took himself off to the living room, the newspaper tucked under his arm. In a moment, the three in the kitchen flinched as the television blared — Da had cranked up the volume. Tuesday wrestling.

The two women and Frank. Their shadows fell on the same rose wallpaper as in his bedroom. Aunt Audrey carried the plates to the trash, scraped, and rattled them into the sink. She sailed back to the table, plumped herself into the chair. Across from her, Ma spooned minute pieces of coconut pie into her mouth, tiny because they drew dessert out and caused only a little sin.

"Sister, you could eat anything and never gain an ounce. I can't do like you, eating pie every day. I might as well scrub it on my butt, because that's where it'll end up."

"Audra, don't be crude with the boy here."

Aunt Audrey drew out a smoke. "He's practically a grown man."

Ma said, "You don't believe that."

1967 – The Sainted Aunt

Aunt Audrey played with her lighter, spun it around on the plastic tablecloth. "You know, now I'm back in Chicago, I might run down and visit my old friend Beth in St. Louis."

Didn't she just drive through there?

Ma smiled, but Frank recognized those thin lips, the emptiness. "You two were steady partners or *mėgėjai* in the past?" Ma threw out Lithuanian phrases all the time — he didn't understand any of it.

"Roommates for a couple of years, but you know, she turned real clingy, so I relocated to New Orleans for a change. We started close, but grew apart."

"Yes, that's what I thought."

Frank knew something had happened in the room, but he hadn't caught it. Nonchalant, he glided the pie plate towards him.

"Hmm," droned Aunt Audrey. Her eyebrows welded themselves together, a flag of irritation.

Frank glanced at his ma. She gnawed on a secret amusement.

Aunt Audrey picked back up. "So a day or two in St. Louis and back over to spend Thanksgiving with you and your wonderful husband."

He'd shift from the couch back to his bed. It would smell like Aunt Audrey, the perfume and the cigarettes, as he nested back into his own space. That gave him a shiver.

Ma said, "This visit is your vacation, Audra, so you should choose."

"You make me sound like the selfish one every time."

"Tcha." Ma fluttered her hand, a bird warning off her sister. "I'll miss you, and so will Frank's father. Maybe him more than me, though he has no chance with you."

"Why, it sounds like you're glad to get shut of me! Sweet little ol' me."

"Nonsense, Audra. And stop with that ridiculous accent."

"Um, I thought I might take Frank with me. You know, a road trip and all. He's such fun, and I'm sure Beth would like him."

The Moth

He perked up, all attention.

Ma raised her eyebrows. "I think he would be in the way."

"I don't intend anything out of the ordinary, sister. As a matter of fact, the boy would be kind of a buffer, if you see what I mean. Beth and I — it could be an itsy-bitsy awkward."

"I understand." Ma turned to Frank. "It is up to you. You have the small holiday now, before you are back with the nuns."

He shrugged, cool as ice. "Sure. Sounds okay." But the blush swept up his neck into his scalp, hot and tingling.

Aunt Audrey spanked the table, her face glowing and open. "Good. All settled. I'll call Beth in the morning."

Aunt Audrey owned a red 1967 Mercury Cougar, with a chrome front end like a vertically barred gate. He had never beheld such a dashboard, a swash of padded red vinyl. And the wheel, a wood and chrome rim in her hand.

She rattled on. For miles. "Of course I love the theatre. In New Orleans, I belong to a supper-house theatre, one that stages a comedy or a romance and people watch after they eat. All very white-table-cloth, you see." She barreled down Route 66. The mile-long red hood pointed the way, the plump white hand on the wheel whizzed them around trucks and past the farms and light industry of rural Illinois. "I married a man named Jeffrey — lasted a couple of years. My leading man in two productions. My, he was good-looking. Wavy blond hair, thin and as supple as a reed." The bucket seats, slabs of red vinyl, clung to their backs. "Of course, I can't make a living as an actress in poky old New Orleans. I really ought to relocate to New York. What would you think of that?"

The finest thing in the world, an aunt in New York City. *I could take the train.*

1967 – The Sainted Aunt

"You're awfully quiet. Cat got your tongue?"

He couldn't take his eyes off her.

Aunt Audrey drove with her legs far apart, her knees up and one foot back. Her soft flowing dress draped into her lap and hung in an arc between her cocked legs. Frank, his back to the door and his face to his beloved aunt, couldn't help but glance at those gentle folds.

Aunt Audrey and her friend Beth embraced at the top of the stairs on the landing, a hug shrill with singing voices and giggles, the sound piercing. He hung back two steps, struggled to win his breath back from the flight up with two suitcases. His Aunt Audrey's beautiful calves posed before him, propped up her bounteous behind. He peered around her to make out this Beth.

Beth appeared to be a medium-size office building, rooted on the landing. Short, stout. She wore a sweeping skirt that brushed the floor and a white blouse all frills and puffy sleeves. Her round eyes glimmered at him. "Who's this?"

Aunt Audrey swept her hand towards him. "My nephew Frank. He's protecting me on the road."

Glancing full in Aunt Audrey's dark eyes, Beth said, "What a nice surprise. You've brought us a part of your happy family." Her voice measured out smooth, toneless.

"I'm sure you'll like him."

Beth circled around Aunt Audrey and touched his shoulder. "Come in, come in. Frank, is it? We're a little cramped here for space, so we'll have to see what we can do." She swept the two into her apartment, shooing them down a narrow hallway like geese.

The Moth

A small apartment indeed, with a fold-out love seat in the living room and a single bedroom. Dark green walls. Wide pine flooring. Beth said, "I live here quite alone. I decided that was best for me. It's a small place, I know."

Aunt Audrey said, "It suits you, Beth. You know your own mind."

Frank wondered if he'd sleep on a pallet that night, like a little kid. Beth said, "Drop those suitcases anywhere. It's nearly six — who's for dinner? There's a café close by — they know how to feed a growing boy like Frank."

After meatloaf with thin gravy and freezer-burned rolls, Frank followed the women home, clandestinely releasing a percolating flatulence. Now he perched on Beth's vinyl-covered kitchen chair, tried not to shift his weight and generate plastic squeaks. The two women had stuffed themselves into the love seat together. They relived their history. On the coffee table in front of them — a basket of limes, a paring knife, seltzer, a bowl of ice and three glasses. A quart bottle of Gilbey's Gin lorded it over all.

Beth said, "I thought gin rickeys, for old times sake." She squeezed half a lime into a glass, hit it with the gin, added ice and carbonated water. "Do you remember the cast party after *Lady Windermere's Fan*? We consumed more than enough of these things that time. Maude fell from grace that night, didn't she?"

Aunt Audrey's fluid laugh pealed out. "Only if your clue was her dancing around in bra and panties. I was shocked. Most of you giggled yourselves sick."

Frank tried to picture Maude in undies. Was she shaped like Aunt Audrey or like Beth? He did what he always did — he waited. Something would happen.

1967 – The Sainted Aunt

Beth stirred up another gin rickey and, arching an eyebrow, leaned into her friend while she watched him. "How about one for Frank? We can mix it virgin, or we can add a teensy taste to it."

Aunt Audrey flapped her hand. "Frank is getting so grown-up. I think he'd like one with a hint of gin in it."

I certainly would. His head pumped up and down.

Two more gins, and the women were rolling in laughter, hooting on the couch. Beth angled the eyebrow up and asked Aunt Audrey, "Does Frank know about me?"

Aunt Audrey leaned her head into Beth, planting them brow to brow. "Oh, I'm sure he does. Frankie is fifteen now. He knows all things."

"And does he know about you?"

Audrey reached across the table and clasped Frank's knee. "Of course he knows. Otherwise I would never tease him. Right, Frank?"

Frank didn't. *I really don't know anything. Except my willie is awake.*

The light from Beth's two sofa lamps blazed out bright. A buzz in his ears, under the women's voices. Across the coffee table, their heads leaned together.

Beth said, "Bedtime, don't you think, dear? Shall we snuggle into my single in the bedroom? A cosy fit for us."

"Oh no, you sweet darlin'. We're so much larger than we used to be. I hardly think we could wedge both of us on that narrow thing."

Beth's eyebrows arched. "Hmm. If you sleep on the fold-out love seat, that leaves the boy to me. He's a small package.

"Beth, you bad girl! We'll plunk him on the floor with a blanket and a pillow."

"No, no. I'm serious. We don't have to make him uncomfortable, do we, Frank?" Her hand swam towards him out-of-focus, a huge

The Moth

pale fish. As the hand caressed his knee, he quivered. Maybe Beth wasn't so bad.

"Why you, Beth? He's my nephew."

"Exactly, Audrey. It wouldn't be proper. Besides, you actually got married once and I never did." She patted Frank's knee again, glanced at Audrey. "You know you can trust me, dear. You know my history so thoroughly, don't you?"

He was about to sleep in the same bed as Beth. A single bed. His blood pounded around his skull.

Frank struggled into his pajamas in the bathroom. He leaned against the sink and wiggled his second leg into the pants. Glided sideways to smack into the dark oak wainscoting, recovered his balance. Gazing down, he spotted the embarrassing wigwam tented out in front, so he fumbled his willie up and double checked the string tie to keep it pointed skyward.

He pried the warped door open — Beth hovered waiting. A blockhouse dressed all in white cotton, a set of knobby buttons from chin to waist. She held out her hand. "Come dear. You take the side against the wall, so I don't have to crawl over you when I get up in the night." Her hand warm, tugging.

He wormed into bed against the cream-colored wall and she heaved herself in after him. A tight fit, but it worked if they both lay on their sides. He wondered if he could sleep. She snapped off the light, turned, and breathed on the top of his head. "There, dear. Isn't that all comfy?

Yes it is.

1967 – The Sainted Aunt

Close to dawn, he snapped awake. Beth had rolled half over onto him. Her thigh pinned his hips and legs. A sticky mess in his crotch. It must have soaked through to her nightgown. No way to hide it.

Her bosoms buried his face. Heat poured off her, as hot as a basement furnace. She softly snored. He slipped his hand between her breasts, to free his mouth from the smothering nightgown. Trying not to brush her. He gasped for air. She smelled of violets and Noxema.

1969 — Lust

More than anything in the world, Frank lusted after a car. Any car, anything with wheels. Something his new friends, whomever they were, would fill; something the girls would admire as it rolled past, sleek, real. He needed that car like a dog needs love. Frank lusted after a car even though he had watched the Driver's Ed film, *Bloody Streets, Bloody Teens* — through half-closed, wincing eyes. If he had to die in a tragic accident, so be it.

But at age sixteen nearly seventeen, he lived under Illinois law. He couldn't legally drive this imaginary car, except with a parent in the front seat. But he didn't need a permit to park in the driveway and wait for manhood.

No chance with his mother. She drowned in the tears of the family budget, short that few dollars most months. "A car was impossible — how could he ask? — they would all starve...."

He decided on a Saturday morning at the breakfast table; his old man could be convinced. Da hunched over his cereal bowl across from Frank; his mouth hung low for the Wheaties and milk he spooned in. This Saturday — the fourth Saturday of the month — Da had the weekend shift in the power house at ComEd. Soon he'd leave, and Frank would work the whole day to prepare.

Frank needed a job and a wheedling argument. He needed to tell his da what the Old Man wanted to hear. His brain burned with the plan.

Da pointed his spoon at Frank. "Playing ball today?"

"Maybe." Maybe he should be more cooperative. "Sure, Da. There's a pickup game in the park."

"That's good. You need to spend more time outside, away from that priest-ridden school and the library. You're like a ghost." His da leaned over to seize Frank's forearm and yank it forward. He laid the boy's pale flesh across his own brick-red arm. "Look at that. White as a sheet."

Distract him. "I wear long sleeves all the time. My arms are too skinny to show off."

"We'll get you a summer job at the Utility. That'll build you up. Get you some muscles, get you some bimbos. You know?"

Frank knew. He knew his father was a dick, but muscles could help.

Da lurched to his feet, a giant inside the small kitchen, dressed in canvas pants and khaki shirt — he dug for the pack of Camels in his breast pocket. "Got to go. See you later, kid."

The day did the trick, succeeded like nothing he could have dreamed. He acquired a job at a grocery warehouse on weekends. No more Sunday Mass — an extra benefit. He worked a half-day right away, stacking cases of Vienna Sausages that had rolled in on a truck. Three employees toiled to store the chemical-saturated pork and beef as they built a castle of processed meat in the warehouse dimness. His arms trembled like sore rubber.

He practiced his argument over and over. "I've saved a hundred from raking leaves and washing windows. I can pay the gas, and as I get older, the jobs will pay more and I can pay for the auto repairs. I'll ditch the Junior and Senior trips and that will save some money."

Mom arrived at the house from the cafeteria about the same time Frank did. She toted a shopping bag that habitually hung by her side, a wax-paper packet buried deep within. Her manager always slipped her something out of the meat locker. This time a roast?

His da never showed for dinner on Fridays and Saturdays. Instead he met his friends at the bar, or "saloon" as he called it. Mom served a thin, brothy goulash, with a few egg noodles that chased each other around the pot as they spooned up. Mom watched TV until ten — *Family Affair, Beverly Hillbillies*. She asked him as she shuffled off to bed, "Staying up?"

"I thought I'd read some." Time seeped through the room.

"Don't stay up too late, and don't worry about your father. He took the bus, not the car." She plodded down the hall to bed. Tomorrow she'd attend early Mass and be at the cafeteria by ten thirty to serve lunch to all the old people and large families — people who thought a cafeteria a treat compared to home.

He did try to read, Zelazny's *Lord of Light* — too unreal compared to the steel and vinyl of a car. He perched in the open front window, a vigil. Da's intoxication would help — his da was a lovely man when drunk, a claim the Old Man routinely asserted. Frank hummed *Crimson and Clover* to himself, over and over.

He spied his da under the streetlights, weaving along from the bus stop. On his arm Da piloted a neighbor. Mitzy. Smoking hot Mitzy. All the boys dreamed of her, her frizzy blonde hair, her fat Polish lips. Those loose summer dresses, restraining those buoyant breasts.

Mitzy and Da stopped to confer. No, to guzzle from a bottle he carried. Frank stared as they interlaced their steps, advancing up the block. He goggled down as the two stopped by the steps, snuggled back into the corner by the house. Glorious Mitzy hung around the Old Man's neck as he reached down to adjust them both. She brought her leg up over his hip, leaned her head back to the sky, and closed her eyes. His da led with a deep grunting sound, and she chorused with a long sighing exhale. Frank gazed at his father's bald spot; Da began to plunge.

Dizzy and sick, Frank slipped to his feet, wove his way across the cluttered living room in the dark. His head sang and a taste of bile invaded his mouth. He tiptoed past his parents' bedroom, with its dark open doorway.

Out of the dark — "Is your father home?"

"He just got in, Ma. He'll be in bed in a few minutes."

"Is everything okay, little man?"

Tell her what she wants to hear. "Yes." He'd never ask his old man for anything. Ever again.

Frank wouldn't possess a car until Los Angeles, and it would be one he appropriated from the curb.

1969 — Up and Out

Ma and Frank huddled together on the couch. The words spilled from the mouth of the fat man in the tie and puddled in their laps. "Mrs. Mahoney, I am so sorry to tell you your husband died today in an accident. He and another employee were working in a utility ditch when the wall collapsed and crushed them."

Frank could imagine it, play it out like a movie in his head — anybody grown up in Chicago knew this type of ditch. Ten to fifteen feet deep, lined in places with steel slabs that were supposed to prevent this collapse. The pipes and the power cables in the bottom, drowned in the muck. Men at the new end of the ditch, at work under the huge yellow claw, confident of the operator. The back hoe would have been run by Da's best friend, Raphael. Dug close to the River. The water in the River would have broken through, turned the walls into slurry, flooded the ditch with his father's death. That's how Frank watched it in his head.

"Did he suffer?" His mother's voice jerked Frank back into the room. A Lithuanian singsong to it, a foreignness even after all these years in America.

"No, no, he... the... it must have been instantaneous. He might have experienced a momentary shock, that's all." The guy would do anything to avoid saying "died" or "death" again.

She asked again, "He didn't suffer?"

Frank clued in. *She wants the suffering.*

The guys at work took up a collection to help pay for the funeral. Insurance cashed out, a meager trickle into her bank account. A pitiful pension would grease the future.

She sold the house, dragged them to Los Angeles. "We will never pay for fuel oil again. I will never be cold again."

How could she have wandered away from the neighborhood, her church, her two or three friends? He didn't understand it at all. He lost a year of school in the two weeks the moving van wasted to deliver their quarter-load of furniture. A meager living room, two beds. A sagging couch, doilies, and other knick-knacks.

Their new house was shaped by four rooms arranged in a square, with a bathroom out the back wall. It hunkered low with a fence four feet away, a fence that separated them from three other flat-roofed squares. An open porch ran across the front and stuck its face out against a dirt road. Home was located on a flood plain below the mountains on the east side, and mud sloshed up to their ankles when the rains arrived.

California rain, California sun, California dreams. The first L.A. pounding Frank collected sprung from loitering on the wrong corner of the right boulevard. On a scale of one to ten, it ranked as a three, but he didn't realize it at the time.

Julio's scheme placed Frank on that corner. Frank hooked up with the Latino in school because they both were the usual shat-upon-spat-upon. Julio weighed in at one-hundred and twenty, like Frank himself.

Julio wore his hair high and greasy, but his sideburns stuck straight out from his face — he resembled a cat with big sad eyes.

Julio knew a guy who knew a guy who knew. The bus ferried them into the Valley with three changes. They arrived at a big metal shed behind chain link and barbed wire. The windows in front had been spray-painted white. Inside, Frank discovered a barn dedicated to eight-track-tape bootlegging. Banks of machines recorded many cartridges at a time. Tapes labeled, sealed in plastic, stacked in boxes. Stretching back into the darkness, cartons bunched together in narrow ranks, their tops open, the music on display. At least a hundred degrees inside. Only one white visible in the place, and he ran the operation.

The head man took them aside after they finished checking out the place. "This's the way it works here. You can buy anything you want from me for three bucks a pop." The boss had once been an athlete, but he had morphed into a tower of flab. His face shone iridescent with perspiration, bleached as only a night dweller's can be.

Frank had fifty dollars on him, borrowed from his mother's purse. He figured his backpack could hold twenty, twenty-five cartridges. "Can we run a line of credit?"

The head man snorted.

Julio asked, "What days you open?"

"We run pretty much 24/7. But you pick a day you show up regular. You show any other day, I'll know cops you brought are in the parking lot."

Frank stared at the boss, at the serried ranks of double chin. "What if we can't sell one, like nobody wants the tape?"

"Tough shit. You buy it, you move it. When you've picked out your choices, you carry your cartridges to my desk in front."

That first day they bought sixty-three dollars worth between them, and they settled on Thursday night as their resupply. For the next two years they rode the buses into the Valley with backpacks and shopping bags. Frank and Julio counted dozens of teenagers with their wrinkled ten dollar bills and their carriers. Dozens — the problem that hung over their heads. Street vending had exploded all over L. A.

They staked out a street in Hollywood, three blocks away from the Palladium. Frank figured the streams of tourists that wandered about in search for the long-disappeared sweater girls of Hollywood would be good for business. Close to right. Tourists didn't buy eight-tracks and haul them back to Nebraska, but their kids did. That block rated as prime real estate. Within the first two days, the street doubled up as a prize ring.

First, Julio suffered at his end of the block — safer to pound on a *Messican* than a white. Frank discovered Julio against an alley wall, his T-shirt jammed into his face to catch the nose bleed. Eight-tracks surrounded Julio, the tape ripped out and strewn about, cartridge bodies in broken pieces. Thirty bucks of merchandise trashed, all because Julio's corner belonged to a guy who sold wind-up toy dogs.

Frank's turn transpired next. He had squatted down on the wall and laid his tapes out on a brown towel. His nearest neighboring huckster sold women's scarves out of a shopping cart. Underneath the scarves lurked nickel bags of pot. Scarf Man snarled at him, "Whatcha looking at? Who the hell are you anyway? Fuck off."

Frank sang out to passers-by, talked to a few, sold a tape or two. "Glen Campbell! Dionne Warwick! Get yer Neil Diamond!"

An Elvis impersonator stopped by to talk to Frank's neighbor, Scarf Man. Elvis wandered off and showed up with a third, a redhead. This guy was constructed out of string and sinew, a broken nose with a bump half-way down. His hands like rocks, knobs of bone on the end of skinny forearms. He sloped across the sidewalk, edged in towards the towel and the tapes, and adopted a guard position on the flank. Frank jerked upright, his back against the brick. Elvis wheeled towards him, crowded right up. He bent down right into Frank's face — Frank hadn't realized Elvis measured six inches taller. "This ain't your corner."

Frank swallowed, his mouth spit-less. "Public sidewalk. But I can move on."

"Move on, huh? Pay the rent first, like a good boy."

Bad. Awful. "I only got fifteen, for change. All in ones." Frank held the money out.

"I can take the rest out in trade, can't I?" Elvis stomped an eight-track. Plastic pieces flew left and right. "Red, introduce yourself to this cum bucket here."

Clear overkill. Red swooped in fast. Elvis pinned Frank while his partner pounded Frank like a body bag. Those huge hands flashed an amazing dance, pulverizing Frank's midriff. Red stopped for breath, and dodged aside when Frank's vomit splashed across the concrete.

They shoved him against the bricks; one pinned his forearm across Frank's throat as the other jerked his knee into Frank's crotch. When they dropped him to the ground, he puked again and rolled into a fetal position. His head caressed the sidewalk and his vision warped. He could smell the cement and dog piss. He blinked. His competitors up-ended a can of lighter fluid and set his inventory on fire.

Frank and Julio tried other corners around Wilshire, tried to negotiate with the unofficial owners, tried spots outside the hotels, next to news stands. In his own neighborhood Julio discovered the groove, pinpointed the winning combination. Julio and Frank shifted to Mexican music — specialized in Rancho Grande, with a little Tijuana Mariachi and Big Band. Their preferred location — a spot under the awning of a Mexican grocery. They worked together, both for protection and so one could pee in back by the dumpsters while the other minded the merchandise. They cleared three hundred bills a week. Frank's commercial Spanish improved, and his sign language. Frank liked the gig — Julio dreamed of something more.

They squatted on their heels, backs against the grocery store plate glass. The sun danced in their eyes, the heat intense. Droning flies, probably drawn by the meat market inside.

Julio had picked up a sunburn under his Mexican patina — his cheeks appeared to be red apples sheened in brown varnish. His voice clotted with sleep, he said, "Sales are slow. Maybe we could give away something with each eight track."

Frank, broke except for the change in the cigar box and the inventory on the blanket in front of him, hated that idea. "What do they need that we have?"

"You're right. Besides, the most popular thing we could give away here would be a one-pound can of lard."

"I can't work tomorrow. Got an English test."

"You haven't been to an afternoon class all semester."

Frank stifled a yawn. "I'm what you call self-taught. The material isn't so hard. Tests are multiple choice."

To wake himself, Julio drummed first on his knees and then on his cheeks as he held the oval of his mouth open. The noise that spilled out of his mouth varied from a bass drum roll to annoying pops. "Have you told tú madre what we do?"

"Nah. She's holding down two jobs, so she doesn't even know I'm not home."

"Mothers aren't stupid, you know."

Frank considered. A couple of times where she had raked him through the "where-have-you-been" inquisition. He allowed, "Maybe she knows."

"Mi madre es old-school Mexico. She thinks it's more important I bring in some money."

Frank picked up a pebble from the sidewalk. "I been giving my ma half my haul. Maybe we're so broke she's decided to close her eyes." He flipped the rock out and hit the tire of the nearest car. The bald tire held up a piece-of-shit Datsun, rusted out, from the beach maybe.

Julio said, "We need to know what the next step-up in gigs is. We can't do this forever."

"We graduate in two years this June. Then I'll find a real job ." But neither of them would finish their Senior year.

Julio levered his way off the glass and glided over to the Datsun. He peeked in the window. "Real job? What do you think about stealing cars?"

Frank refrained from an explanation of how much the idea sucked. Serious jail if caught. Their neighborhood full of crap cars anyway. Adrenalin used up like water, all for what? A couple of hundred *maybe* when they turned the car. "I'd have to learn how to drive, wouldn't I?"

Julio wrinkled his face. It would require a couple of years in close relationship with the State of California to wean Julio of cars.

1972 — Decency

Da smoked until the exact moment he died, as he drowned in a wave of mud. Frank wouldn't have been surprised to see him stretched out in that cheap coffin on shiny rayon with a Camel bobbing from his lips. But Frank's ma got the cancer, not her cigarette-puffing husband. The long road where her organs swelled until her abdomen dimpled and heaved — something alive in there that couldn't be her.

For weeks she huddled in the ward, her hands gripping the sheet like she held the bed down, kept it from flying away in pain. He'd doddle down the hall, peek into the room praying she was asleep, stare over the bulk of the three other women to spot her marooned in the corner.

Even with the morphine she didn't sleep — just a doze or two during the day. Her hand came up, beckoned him. "Little man. How good. Come to me."

He marched across sticky linoleum, drew the plastic curtain around them. He dropped into the chair, leaned forward to clasp her hand. Pale, as dry as chalk. "Hey, Ma. How are you?" He didn't wait to hear the real answer. "You're looking pretty good."

She knew. "I'm so glad to see you. I feel fine. Better than yesterday. I think about going back to work soon." She squeezed his hand. "Thanks for coming."

Back to work? They both knew she wouldn't be leaving this place. "Sure, I came over as soon as I got off the job."

"You're so good to me. But.... Lean over. Let me smell your breath."

He lurched out of the chair close to her face. "Ah, Ma. I haven't had a drink in two weeks." The two weeks since she had caught him with a cheap sweet wine hanging on him like guilt.

"Good, good." She eased back. "My mouth, so dry. Could you reach me the glass?"

He grasped the aquamarine plastic cup, fed the straw into her cracked lips. "So. What did they bring you for dinner?"

She gazed into his face. "I don't really remember. I wasn't very hungry. Frank, you have turned out a fine young man, so handsome."

Frank knew she deluded herself. He had only weaseled his way into two dates in his entire life. But she had so little left. "Ah, Ma. Thanks, though." What else could they talk about that concerned the hospital but not the basic goal of the rooms, the nurses and doctors of this wing. He could smell her, the sour smell of a neglected patient. Her hair hung limp, tucked back behind her ears.

"The television is good here. More channels than at home."

He should locate a basin and a washcloth. At their house, before they had to come here, he had bathed her every night, changed her nightgown. Helped her into the tiny bathroom. "I bet you fight over what you all watch."

"Yes, and at least one of us has to have it turned up louder than a marching band."

"And that wouldn't be you."

Silence stretched out between them. She seemed okay with that, with lying there holding his hand. Maybe she had dropped off to sleep. He glided his hand back, slid up to his feet as quiet as a mouse.

Her eyes flicked open. "Pranciškus."

Lithuanian for Francis. Maybe the old language wasn't so bad after all. "I'm here."

"Pranciškus, pay for the hospital, after I'm gone. We have always paid our way. Don't let me die in their debt, like a beggar in the street."

He didn't have to pay. The goody-two-shoes supplied relief funds, indigent resources. He didn't have to stand up for her debt. But she had asked directly — he was trapped.

He did have to honor his mother.

1974 — Ripping off Ralphs

When Frank turned twenty-two, they promoted him. He became the youngest Assistant Manager in the Ralphs California empire. Twenty-two carat gold. Being a winner left dust in his mouth, an unfocused sense of a universe gone awry. As he tried to pin it down, he decided he had peaked too soon, his career plateaued out. Where could he go from here?

Gerry Ford lived in the White House and things hadn't deteriorated like they would seven years later. Frank's attitude could be summed up as "work hard and keep your mouth shut." The guy that carried the cash register key could steal all the cheddar cheese he wanted, and Frank had transformed into that guy. Anybody could work hard, say "yezzer" constantly, and be a success. He sneered at the poor, even though they included his own mother, or had, before the cancer killed her. He believed the poor should all leap on the Ralphs gravy train.

The smoking years — he favored menthol. The grocery store loading dock backed out onto a large dirt lot, complete with dumpsters and a line of businesses on the other side. The first time the Grant family trundled into view, he spied the loaded shopping cart first. Father Grant shoved on the cart, tried to plow his way across the lot from nowhere to nowhere. Frank recognized the cart by its colors as

1974 – Ripping off Ralphs

one from Kroger — to differentiate between supermarkets came with the territory. He breathed a sigh of relief — one less Ralphs cart in bondage to poverty, one more for Kroger. He leaned against the man-door beside the roll-up, sucked away on the filter and tried to siphon one into his lungs as fast as he could. *Why isn't this dude with the shopping cart in some shelter somewhere, or in a work program?*

Two kids and a woman shared his journey. The smallest child rode in the cart seat. His father, head down on the back bar, grunted as he forced the cart step by step forward. Mother lagged behind, clutching the hand of a girl who scuffed her feet in the dirt. Father appeared thirty, Mother might have been twenty-five.

Mother spoke — to her husband or to the unfairness of the dirt lot. "Stop. Take the child." Father slowed for three steps, like a train making up its mind. He ground into the dust at a full halt. Mother latched the girl's hand to her father's belt, wheeled on Frank. She sidled towards Frank, all humility, and said, "Can you spare any change, mister? The little ones haven't eaten in awhile."

He gave her a dollar and stared down at her as the grubby piece of green and ivory passed into her hands. She had been pretty once, before life had ground it out of her. Not beautiful — her nose beaked out too sharp and Appalachian for that, and her forehead showed an inch too high for her to have been a princess. But she had been pretty, and now her life ensured no one could accuse her of that. He said, "Hungry, huh. Wait here." Something she couldn't fritter away.

He dodged inside to his employee locker, dug in a bag in the bottom, and rediscovered stolen Ritz crackers and sharp cheddar cheese. He could boost more later. As he hurried back out, he ran into her poised at the dock edge, as obedient as a dog that smells a biscuit. "Here." He thrust it into her hands. Her eyes — a startling blue, surrounded by a clean white. She cradled the crackers like they could shatter.

The Moth

During break on Thursday, slow Thursdays, he could linger. He had a book by Sartre, a cheap paperback by a cheap Frenchman, jammed in his back pocket, but he didn't feel much like all that brain exercise. Perched on a stack of pallets he inhaled as slow as a tortoise on the cancer stick, let it smolder in his hand. An eddy carried the smoke up, teased his left eye, and settled it into his right like a smog bank. He flapped a hand. Across the way, across the dirt lot, a hand waved back.

The hand connected to the older child from yesterday's foursome, perched on her loading dock. Frank and his break remained sacrosanct, safe — the child a hundred feet away. He turned his head left and pretended to scan the four-lane past the lot. Out of the corner of his eye he peered at the child. She waved her hand again. He could discern small scraps of song. She sang — what? Her hands raised to her face; she cupped them in a trumpet. The song sounded clearer — he could pick out phrases. "Good Morning." She sang good morning to him, a grade-school song he had known back in Chi. Wretched midget thing sang. Buried in dirt and hunger, and she warbled a greeting. *Shit.*

Beside Frank a brown paper bag held his lunch, food he had grazed off the shelves. He hopped off the pallets and toted it across the rough lot. The munchkin's loading dock, creosote timber, stood shoulder high to him. He squinted up at her. "I'm Frank."

"My Daddy's name is Merle."

He reached in the bag and ripped off a banana. "Daughter of Merle. What's your name?"

"Cindy."

"Well, Cindy, here's a banana." He handed it up.

With great concentration, she peeled it and caused it to disappear. He watched her quick minute teeth as she minced away. But she didn't gulp it down. With great dignity, she said, "Thank you, Frank. Can I have another?"

Polite little beggar. A real beggar. He tore off another banana and handed it to her. "Where are your folks?"

Instead of an answer, she gave him, "That's my baby brother, Bruce."

Frank jerked — something had grabbed his pants at the knee. He stared down — a pint-sized blond stared back at him.

Cindy said, "He wants one too."

Frank threw the sack on the dock, picked up the boy, and set him beside his sister. He hunted out another banana and gave it to Bruce. "Sorry. That's the last one." The boy couldn't manage the banana stem — Frank tore the peel top and handed it to him.

Cindy stared into the bag, without reaching in.

Frank had stolen more than bananas. "Do you like M&M's?"

Her head dipped with such violence her hair flew.

"Just a minute." He hiked down to the edge of the dock, crawled up a ladder. "Scoot over." He landed between them, the sack in his lap.

Cindy received the M&M's, a shining handful of color, with graciousness. Holding them in one hand, she picked out one at a time for transport to her tastebuds. Bruce crammed all ten into his mouth straightaway.

"Where's your Mom and Dad?"

"Downstairs."

Frank bent his head, spoke to the part in her hair, "Downstairs?"

"We play house here, and there's an upstairs and a downstairs." She pointed down. "We're upstairs right now, and Mommy and Daddy are downstairs."

Bruce confirmed, "Sleeping."

"Have they had anything to eat today?"

The Moth

Bruce wobbled his head no. Cindy wrinkled her face and said, "I don't think so. Should I have saved them a banana?"

Frank reached out a tentative hand, patted her on the head like he would pat a dog he wasn't sure about. "No. I have to go back to work, but when I get another break, I'll fetch something over for your Mom and Dad. Here's the rest of the M&M's. Share them with your brother." He dropped down to the ground, and trekked off across the dirt lot. He reached into his shirt pocket to fumble out another menthol. Frank lit up.

Ralphs stocked sandwiches in wedge-shaped boxes, fabricated a day or two days or a week in advance somewhere far away and trucked in. They never stuck in any lettuce in the sandwich, since it would transform into a smudgy green paste before a customer bit into it. But those unknown hands did stuff in mustard, lunchmeat, and a plasticine cheese. The bread could be a bit soggy, since it sucked up the pickle juice. Frank stole six from a pallet in back rather than off the shelves. He dropped them into an empty cleanser box that waited to be flattened and took himself off across the lot. Gazed down as he strode along — in a hurry this time. His shoes covered in a red dust and his own official-black pants tarnished in an red ocher. When he reached the creosote dock, with its stink of petroleum in the hot sun, he sang out, "Cindy, Bruce."

Instead of a child, the woman's head popped out between the posts. She crawled forward on her hands and knees. Hair matted, neck dirty — but when she raised her face to him, her deep blue irises set in a field of pure white eclipsed the grime. "Hi." A quiet, gentle voice. The single syllable drawn out, like a whole note in a world of eighth notes.

Frank's breath caught. "I've met your children."

"Yes and I'm very grateful. You fed them good things they haven't had in a bit." She crawled out, rose, and dusted off her knees. Just his height.

He stuck out his hand. On most days, he wouldn't touch a person, much less a dirty one. "I wouldn't call M&M's good for you."

She gripped his hand — her grasp dry and scratchy, a calloused and abused skin. "Bruce did eat his share too fast, and his tummy hurts."

A pang of guilt. "I brought real food. Maybe it will help. Where's the family?"

She clasped the box, stared into it, and drew a ragged breath. She must be starved. "Under here. We're living here for a bit." She pointed into the darkness. Urban cliff dwellers, hidden under the overhang. "Let me bring them out. We'll eat out in the fresh air."

She called out, and again her voice sang. Mutters and shuffling sounds slipped out of the dark. Sadness infected him that he wasn't to be alone with her. Confused, he filed away surprise at himself. He searched out a smoke, lit it, watched his hands and the dirt, avoided a glance at her.

She leaned close to him and he jolted in surprise. In a hushed voice she said, "You might notice. My husband Merle was in an accident. He had head injuries and sometimes he doesn't seem right."

"Oh." The two children boiled out from under the platform, shadowed by Merle, slow, cautious. When he straightened, squinted into the sun, she glided over and dusted him off, brushed his hands free of dirt. "Merle, this is our new friend." Merle swung his head towards Frank, like a steer that checked out motion as a possible threat.

"Frank. My name is Frank."

She said, "This is Merle, Frank, and I'm Doris. I think you already know Cindy and Bruce." Her voice feathered out slow. None of the West Coast hurry and flatness.

Frank said, "Are you folks from the South?"

She laughed, her voice a lilt. "Kind of. Kentucky is considered Southern by everybody but Kentuckians. Come on kids, let's eat. Merle, stick them up on the dock."

Her family claimed her. He shuffled his feet once, raised a smidge of red dust, said, "The store is calling me. See ya." He turned and as he hurried away, he drew in a big drag on his coffin nail and cupped it in his hand at his side. Just for something to do.

Frank spotted Doris at closing time, as he locked the back. She perched crosslegged on her dock under a single lightbulb on the back of the building across the way, played pat-a-cake with Cindy. The hundred feet across the lot lay out like the battleground inside him, Doris on one side, him on the other. He shouldn't do this. They stopped the game and watched him pace out of the dark. Calm and waiting, for what the moment brought.

"Doris, would you like to get the family cleaned up? We have an emergency shower you can use in the store, but we have to hurry. The night watchman will clock in at the back by ten."

The five of them crowded into an industrial space in the store back. It measured five-by-ten and was constructed of cinderblock twelve feet high. A shower head and the drain crowded one corner — store cleaning equipment filled the rest of the space — brooms, mops, roll-around buckets with ringers. Tripping over his words, Frank said, "Here's a bar of soap. Here are rolls of paper towels. Maybe you can all shower at once. I'll be around the corner."

Doris tugged at his sleeve. "What about laundry? It doesn't do any good to shower and dress in weeks-old clothes." She had a stink like a dumpster and he didn't care. He let her slide right up to his shoulder.

"Okay, okay, I can fix that. We have butcher coveralls. You can throw those on, and we'll do laundry down the road — there's a coin wash. I'll scoop up some soap here and give you five dollars in quarters for the machines." *Deeper and deeper.*

Doris showered behind that concrete wall, with her befuddled husband and two slippery children. Frank knew. Naked, she'd scrub them all with soap, stand them under the shower head. Tear off paper towels and swab them dry. All this before she attended to herself. Frank had the shakes. He gazed at his hands full of white, paper-thin coveralls, all of them size XX. His hands trembled; the coveralls rustled like birds. *What's wrong with you? What the hell are you doing?*

She sent Bruce out naked and happy to fetch the coveralls. After, Frank whisked them out the back door and headed for the laundry, their real clothes in a trash bag. They came to rest in five hard plastic chairs, watched the laundry. Merle's coverall fit, except for the huge folds around his middle where a fat-man's size surrounded a half-starved man. Doris, her wet hair in long dark ringlets that draped over her shoulders, had rolled her sleeves back a half dozen folds and had turned the legs inside out up to mid thigh. Cindy and Bruce were cocooned in theirs — only their heads poked out of oversize collars, the coveralls folded up around them like sheets on a bed — they had to be carried everywhere. Laundry time dragged on and on, and Frank didn't deliver the family back to their loading dock until eleven.

At his noon break, he scurried across the lot to the creosote dock. "Doris, Doris! He crouched and duck-walked under the beams, inward two feet. He plunked the box of food, enough for two meals, behind one of the posts. He thought about crawling back to search her out, but the red dust would disfigure his pants. Out of the half dark, two children popped into his face, and he fell over backwards on his butt. Cindy giggled so hard she slipped towards hysteria. The mirth became more and more of a shriek. The other girl, another half-pint, a tawny black. She chewed on the fingers of her right hand. She had the largest eyes in the boniest face he had ever seen. She didn't giggle or say a word.

Impatient, he reached out and shook Cindy's shoulder. "Hey. Stop for a minute and tell me who this is."

Cindy did slow to a muted sniggering. "It's Amy. Mommy says we have to take care of her and feed her. She doesn't have anyone. She's my best friend."

Frank had Fridays off, because as the assistant manager he worked on the weekends. He hadn't thought ahead, so Ralphs didn't feed his new family — he'd have to pay the bill. A long trek, two city blocks, but he managed to tote the two giant cheese pizzas to the loading dock along with a sack of bread sticks and sauce. For the last block, the loading dock waited with a solitary figure posed on it, out in the sun. Waiting. Doris.

She caught sight of him and hurried forward before he reached the platform. She clutched the cheese sticks. "I wanted to talk to you in private. There's a couple that have moved in with us, the Stubblefields. They're real elderly, and if someone doesn't take care of them out here, they'll settle on a curb and die."

Two more! "And that someone is?"

She gripped his elbow with her free hand. "Me. And you'll help me. Mrs. Stubblefield doesn't seem to know where she is, so I need lots of help."

1974 – Ripping off Ralphs

"I'm glad you warned me. Now I have to buy for two more."

She bumped into him as they paced along. He wanted to drop the pizzas and hug her. She said, "But you're not buying for us, are you, Frank? Ralphs is. You're stealing for us." She allowed a long pause, where the word "steal" hung there by itself. "Thank you, Frank."

He bobbed his head, not wanting her to detect how she pleased him. "I'll have to be smarter when I lift stuff. None of us can afford to get caught."

She stopped him and turned in front, gazed at him across the pizza boxes. "One other thing. We have two teenage boys, Rory and Matthew. They ran away together because they're homos and their whole high school knew it."

Nine. Nine mouths to feed. He was screwed.

Elfin Cindy met Frank in the dark by Ralphs' back door. She reached up and clasped his hand, her fingers ridiculously tiny, soft. He could hurt that hand, just by accident — it frightened him.

She held his hand as they ambled towards the homeless squat. She chattered on, excited with perhaps one of the best days of her young life. They'd had peanut butter and jelly sandwiches for lunch. The grocery sack in his other paw slipped. He mustn't drop it — full of hot chicken strips.

It had seemed like a good idea. He had a bale of chicken strips in the cold locker that had slipped past its sell-by date. He'd spent the hours between closing and the night watchman's rounds in the employee lounge, nuking them in the microwave. By the time he finished, he had learned the lounge would reek of chicken the next morning, the sauce and the catsup wanted to explode out of their packets, and the paper bag heated up to where it burned his fingers.

Doris reached the bag out of his hands. "Thank God. I thought you'd never come. They're all so hungry and Mama Stubblefield is wailing."

"Here." He thrust another paper bag in Cindy's hands. "Two flashlights. We don't stock lanterns."

Doris shoved at him and the little girl. "Quick, quick! Get under cover. It's the night watchman." Back in the dark, away from the security lights that surrounded the dirt lot, they stared at the car, a dwarfish Toyota Corolla with a shield on the door. It jerked to a stop by the supermarket; a fat man in a uniform oozed out and stumped up the stairs onto the dock. He approached the back door, fished out his clock, stuck in a key chained to the wall, and used it to log his round. He represented Security, a force that stood between Ralphs and a lawless world.

Doris said to Frank, "Okay, dear. I'll take it from here. See you tomorrow." She gave his cheek a peck and disappeared into the gloom under the dock.

He slipped out for a smoke break at ten — Doris waited for him. She had been weeping — her sharp nose glowed like a hot coal and her eyes carried remaining tears. "Thank God."

She had begun to say that a lot.

"Frank, Frank, I don't know what to do." She kicked her bawling up to full force.

"What? I can't help if you don't calm down enough to tell me."

"The police took Cindy! She tagged along with old Mrs. Stubblefield on a walk and when they didn't come back, we all went out searching. Matthew and Rory tracked them down — at least they spotted them in the back seat of a police car. And it drove away." She gave out deep piteous sobs.

1974 – Ripping off Ralphs

This rocked Frank back. His beautiful Doris — a blubbering wreck. She couldn't catch her breath. "Why would they take them?"

She managed to gasp out a sobbing explanation. A cracked old woman, moaning and wringing her hands, lost on the street with a little girl.

"Okay, we'll get her back. I don't know how, but we'll track her and bust her out of wherever she is." *Who's playing Bonnie and Clyde?*

Harder than he thought. Frank searched for three days — off work — to discover Mrs. Stubblefield had been incarcerated in a mental ward at Los Angeles General. Cindy had been stashed with Child Protective Services. He located both buildings on his bus map, figured out the stops, and prepared for the lying. Frank manufactured some I.D. for Doris. He entered her as an employee of Ralphs, burned her a salary card with an invented social security number. Wrote up a time clock card. He boosted a smock for her and pressed out a name badge. He dropped all this into his other criminal equipment, a brown grocery sack.

This he showed her, on the Ralphs loading dock, as a truck unloaded close by and four staff bustled back and forth. All the confusion — real anonymity.

He sprang the surprise. "You have to clean up first, before we can ride the bus downtown. You can't use the shower here, not during regular hours. I'll take you to my place."

The journey ate up ten minutes by bus and three minutes on foot. They climbed the steps, he opened the door, she stepped in. "Oh Frank. It's so nice!"

No, it wasn't. He rented a studio apartment where the living room couch folded out into a bed and a drywall nook in the corner with a veneered cardboard door masqueraded as the bathroom. He'd constructed a closet — a pipe rack from a lumberyard screwed together, hidden behind a sheet stapled to the ceiling. The apartment complex had struck him as safe, and besides, he was paying off his mom's hospital bill. Even now. He said, "I'm glad you like it."

She popped into the bathroom to clean up; he jittered in agony on the couch. When she reappeared, she created the impression she had worked in Ralphs Produce all her adult life. He leapt up, she twirled to show the disguise off, and they ended toe to toe. Gaze to gaze. He leaned forward and hunted a kiss. The kiss he so deserved, for all he had done and for all his waiting. His lips grazed hers.

With a stout shove she threw him back and he plummeted to the couch. He lay sprawled out beneath her — a fat history book jutted into his spine. He watched her frowning mouth, despaired of the words she said. "Frank, what are you doing? Why, Merle would pound you into the ground, at least the old Merle. That's foolishness from you."

Confess! "I'm so sorry. It — just happened. I didn't mean for it to."

"I'm so disappointed in you." She jerked in a breath. "All right. We'll forget it ever happened — as long as it never does again."

His soul deflated like a ruptured lung.

Doris flicked both hands, like she slung grease off her fingers. "Let's go get my little girl."

Their rehearsed story involved a senile neighbor who had meandered away with Cindy and an entire neighborhood that searched for them for days. Frank alibied himself as a helpful supervisor. The minimal I.D. held up, though paperwork emerged to be filled out. They also bowed their heads and listened to not-so-veiled threats about County supervision and children removed from their parents. They strolled

1974 – Ripping off Ralphs

out hand-in-hand, the diminutive girl glancing up, at first at her mother, then at Frank.

Not a word in the beginning. Then floodgates opened — Cindy informed them, "They don't have peanut butter and jelly, but they do have Cokes. The other kids were nasty. I didn't like my bed. It was so lonesome. I knew you'd come for me...." " She must not have spoken for days.

Frank glanced over at Doris. She shot him a smile full of... what, gratitude, admiration, love? *I got a chance then?*

To spring Mrs. Stubblefield proved harder. Frank finally wheeled her out of a sunroom temporarily unsupervised because of a ringing alarm at the end of the ward — an alarm that Doris had jerked. Once on the sidewalk he abandoned the wheelchair, nabbed the old woman by her arm, and hustled her to the bus stop.

Bonnie and Clyde had nothing on them.

Frank shared his office in Ralphs with his boss — or vice versa. They worked back-to-back at desks heaped with paper, with inboxes and outboxes, with three-ring binders on the corporate procedures of personnel, cash management, ordering, meat handling, and of course, reporting to Head Office. The space was fenced away from the employee lounge, the Coke machines, and the service corridor with a half-wall and glass rim. He lived a lot of his working life here. He looked across the glass to see two checkers nattering over soft drinks.

Inside the glass, they counted up as three people against one; his boss, the regional manager, and a corporate lawyer versus — him. The new thing, besides the two outsiders, squatted on the desk — a twelve-inch black and white TV with a video cassette recorder hooked to it. Frank had only seen pictures of VCRs. Never one in person. His weary boss cleared his throat — these confrontations sucked the life out of managers, as Frank well knew. This confab carried all appearances of bad news. He faced a reprimand at least.

His manager, a man who carried sixty pounds of comfort hung over his belt opened the inquiry. "Frank, we initiated some security precautions last month when our pilferage levels skyrocketed. We positioned cameras in the ceilings, both front and back. I'm thinking you know what we learned."

Things began with a scene of him as he filled a milk crate with fruit and carried it out the back door. Another scene where he ripped open packages and nuked the contents in bowls in the employee microwave. They ran camera footage of the Grant family in the shower. After all his hopes in the past, Frank beheld Doris nude — but it upset him so that *they* stared at her that he failed to notice any details. Finally, a scene where the Stubblefields wandered around the back of the store dressed as Ralphs butchers.

"It doesn't look good, Frank. Can you explain yourself?"

"They're homeless. They live behind the store. They have nothing and nobody."

The regional manager sniffed. He was trim, golf-tan, so suburban Frank knew he drove a Buick Sport Wagon. "Evidently they have Ralphs. Lots of Ralphs."

"The food was all going bad anyway. It would have gone in the trash in a couple of days."

"Really, Frank?"

His head sunk. Turning into a show trial — how bad could it get?

"The evidence looks pretty damning."

Frank said, "I'm the assistant manager. How come you didn't tell me about the theft levels, the cameras?"

His boss, who had hired and promoted him, had tears in his eyes.

"I realized the big losses happened only on days you worked. Frank, how could you betray me?"

The knife slid into Frank's back. "How could you sell me out to Head Office?"

The regional manager clucked his tongue. "How many are you feeding?"

Frank muttered.

"What?"

"Nine."

His boss actually wrung his hands. "Frank. What were you thinking?"

Frank twitched his head. "I was thinking they were hungry." The screen before him showed the gray streaming specks of an empty tape.

"Why didn't you ask?"

"Because you'd have said no."

The regional manager pointed out, "Ralphs does have a foundation. The company does direct money towards charities."

"To these people?"

The regional manager stood firm, not at all sorry. "No, I'm afraid not. Only agencies."

Asshole.

Now the lawyer stepped up. "I'm pleased to see you have our personnel manual on your desk. Have you read it?" The lawyer dressed in undertaker black, his hawkish face offset by a glabrous hand-width of pale baldness.

What a jerk. "As a matter of fact, I have," said Frank.

"And what did it say about theft from Ralphs?"

"It says disciplinary action if an employee is caught grazing." Maybe he could stop it there.

The lawyer simpered like a kindergarten teacher who had coaxed out the right answer. "And grazing is?"

"Eating from the store stocks."

The legal beagle leaned into Frank's face. His breath smelled like peppermints. "And if it's more than grazing, if it's theft?"

"Up to and including termination."

Teacher had secured the answer he wanted. "Well. There you have it."

The worst possible outcome. His mother's hospital bills like an ax over his head. The people under the dock. Doris. "I'm the best guy you've got. You don't want to fire me."

The regional manager's white teeth shone out of his bronze face. "That's exactly what I want to do. You're done here. You're lucky we're not going to prosecute."

Frank rose, removed his Ralphs vest, drew out the pocket protector with the Ralphs pens. He unhooked the pricing gun from his belt. All these he laid on his boss' desk. "You're supposed to search my locker. There's nothing in it I care about. The manual also says to escort the ex-employee from the premises. Let's leave by the back — I have to go tell my people." *Tell them I got caught.*

He marched out of the office, into the service corridor, to the dock. The mighty three trailed after him. Just inside the roll-up door, he delved in boxes for jelly and peanut butter, snagged a loaf of white bread off the roller rack. Turning to his boss, his ex-boss, he said, "Cindy loves peanut butter and jelly. It's the only thing she wants out of the day."

Onto the dock. Down the concrete steps. They'd all be forced on by the police. He'd lose her.

Well, at least my career hasn't flattened out.

1978 — Molly Legs

You Light Up My Life had soared up the charts. Wildly popular — but not with Frank. He worked on his loneliness in strip clubs, or one in particular. Sully's Place owned neon on the street side: "Exclusive Gentleman's Club" and "The Hottest Stage in L.A." and an "All GURL Revue." Sully's offered no parking in front, since it squatted right on the sidewalk. The customers shared the parking in back with the dumpsters of a Chinese restaurant. For all his life Frank would associate the smell of sweet and sour with an undefinable yearning. Molly liked Chinese and that was enough to key his lust, his sadness.

Frank met Molly one June night on the back step next to Sully's. He had slipped out of his apartment on the hill behind Sully's boulevard about eight. Scrunching down the sidewalk on the L.A. grit under the streetlights, he watched the shadow of his Afro stretch out on the ground before him, slide under his feet, and start back home. He no longer tried to slick the snarl of his hair back. He'd decided if Art Garfunkel appealed to women, he'd try the trademark fuzz-bomb. He slipped in the back door of Sully's, plodded past the dressing rooms and the pisser, and spent two-and-a-half hours by the stage — all he could afford. He propped his forearms on the scarred counter that circled the stage and leaned forward in his chair. For two-point-five hours.

He didn't spot her at first, as he sidled out of the bar, because the metal fire door struck his elbow. Pain lanced through his entire arm. As he massaged his elbow, he turned his head and froze. One of the hookers from around the corner perched stoop-shouldered on the concrete step behind the restaurant. She ate Chinese out under the two mustard-yellow lights that lit the back, poked with chopsticks into a humble white box. In the L.A. summer night, she dressed in a crimson shiny top, slashed in front clear to her waist, and lemon-yellow loose shorts that showed off her best asset, her long legs. Her hair, not so great, ran to bottle-blonde and crinkled. She tugged it back tight on one side and let it run wild on the other.

Klaxons blared in his head. *Here's a chance.*

Frank slowed to an amble as he drew near. She angled her head towards him and showed her forehead, her chin, her nose in the flicker of shadow and light. Her face displayed too much character to be pretty and a weariness that held back beauty. From his towering five-feet seven-inches, he could make her out, haggard in the restaurant's parking lot lights. *But not bad features, really.* He sucked in a deep breath, and his entire chest filled with a longing. Or maybe just craving.

She cocked her head, a defensive evaluating gesture. "Hey there, Garfunkel. Where's Simon?" She snickered, and dug at the cardboard carton with chopsticks.

He mumbled, maybe said, "Nice evening," or "Not too hot tonight." His mouth formed shapes. His lips on autopilot.

Her eyebrows creased in a question. "What?"

"Nothing. Eating Chinese?" Even to himself he sounded lame.

"You're a bright one, you are."

"I only meant, is it good? I've never eaten here." He ducked his head. He must look like Opie on *Andy of Mayberry*.

1978 – Molly Legs

"S'all right. Want a bite?"

She had offered him — something. He bobbed like a bird pecks, stepped forward, and tripped on the smallest rock in California. He fell towards her, his arms open, his neck craning down. His hand smacked onto the step and drove his wrist back. The pain ran clear up his arm into his shoulder. The same arm slammed by the steel door a minute ago.

She shoved at him with both hands and threw him back like a rag. "Give it a rest, big boy. I'm on break here. Give me ten minutes."

Hot blood rushed into his face, enough to make it burn. "No, I fell — I didn't mean — it wasn't any.... " He gave up. "See you around." Staring over his shoulder, he strode manfully away across the parking lot into darkness.

She shouted after him, "Hey, Garfunkel! Don't go away mad."

The second time he met Molly, he fell into apocalypse. He left Sully's an hour early with forty dollars in his pocket. Forty could be an impotent amount, or it could be enough for a transaction of mutual satisfaction. *I need a chance, at something. Someone.* As he hesitated in Sully's back door, he cadged a glimpse, but didn't spot her. He retreated into the bathrooms where he took an over-long time grooming himself at the sink with a paper towel — he ensured nothing could be interpreted as, well, disgusting. He fed eight quarters into a machine on the wall to squirt out a liquid dribble into his hand. Once he rubbed it over the back of his neck and dabbed it on his wrists, he decided it smelled more like machine oil than cologne. For next time — if he lucked into a next time — he'd buy the witch hazel product at Walgreens. He stole out of the crapper and angled his head out the back of the club to check again.

The Moth

She had planted herself behind the Chinese joint. He sidled across the lot. He bobbed and becked — an image in his head of a crane that stabbed its beak into a clear pond.

In spite of the wrinkles that ran back from the corners of her eyes, she appeared magnificent. He noted for the first time her long elegant neck. Her breasts, cloaked behind a tube top, jumped towards him as if his to touch. Her grin, guarded at first, flashed out like a matador's cape that summoned the bull. "Why, it's Artie. How's Mrs. Robinson?" She drawled, the words elongate and sweet.

He stared at her ankles, strapped in a hot blue web that bound her high heels to her feet. Could he have developed a shoe fetish? "S'okay I sit down?"

"Depends. You want to share this sweet and sour? If the answer is yes, plunk your ass down. If it's no, trot yourself inside and buy something off the American side of the menu."

He said, "Sweet and sour is fine." He fell from a great height, like a pelican that dove on a fish, slapping onto the concrete.

She offered him chopsticks that pinned a fried-up piece of pork coated in a sticky glaze. She popped it into his mouth, stared into her carton. "I recall the last time we met, you interrupted our business by a sudden acrobatic gesture." Her voice, now that the sarcasm had dripped off into the dust, had slowed even further, into a smoky Southern sound.

"When I fell."

"That disappoints me. I thought you were leaping into my arms."

He cleared his throat. "I would have. But I fell."

"Hmm. Want a leap tonight?" She darted a peek at him, and down into the carry-out carton.

"Uh, yes. I don't have a lot. Is forty enough?"

She hooted out laughter, like a shattering window. "You have less than half! We couldn't hump until we're half-way to heaven and then

1978 – Molly Legs

quit, now could we?" Her chopsticks excavated another bite and stuck it into his mouth. She allowed his lips to close, teased back the chopsticks. "Sure that's all you're holding?"

He nodded like his head was spring-loaded.

"Damn!" The word ran out two syllables, *daiyumm*. "Tell you what. I'll do it as a special introductory offer. Next time, full price — a hundred for a half hour, one-fifty for an hour. I'll just have to do two guys later like the Kentucky Derby. Over in three minutes each."

"What?"

"Lucky that's no problem. Most of you guys are quick on the trigger."

He didn't want to be quick. His pants squeezed him tight, not in the prime spot, but around the waist. He had bought them on sale an inch too small. Time stretched to an eternity as he wedged his hand in his pocket. But he couldn't jump up and dig for the money. He fumbled out the forty bucks, proffered it. Did the business deal begin like this? *Or does money come last?*

She flicked it out of his fingers and tucked it inside the tube top, the most sensual gesture that Frank had ever seen. "Deal. Once we finish the Chinese, we'll skedaddle off a block to Hotel Hump'N Bump and do a little party." She chopsticked an immense wad of rice into her mouth and offered him another piece of savory pork.

Four words scratched out behind Frank, a huge shock to his system. "Goddamn. This is homey."

Frank jerked halfway off the step. A bass growl. And the man who loomed there with his own carton of Chinese — even worse. Frank wanted to run or hide.

The barrel of a man parked right beside him. Landed so close their hips touched. He stank, stained the air with hair pomade, with bay rum cologne, with days of sweat. The stranger opened his carton and with a plastic fork ferreted out something pasty white and unrecognizable. Three times he did this, crammed his mouth full. Frank watched for the swallow. The five-o'clock shadow chomped, the black hair flopped out as the head plunged down to the carton then jerked up, porpoising food. The fat, sensual lips, muffled by food, said, "My name's Little Wheezy."

Under the stare. Frank turned to the hooker beside him. He warped his face into what he hoped was a beseeching plea.

She leaned across him and handed Little Wheezy a fold of money. "Here's for three, dearie."

Little Wheezy threw his eyes up and down her, from the crinkly hair to the gorgeous legs with the dark blue heels. "And for this john?"

She coughed, reached into her tube top. She handed the forty across Frank like she would across a store counter.

Little Wheezy fanned the four tens out. "What's this?"

"I gave Garfunkel a discount here. You can tell it's his first visit to the amusement park."

"Wrong, girl." Little Wheezy rose. He possessed a torso like an oil drum. He twisted around, shins to Frank's knees. He leaned into Frank's shoulder, crushed down with more and more weight. "When you short her, you short me. Just cause you worked up a stiffee, don't mean you can stiff me." He raised his foot and pressed his heel on Frank's hand, pinned it to the concrete step. Little Wheezy ground his heel in, his hand shoved hard on Frank's shoulder to keep him trapped. He leaned his full two hundred pounds into his foot — pancaked Frank's hand.

The tears rushed into Frank's eyes. His whole being curled around that hand. First one knuckle, then another cracked and popped. He didn't so much as whimper.

Little Wheezy slacked off, stepped back. He yanked Frank's chin straight up, so he could stare into his face. Little Wheezy's voice dribbled into his ears like an oily, satisfied chuckle. "I'm keeping your forty. You want it, you root it out." He jammed the money into the front of his pants and scrubbed his crotch into Frank's chin. He gestured at the woman. "C'mon, baby cakes. You're trottin' back to work on the Boulevard."

The third time he met Molly, Frank fell into her grace. But for four weeks he didn't bump into his beautiful whore — time stretched out flat and bleak.

In the meantime, he carried a knife. Every time his hand throbbed, he'd dip his fingers into his pocket, caress the switchblade. *Could I use it?*

He fell back into his old ways. He left Sully's later than usual — one of the girls had danced at his bit of stage. She ignored the two fat men to his left and the shoving, yelling blue-collar foursome to his right. *I'm golden, or she's pissed at them.*

After that bit of kindness in the club, the back parking lot stretched out empty, the air sour from the smell of dumpsters that hadn't been emptied in a week. He scuffed his feet, too depressed to bother picking them up. Pebbles shot away from him. Frank shuffled right up on her before he caught sight of her. He jerked to a stop.

Molly cocked her elbows on her knees, her face in her hands. A carton of lo mein was balanced beside her, chopsticks jammed in like the naked stems of dead plants. She popped a sideways glance at him. "Hello, Garfunkel."

"Frank. My name is Frank."

"Okay, he speaks and everything. Take a load off, Frankie."

He jerked his hands out of his pockets, scuffed one shoe, dropped heavy onto the step. A foot away from her. "Thanks."

"The way you moped out the door, across the lot — looked like your faithful dog just peed on your pants leg."

"Yeah, well." Here she lounged, back after a month, and his hand still hurt. A *reminder.*

"I've had a rough week too. My feet are killing me." She dropped her hands from her face, leaned back, and held out an offending foot.

She wore spangly red heels, five inchers, not the platforms he had observed on the other women. They gleamed out at the end of her long legs like beacons in the harsh yellow light. He glanced at her face, sneaked another peek. The side of her face showed mottled and blue, disguised by beige base pancake. It resembled paisley drapes behind a foggy window.

She caught his stare, reached up to touch her cheekbone. "Rough week, like I said."

"Does it hurt?"

"Only when I open my jaw."

"I might have some aspirin on me." He dug in his pants pockets. "I gotta problem with these headaches."

"No, don't bother. I can't swallow crap like that without water anyway." Her Southern slow-motion strung out the word "crap" into a two-syllable pronouncement.

He stared straight ahead. His peripheral vision showed her stroking her cheekbone. She allowed the courtesy of silence. He settled into it, let his spine curve into a slump.

She turned toward him. He rotated his head her way. *God she's beautiful.*

She gave him a sad grin. "How about it, big guy? Ready to party? Want to take a girl out for a little boom-boom?"

Abashed. His first — well — professional, and he couldn't. "I'm so sorry. The club there." He twitched his head back. "I spent all my money for the weekend. I'm tapped till the next check."

1978 – Molly Legs

She shrugged. Her gaze fell off across the parking lot. A long sigh.

He imagined the camera panning back to show two figures on the step. The yellow light shining down from two metal shades, the moths flickering around. *This movie is called Lonely.* Attracted by the gleaming white of her satin blouse, the moths descended around them, first as a few flitting points of light. They gathered round in a roiling cloud. She batted her hands in front of her face. "Goddamn moths. I hate 'em, just hate 'em!

"They hatch out this time of year." He didn't mind their darting chaos, but he felt bad for her.

"I tell you what. You live alone? You give me a shower and a place to sleep, and I'll give you a free jobber." She pumped her fist up and down.

He should have been enchanted. A first. More than one first. His first hand job. The first time a woman visited his apartment. Maybe coffee, maybe breakfast. He asked, "What's your name?"

She grinned. It made all the difference. Her face brightened and she transformed from maybe thirty-five to twenty. He wanted to laugh out of sheer pleasure.

"It's Molly."

"Pleased to meet you, Molly."

They climbed the hill to his apartment complex, a foot of companionable darkness between them. All the way he listened to the scrape of her five-inch heels on the pavement.

1978 — Hustling The Finance Company

By late '78, Frank had picked up a GED and two years of community college at night. Those years had frittered away while he chopped out car loans for a General Motors car agency. This office job paid for Sully's with a little left over from each paycheck, and of course Chinese for Molly.

His detractors nicknamed him the Moth. His afro, his bad teeth, his eyes hidden behind big square glasses. Molly hated moths.

Frank never worked anywhere that he wasn't plagued by a dick. At the car dealership, this prick bore the name of Cornell, and was built like the double front doors of a prison block. He wore a glossy shell of hair like Bobby Sherman. Cornell loved the ladies, and enjoyed long monologues where he detailed their anatomical differences.

The day the Moth became Cornell's enemy, there in the office bull pen, they had all been seized as hostages. Their captor Cornell forced them to listen to baseball.

During the seventh-inning stretch, Cornell ambled by the Moth's workstation with its bulky monitor. He leaned over the Moth's back, grasped his shoulder. Cornell spoke into his ear, "You know, Frank, we agreed the loan would come due next week, but I could use the scratch this weekend. I'm taking Carmelita down the coast and four hundred would about cover it. Can you bounce it back on Friday?"

1978 – Hustling The Finance Company

His breath, sibilant in the Moth's ear, stank of beer and an aromatic like fried onion.

His head nodded on automatic. His own voice joined the agreement. "Okay, Friday." Cornell lumbered off to rid himself of lunchtime booze. The Moth dropped his head into his hands. He carried sixty-seven dollars in his wallet and nothing in the bank. Yes, he did have ten pilfered grand, but he had tied it up in something he called "interstate trucking." Trying to weasel even four hundred back from his partner before the load of TVs were on sale would be worse than anything Cornell could do to him.

He could smell another problem coming. Sales had slowed — fewer cars to finance. And the dealership needed fewer people anyway because of technology. Computer terminals from General Motors Acceptance Corporation had infected the dealership and all Finance was plugged into Detroit. The rumors of computer-caused layoffs flew around the place. He believed these rumors, since nobody had enough to do in front of the glowing GMAC tubes. He asked himself every day how many would leave — the second question he asked. The first — was he one of the doomed?

The Manager minced back into the room, and Cornell switched the radio off. Their boss, Delilah, a tough old biddy, had been at the dealership since the first cars rolled off the assembly line. She had a mouth like a prune and a stick figure so skinny that her double-duty ass and a small pot belly seemed pasted on.

The Moth had no idea why she had dumped him into the wilderness. He groveled as much as everyone else and told her what she wanted to hear. He even contributed the full amount when she clomped around for United Way. He toyed with the idea she'd be one of the staff with a severance. Not likely — an agency owner admitted he was her cousin. Her close cousin, like play-bridge-on-Wednesday-nights close.

The Moth

He stared over the partition, first at Her Highness behind the mahogany desk and then at Cornell, caged like a bull in his office nook. Nothing for it. He had to act, to save his teeth — and maybe his job.

He fished a folder out of his drawer, the one drawer the company allowed each employee, and journeyed up to her desk. "Delilah, can I speak to you?"

Without attending, she opened another file. "Go ahead."

"I mean, can I speak to you in private?"

She closed the folder, gazed over her half glasses at him, said, "Huh." She humphed out of her chair and led the way out of the room, down the hall into the showroom, and into a salesman's empty office. Trailing, he watched her quick steps, the skirt that pinched at the knees and flared in a ruffle. She took pride of place behind the desk. "All right. Here's your privacy."

The Moth closed the door. "I stumbled across something and I thought you ought to know. You know how we sell the car loans to GMAC and the customers pay GMAC on their notes every month?"

"It might surprise you that I do know. I run Financing, remember?"

"I figured out some of our GMAC money ships out, to a vendor who doesn't exist."

"Can you prove this? And why hasn't it shown up in bookkeeping?"

"Because the money siphoned out is matched by unexpected money flowing in from GMAC. They're paying us too much."

"How can that happen?"

"Somebody made up the files, somebody passed fraudulent loans back to Detroit. I dug them out of the system. There are at least four car sales that never happened this year."

It rocked her back. "That can't be."

In a quiet voice, he said, "Yes it can." *I've done more than four, you blind old hag.*

"How?"

"Someone invented a car — four actually. Somebody created four phony VIN numbers. GM never built those four cars, but Detroit doesn't know it. Nobody pays GMAC on the notes because the cars and the customers aren't real. Someone zeros the shortfall on the computer every month, marks the note as paid."

"So you say money is paid to us because of phony cars, but where does it come from?"

He had assumed she would twig it sooner. "GMAC pays us because of the files we built on their computer. Everybody believes the computer — it's like a god."

"Who cut the paper?"

"Cornell." At least Cornell's computer terminal account and password had.

She must have liked Cornell, based on the sad eyes, the slump in her shoulders. "Are you sure?"

"Yes. Let me show you." He opened the folder.

To Frank's surprise, Cornell had slept with his boss, Delilah, as well as his blazing Carmelita. His firing escalated to DefCon 4 — the bull roaring and the hawk screeching. The Moth's betrayal sprang into the overheated air that boiled between Cornell and Delilah, and the entire staff caught an earful. The words bouncing around the echoing ceiling and walls convinced the Moth he had miscalculated — he wasn't going to duck this one. But Cornell would — no one prosecutes office thiefs; they just get fired.

On his way out the door, Cornell allocated some time to discuss his job loss with the Moth. This encounter occurred in the employees break room, up against a Pepsi machine. On the Moth's beating scale of one to ten, he ranked this as a two. Not too bad. All the physical activity distracted Cornell enough he forgot the 4 C's until the next day. By then Moth, a purple blotched foreground on a gray wash, had pawned his deceased mother's recent-vintage TV and her antique china. Maybe he should have done that sooner, but just paying Cornell wouldn't have saved the Moth's job. A bruise taken, a debt settled, guilt cast elsewhere. All was well that ended.

1979 — Molly Redux

The Moth still carried the name Frank around, mostly. That year, after he had first met Molly and she left her scent on him, he let woeful yearning and a cheap watch run his life. This digital watch possessed an alarm. He set it for 9 p.m.

On most nights when it sounded, he'd stare at the watch for a few seconds as its annoying Japanese beeping chattered on. With a sigh, he'd turn it off. But on Saturday nights at seven, he strapped on the watch and hiked down the hill to the strip club. He visited the club as a warm-up to his week's high point.

He slipped in the back door, past the johns and the office. He claimed his place by the stage and nursed his virgin Tom Collins, and another and another as he fumbled his one dollar bills into the side of Loretta's or Carol's G string. Occasionally he could spirit the dollar straight down the thong front when one of them simpered and held it out — a peek into shadow and ambiguity.

Off-and-on for two hours, he lit up the watch and checked the time, until the alarm chattered. He popped up sixty-five dollars poorer, grinned and bowed to Loretta or Carol. He hoofed it out of the front door and next door to the Chinese restaurant, thirty minutes before they closed. He ordered General Tso's chicken for her, sweet and sour pork for himself, and carried it through the kitchen out the back door.

The Moth

Sometimes he waited ten minutes to an hour while Molly entertained a client elsewhere. That's what they both referred to — clients. Sometimes she was already parked on the concrete stoop, gazing dreamy over the gravel lot. He'd linger behind the screen door and stare at her, at the narrow set of her shoulders, the knobs of her spine where the back of her blouse scooped down, the dusky white of her skin. And only then would he deliver her dinner.

She had ten years on him. She had crinkly lines running back from her eyes and hair bundled into two pigtails — a laughable attempt to pass as an adolescent. In contrast, he might pass as a Boy Scout working on his chopsticks merit badge. He wore his anachronistic afro — high and fluttered by passing breezes. She dressed in the shiny blouses, the hot pants, the high heels of her profession. He wore baggy black pants and the unpressed shirt from his job at General Motors Finance.

He'd hand her the carton, the chopsticks hygienic in their tissue paper wrap. He'd thump down beside her. His week could begin. And end a half hour later. In only thirty minutes, she devoured the chicken, sauntered through the parking lot, and back to work on the Boulevard.

But for that half hour they visited. She mocked him. He told her about his job at the finance company. She drawled on about her childhood in Tupelo. "We rode our bicycles everywhere. Big ol' tree-shaded streets. We'd never heard the words danger or beware — at least we were too young to hear the whispers."

"My neighborhood was Chicago working-class. Plenty of trouble on our streets."

She murmured out a sigh. "My trouble was at home, with the family. My mom."

He recited weak jokes. He abhorred human touch, at least from normal people, but Molly handled him like a pet poodle. She shoved his shoulder at the punch line, dropped her hand onto

1979 – Molly Redux

his knee as she leaned forward to tell about fishing trips at night on a back river. Molly reached over and pinched his cheek if he didn't appreciate what she said enough. She scratched the back of his hand if his pun ran more than usually atrocious. "A bike can't stand alone because it's two-tired" cost him a dotted line of oozing blood. He watched the crooked grin tease the corner of her mouth and imagined his own smile as a hundred watt beam lighting his imbecilic face.

Four times that winter when the temperature dropped too low for her to work, she commanded the warmth of his worn apartment. Little Wheezy's supervision had loosened up — and besides, Wheezy's Italian ass froze too.

They would tramp up the hill together, his arm around her because — he told her — both man and working girl could freeze solid.

Three in the morning, the coldest day L.A. experienced in '79. They nested in his bed after the sex. After a while, he prepared macaroni and cheese from a box. Molly perched on an old metal stool he had snagged in a garage sale, her elbows on the counter. Snorting, she had shoved his tattered copy of Michener's *Chesapeake* aside.

Her hands cradled a cup of coffee. Draped in his seedy blue-striped bathrobe with her makeup scrubbed off, she showed her age, but regardless, he sneaked peeks at her arms, her hands, her legs. She swung her head around the room as she gauged and catalogued. "My Momma and Daddy had a big ol' house, with two hundred years of furniture. Did I ever tell you my Daddy ended up a preacher?"

His head twitched, like electricity juiced his neck. "A minister?"

"Sure. Granddaddy fixed it such that Daddy would be assigned to a Baptist Church in our poky town, because Grandma wanted him close. Not *the* Baptist Church, just *a* Baptist church. Tupelo. Nothing there ever changed for the worse."

"In L.A., nothing ever changes for the better."

Her Tupelo voice drawled out, "I don't know. Bad things happen even in a world that seems perfect. And good things happen even in the garbage pile." She rubbed at a place on the counter where the Formica had been scratched to white. "Did you ever hope for anything better?"

He knew what she saw. Besides the couch with the sinkholes in the cushions and the two lamps rescued off the curb, he owned precious little to brag about. He had liberated his only painting from a motel while they were closed for a bedbug infestation. As for the apartment, the kitchen hunkered smack dab in the front door and the breakfast bar separated it from the living room. Two inside doors led to a bathroom and a ten-by-ten bedroom. The apartment boasted no closet, just a clothes rack behind a sheet. But it did possess an immense water stain shaped like a nebula across the ceiling, and also a front window darkened by ligustrum bushes. He said, "Maybe we could spend the night at your place instead."

"Are you kidding? I share with two roommates and they use the place for business."

He refilled her tea glass. "I'd like a nicer apartment, but I'm paying off the hospital for Mom. I'm only twenty-seven. It'll get better."

"My place is a dump too. It drags me down sometimes. The only nice things I have are my working clothes, but I can't wear those to the supermarket."

He could well believe her place resembled a dump, as he gazed around at what she had done to his. While searching for her lip gloss, she left her carpetbag of a purse with its contents spilled across the coffee table. Her short jacket she dropped by the front door. Her blouse and miniskirt lay balled up on the couch. One shoe capsized on its side in the bedroom doorway. In a few minutes, when she slid off back to bed, he'd gather everything and launder her underwear and her miniskirt in the kitchen sink with Woolite. They would half-dry in the bathroom and he'd press them crisp. His secret scheme imprisoned her semi-naked in his apartment, even though she would spend most of the time asleep.

She picked at the imperfections in his counter with a red fingernail. "God, I wish you owned a nice little house. I'd love a bungalow I could run off to, disappear from my apartment — my job — my pimp."

Aah! *Need a house.* Money. General Motors Finance could afford it, wouldn't even miss it in the bigger picture. He'd need a better credit rating too. Yes. A cottage, a lawn, a life.

1980 — You Bet

The Moth didn't like bars much, but every Friday at noon he scrunched into a booth in Uncle Sandro's. Besides claiming the title "Uncle" for East L.A., Alejandro *was* Julio's tío. The bar lit up with harsh fluorescents that painted a dismal picture. Cheap vinyl paneling in a chocolate brown covered all the walls and the base of the bar, so walnut-dark, it caused Julio to appear white, or maybe yellow — the lemon-green color on corpses in city morgues. Julio leaned over the gouged wood table, showed the Moth a piece of lined notebook paper with dense black scrawls. The page corner had trailed through a beer ring and hung limp and translucent. Julio said, "We'll hit Rosarito and the warehouse about five, load up, and head back north. That shoots Saturday. We'll deliver Sunday. Here's the list of the guys who called for a restock."

For a year the Moth had partnered with his old friend Julio, who was off on holiday between jail terms. They reinvented a simple enough scheme — they drove cases of tequila and mescal from Rosarito and handed them in the back doors of bodegas. They stocked barbecue restaurants with ersatz bourbon. They dumped Mexican scotch and vodka into circulation in bistros, saloons, upscale restaurants, and cheap Italian eateries. The Moth said, scratchy for once, "That many drops, we'll be working through Sunday night. Monday I'm back at work — worn out and with no sleep."

Julio laid the list out, drew a line between two names with a Sharpie. "We'll quit after Arnie's. Stack the rest of it in your apartment until Monday night. Deal?"

"Sure. Deal." That whiny sound in his own voice. Huge margin, because the booze was created from grain alcohol and flavoring. The Moth needed margin. It had paid off the colossal debt he had owed to County General for his mother. Now it piled up until he had enough stake to buy Molly a house.

Solemn and sad women in a warehouse across the border doped and diluted the alcohol and filled the empty high-end bottles Julio and the Moth transported across the border to them. Julio piloted them down; the Moth drove back from Mexico, since he was the white. Sometimes a bottle would tour to Mexico and back five times before it turned too grungy to pass inspection. Julio used a simple criteria. "Beat to hell, like shit, man. We throw this one out."

The Moth asked, "Should we swing past your cousin's for tax stamps?" Julio worked through every case in the back of the van to paste on counterfeit labels.

"Nah, still five hundred in the truck." Julio insisted on these tax stamps as camouflage. He repeatedly said, "I tell you man, if they think it's the real thing, you can bribe your way out of anything — just hand them a case."

"Okay, we're set. Pick me up at the apartment the usual time." The Moth acknowledged Julio did most of the work and knew the southern connections. But the Moth brought his share. He had developed the list of L.A. customers when he had crosschecked profession with late payment in the GMAC system. A bar owner behind in his car payments — a friend for life.

The Moth

The night beat cool and dark against his cheek, the window down as The Moth drove north on I-15 after he had skulked along on Highways 1 and 125. As they crossed under the freeway lights, the stars hung in the beyond, invisible. At least he believed they swept the night sky.

A long haul, but they planned two stops before unloading the van — big orders. He and Julio would have less to empty out of the van into his apartment. He wouldn't eat Chinese with Molly tonight. *Money or Molly — a harsh choice.*

The route down the alley stretched two hundred feet. The Moth steered down the dusty track — his van crushed a couple of bags dragged out into the path by crows and spread out for the picking. A dumpster across the alley stopped him. Julio leapt out, trudged around, and banged on the back door of the bar. A bright light hung off a utility pole overhead.

The Moth wrestled cases to the sliding van door, checked the list as his heart thudded from the work. He straightened up as erect as he could within the van — Julio hadn't showed, was taking his own sweet time. Through the windshield the Moth could peer through a narrow slot across the dumpster top. Julio — braced in the alley with two men, at attention.

Slump-shouldered and with a lizard's horizontal neck, Julio never stood upright like that. He held his hands interlocked on top of his head. A long barrel swept into view — a shotgun! Rip off!

Glancing back over his shoulder, the Moth discovered a man in the van door. A guy with a triangular face, a ridiculous mustache. A black pistol waved back and forth in a lazy arc.

The guy's voice boomed out an improbable bass. "Hands in the air, asshole. Drop to your knees."

Drop to my knees? And get shot in the back of my head? The Moth dived over the back of the driver's seat, clawed at the door handle with both hands. A shockwave buffeted the van. His hearing cut out. *Have I been hit?*

The Moth spilled headfirst into the alley, windmilled to his feet. The alley, bereft of anything but loose trash, stretched out in a long skinny death zone without any cover. He scooted around the driver door, glanced up where the windshield had shattered like white cobwebs. The dumpster lids were thrown back, the garbage heaped high. He flung himself over the edge like a teenage high jumper. The trash cushioned his body and tore at his legs. Something sharp grazed his skull — he glanced at a snapped-off broom handle. He burrowed.

The more shouting, the more noise he caught, the more he willed his heart to slow, his breath to wait a minute, an hour, a day. The van roared, doors slammed. It backed down the alley. The loud engine, the metallic scraping of fenders against the cinderblocks.

Quieter in the dumpster. The trash pressed against him; its cacophony of smell dug into his nose, forcing him to dizziness. Unhooked from gravity.

Dragging feet, scraping gravel. A bang on the dumpster edge. A panting voice — Julio's. "Ju in there? Ju alive in there?"

The Moth raised his head, a turtle emerging from his garbage shell. "I'm here."

"You been shot?"

The Moth inventoried himself. Nothing hurt. He kneaded his chest — no pain. "No, man. He missed. How did you know I was in here?"

Julio had a black patch smeared across his forehead, a slash of blood caked over his cheek. He reached up to it, his hand vague and wobbly. "I know you even if they don't. You'd hide before you'd run."

The booze, the van, the paper bag of money. "Sorry, Julio. I quit. I can't do this anymore."

Julio sagged against the dumpster. "Bueno. Believe me, I understand."

"Good. It's not worth it. I'm ten years older, all in five minutes. I actually shit myself."

Julio's grin twitched into his face, slid to a grimace as he dabbed at his forehead with his fingertips. "But."

"But what?"

Julio shook his head, winced. "You owe me for your half of the van."

The van someone else was driving.

This year alone, the Moth had scratched up twenty G's. Not quite enough for a house with his credit rating. He wanted the money to grow.

For a short while the Moth believed in regulated, legal capitalism and invested the twenty in the stock market. Within fifteen weeks, the Moth's broker bankrupted him and his belief in legal enterprises. Maybe the broker bled him dry through the commissions, maybe he had shit judgment. Either way, the Moth was tapped. His conviction? — "legal" meant rigged and "illegal" understood its own methods and goals. He commenced again with a new night job, as far from Julio and gunfire as he could arrange.

The Moth showed up for work for his second job at 11 p.m. and worked until 4 a.m. Work occurred behind a steel door off a back parking lot. The lot bordered back doors for a package liquor, a dry cleaners, a thrift shop, and an auto parts store. Opening *his* door revealed a man with a gun and a baseball bat who either damaged you or let you in. A dim staircase ascended to a busy office over the auto store. The loft held ten or so desks, each garnished with a phone and small yellow tablets of paper — the betting slips. Three walls were ornamented with the regime of betting — the fourth held two windows covered in dusty venetian blinds.

The management had shoved a copy machine, three shredders, and a table against the left wall. On the table, two guys packed bundles of cash into book cartons. The table also held bill counters — machines that could riff through a thousand dollars in twenties in a second. Men trooped up the stairs throughout the night, with gym bags full of green, and exchanged the money for new names. They slid off into the night to collect or sometimes to pay off.

The Moth worked in a book — a bookie shop in a town where authorities seldom discouraged illicit gambling. The Book was big-time, competed with three others that all lay within ten square miles.

The phones, the voices, the money counters all created an appalling racket, but the Moth endured. He had to earn more than the twenty grand back; so far he had racked up 5K out of the work here. The twenty plus represented his future and the key to romantic dreams. So he suffered through the exhaustion, the unhygienic co-workers, other people's incessant need to share their lives with him. At least border guards weren't jerking him around and he wasn't robbed of bartenders' cash.

His desk squatted close to the long wall, back in a corner. Track lighting splashed the wall in front of him, revealed the games and the odds — this book specialized in college and professional sports and left horse racing to the legal OTBs. The phone rang — he picked it up. "Abercrombie's." The code name this month.

"This is Slidell 22. Put me down for the Rams." Slidell called in regular, had a credit line, and currently carried five G's in debt.

"Hey, Slide. How much?"

"A deuce. What's the spread today?"

The Moth

The Moth peered at the crisp board, white chalk on black. "Ten against the 49ers."

"Jeez. Give a guy a break. The Rams aren't that good and the Niners aren't that bad."

The Moth grinned into the beige phone. "Yes they are. And you know I don't set the odds."

"Bastard. I'll call you later tonight."

"Sure thing, Slide." He had scribbled "June 20 80: Slidell22, $200 on the Rams." He handed the slip to the black kid close by. "Eustace, pass this back."

Eustace's hair showed as a three inch rise with a lightning bolt cut into the side. He grinned and handed the Moth two sheets of paper. "Sho. Here's an update on the guys we don't cover 'cause they owe us."

The Moth waved his hand. "Okay." He tore the old two pages off the desk top, wadded them, and dropped them in the can by the desk. He seized a roll of Scotch Tape and installed Eustace's pages in front of him.

The phone rang. And the phone rang. At 3 a.m., he crumpled his paper coffee cup and dropped it into the trash. His stomach simmered, a boiler of acid that worked up an excuse to hurt him. The coffee tasted like iron filings in his mouth. The phone rang.

Like the phone bell had triggered it, the door blew open with a eardrum-busting detonation. It flew out of its frame. The door struck Teddy the Guard, mowed him down. Buried him on the floor. The men who charged in — each face masked in a bandana. The Moth's eyes flicked across the masks — didn't count the number of men. His sight focused on the guns they carried, as if the metal threatened him.

Achiote, the boss on the money table, lit up the room with his semi-auto pistol. He crunched off shot after shot. A shit aim — he only clipped one attacker. Achiote fumbled with the magazine, struggled to reload — he caught a shotgun blast in the chest. That did it for the Moth. Sprinting across the room away from the back door, he tucked his chin down and leapt. His slight frame crashed into the front window; his forearms absorbed the crumpling blinds and the glass as it shattered. The metal crossbar hammered his ribcage but ripped loose.

He tumbled to the metal auto store awning. The cheesy tin split and he crashed to the sidewalk, his toes and knees first, then his extended hands. His wrists ached like they were being electrocuted, but he struggled to his feet anyway. Blood had slicked his arms, and he stared at them. Blackish in the half-light, adagio dripping onto the sidewalk.

Sirens moaned, grew louder. The Moth ran. Bolted towards safety and away from the twenty G's.

1981 — Mortgage on the Bungalow

By late summer of 1981, he possessed the house, a mortgage, and a battered AMC Gremlin — because of the distance between work and the cottage. Only six years old, the car had eighty thousand miles on the clock. Somebody had run it up and down the beach and the fenders rusted from the inside out. But he had to buy it. Once he dumped his apartment and relocated to the house, he could no longer hike to the strip club or the Chinese restaurant.

He wanted to spring the surprise on her, a car and a house. At ten in the evening — a warm summer night with a fragrance of passion, he rumbled down the hill. An obnoxious smoke, he knew, oozed from the tailpipe. He drove back and forth twice, on watch. Little Wheezy not yet there to suck up her money — why bother, since she always turned it over?

She hated the car. Hip cocked out in an uncompromising stance, on the curb by the boulevard edge, under the glaring streetlamp, she said, "God, Frankie. It's snot green. I'll never ride in it."

He caressed the hood, looked at her standing under the light. The women hung back. Either they believed him a paying customer, or they had a soft spot for Molly. He sidled up to her, taking advantage. "At night, when it's dark, no one can see you. No one really sees the color."

1981 – Mortgage on the Bungalow

"I see it."

"I'll buy spray paint. What color do you want?"

"Blue. But why bother? As if I hang around with you a lot."

She said she wouldn't ride in it. But she'd admit she sometimes spent the night with him. The Moth considered this a step forward, since she didn't even confess to an off-the-books relationship. *Start small, work up.*

He said, "I could drive you home more, at the end of your shift. *My* home that is. At least on Sunday mornings."

"It ain't winter, Frankie. I work until two, meet with Little Wheezy and turn over his take. He drops me at my apartment. The regular drill."

Little Wheezy — her pimp, also head panderer for her two roommates and another girl. The Moth had spied on him from afar. Little Wheezy had everything the Moth didn't: a barrel-shaped body of fat and muscle, a deeply Italian flair, fat glistening lips, an evil and intimidating smile. The Moth no longer dwelt on Little Wheezy — it upset him so much it gave him the shakes. The knife in his pocket was no comfort — he had cut himself once fiddling with it.

An impresario, the Moth flourished his hand. "I could pick you up at your place and drive you back to my new house."

"House." A flat voice.

"House. It's about ten miles away."

"You bought a house? No shit?" She linked her arm in his, leaned into his shoulder. "When can I visit?"

"It's not ready to live in yet. I'm still painting. But I could show it to you right now if you want."

She laughed, a burst of glee. "A house! I'd love to check it out. But I'm working."

Now she'll ride in the car. "Maybe I could cover the half hour for you."

"That could work. I'll need seventy-five for Little Wheezy. And we have to be back quick."

"Let's make it an hour. I have your Chinese in the car — you can eat dinner early — he allows that and he doesn't have to know it's in the car." *The world run on Wheezy's rules.*

A dropout, the Moth had never squired a date to the prom in high school. He imagined the prom date would have been something like this. He peeled the passenger door open — it groaned. She stepped forward, slid her bottom into the seat, clinched her knees together and swung them. Those calves and the green glittering shoes flashed at him. He eased the door shut, hopped into the driver's seat, and drove her off on his adolescent adventure.

Now that he had her at the house, he could view it the way she did. It had suffered worse than the neighborhood. It boasted no porch, only a concrete stoop that shouldered out into the yard, with a shed roof overhead that peeled away from the house-front, about to fall. The screens over the windows sagged, rent with holes. A dead tree towered over the house like an omen. He parked on the naked dirt before the stoop.

She said, "Jesus Christ, Frankie! It looks like the Bates Motel."

"It's better inside. I haven't touched the outside yet." He ran around the car to open her door. He snatched his reward — a snapshot up her miniskirt as it hugged her lovely legs.

He unlocked the front door and seized her hand as they crossed the threshold. He flipped the light on. "Living room." It lay naked before them, all the molding around the doors, the floor and the cornice an old varnished brown, the new paint a shiny ivory that perfumed the air.

1981 – Mortgage on the Bungalow

One wall had yet to be touched — the wallpaper, covered in bursts of faded roses, drooped off the wall or had been torn off in patches. She ambled over to it and tugged away another tatter. "Was it all like this? You've accomplished a hell of a lot."

He inclined his head. "I slap up a primer. And I use enamel for good coverage."

A small living room, just like his resources, about sixteen-by-twenty. The dining space lurked at the end, illuminated by a fake Tiffany hanging lamp. No table crouched beneath it.

He escorted her through the entire house: the tiny kitchen with an old-fashioned refrigerator, the enclosed back porch, the backyard full of junk and a rusting hulk of a 1950s car, the two bedrooms. Everywhere they skirted brushes and rollers, paint cans and trays.

The master bedroom held the only thing new in the house — a king-sized extravaganza of a bed with an upholstered headboard of tufted cloth, inset with gold buttons. He had bought six big pillows and three small ones, heaped up like a mountain range at the head of the bed. She nudged him, "You slap satin sheets on this baby?"

He bobbed his head.

"Black or white?"

"Baby blue. I'll paint the walls blue."

She plumped herself on the bed, leaned back and crossed her legs, to show them off like a pantyhose commercial. "Oo, I could do this." She flopped back and stretched her arms above her head.

He yearned to lie beside her. He eased forward a step, leaned near with his hands on the coverlet.

She leapt up. "God, Frankie, it's wonderful. Or it will be." She spun around in a pirouette. Her hooker heels flashed under the bare lightbulb.

"I hoped you'd like it."

"The thing I like the most is that it's miles and miles away from the Boulevard."

"Will you stay here some? Or a lot?"

She swept down the hall into the living room, the Moth trailing behind. "Gee, I don't know. It could be like a mini-vacation once a month on Sunday. From the hooking. From Little Wheezy. I could sleep all day here, wrapped in a cocoon of sheets and blankets."

"Maybe more than once a month?"

"I can only give you one of my days off. The other three days my real life hangs over me, all those things piled up to do. But you could pick me up after work on Saturday, maybe mid-morning and I'd hang around until evening. Or we can run errands." She sneezed from the fumes. A messy sneeze. She cupped it in her hand below her nose.

He dug around in his pockets. Nothing. He dashed into the '30s bathroom and trotted back with two feet of toilet paper. She snuffled, wiped her hand, blew her nose. She handed the white gauzy paper back to him.

He cupped it in his hand, her snot-covered toilet paper dampening his palm. "Maybe go one better than Saturdays. Maybe you could quit and move in full-time. Give up the streets before it's too late."

Her amusement rang out like a clanging bell. "You're kidding, of course."

He dropped his head as the blood rushed into his face.

"Awww, you did mean it. That's sooo sweet."

The sugary, slow Mississippi voice melted his heart. He could feel his binding ribs, his breath locked out of his chest.

"But I don't think so. I'll never actually *live* with a man again. My ex taught me that."

She'd never mentioned a husband or a long-term boyfriend. He

1981 – Mortgage on the Bungalow

could endure the clients, and choked on the pimp added to it — but a husband? He'd forever be last in line. "Molly." Her name ground out as a croak.

She grabbed him by the cheek, nipped him with her grandmother pinch. "Silly boy. Did you think we'd be June and Ward Cleaver? Now, the street's calling me back. Give me the seventy-five and drive me down the hill."

So ripping off GM's money for the down payment hadn't changed much. Not that he could stop, now that he lived with the payment. He'd settle for one Sunday a month. Only twelve nights a year, plus some Saturdays.

1981 — Molly Comes To Stay

In 1981, a two-year-old song about a whore named Roxanne hung in the charts like an angel hovering over Bethlehem. The Moth hated it. He had romanced his hooker for three years. He had discovered that this long-legged horse of a woman wouldn't surrender her independence. He accepted it, but he couldn't understand. After all, she yielded her sovereignty to a dangerous toad named Little Wheezy. It was so bad, Wheezy now kept everything and paid her bills, slipped her pocket money when *he* deemed she needed it. But she did put out for the Moth, a kind of recreational sex.

Christmas time in a couple of weeks and the temperature hung in the low 80's. Like many Sundays, the Moth perched on the dresser four feet in the air at the foot of the bed, for no reason other than to contemplate her. Asleep, she appeared vulnerable and sweet, with no trace of the hardness and edgy fleeting expressions of her waking hours. Asleep, her hair — a tangled yellow — floated across the pillow. It resembled the water grass from a city park of his childhood, flowing out from the dark brown part on the side of her head. Asleep, she might have been his.

Genetics left her face more round than the angular Scandinavian style, but the cheekbones stood out like carvings. He believed her nose a bit pug and her skin color, untouched by sunshine, dusky rather than white. Probably Slavic. Or Genghis Khan's many-times-great-granddaughter, to bring in that olive tone. But she might be descended from a rich slave owner and a housemaid long ago — the South had its patterns.

He hopped off the dresser when the chime rang quiet through the house. In his enclosed back porch, he rummaged her clothes out of the dryer and sorted things out into his paper grocery sacks. He lingered over her everyday underwear — he claimed the soft cotton. The silkies belonged to her profession. Using a warm iron, he pressed out the wrinkles in her hot pants and her favorite miniskirt, and folded everything before he nestled it into the bag.

In the kitchen, as the clock signaled six, he heated take-out minestrone soup. He ladled it up, carried it into the bedroom, and woke her. "Molly, it's time."

Her eyes snapped open, vigilant. Reassured by his geeky face, she yawned and flitted back the sheet. She stretched; he caught his breath. The afternoon sun streamed through the venetian blind and across her body, outlined her against the headboard. Her voice, now that she had unwound from waking, flowed slow like Southern molasses. "Soup. That's good. Last Saturday that pasta lay in my belly like lead. Obliged me to fart at the wrong time. My customer dropped limp as a string."

"Yes. You told me." *Twice.*

She cradled the bowl on her knees and brought her face close — the spoon traversed a few inches, back and forth.

She handed him the bowl. "Fantastic soup. Barolo's is a great restaurant — wish I could eat there all the time. Gotta hit the shower." She threw her legs over the bed side, sauntered by him as naked as the innocent child, and squeezed his shoulder. "Frankie, you're too good to me. I ought to screw you twice on Saturdays."

The Moth

On Fridays he shopped for her. On Sudays he packed the food over to her place, as he drove her to work. He wanted it all to arrive in her refrigerator as fresh as possible — so he waited till he heard the hair dryer. He filled two grocery sacks: canned tuna, fresh celery, cream cheese, ten cartons of yogurt. Odd bits she asked for, like potato rolls. A dozen eggs and a package of bacon. He worried the protein and fat would end up tucked inside her new roommate. *Are the roommates ripping me off?* He carried groceries and laundry out to the rear seat of his blue Gremlin, plunked himself in the kitchen to wait.

She strode in like marching to war and poured her cosmetics out of a bulky zip bag onto the table. As she peered into a hand compact and applied the garish cosmetics he loved so much, she chattered. "Did I ever tell you about the time Mamma drove us over to Bayou Plaquemine? This was a time when she acted like a normal mother. She wasn't in therapy or anythin', but she had stopped hurting my little brother. And she let me — you know — sleep by myself instead of calling me into her bed and mo-lesting me. She hauled us over non-stop and we checked into this motel down by the water. I guess it was a dump, but you know, when you're a kid...."

"I do know. Everything new has a magic." The Moth had never been on a vacation. "How old were you?"

"Eleven. I loved the varnished pine walls. The TV was crap, but it was summer and we played outside on the grass by the water until dusk every evening, until the mosquitoes buzzed out in swarms."

He inclined his head like a benediction. "Long, long days. The sun sinking down across the water."

"We ate in diners, real old-fashioned diners, all up and down the parish. Have you ever been in that kind?"

"L.A. has a few diners."

"Naw, not those chains, and not that god-awful railroad-car one.

1981 – Molly Comes To Stay

Family places." She painted on an eighth-inch wide bar of eyeliner. "These looked like they'd been built years ago by the daddy and his buddies. Daddy cooked and the sisters worked the tables while Ma ran the register. Fried food, that's what I remember. And not just the seafood."

He leaned his chin on his hands. "I'm partial to fried fish myself."

She glued on the second eyelash. "With hush puppies. And slaw. Anyway, Mamma acted decent to us for the whole two weeks. On the last night she plowed into the wine until she was really drunk and weepy. All about how he shouldn't have left her, our daddy. But he didn't leave us — he died. She turned to yanging about what monsters we were and the trouble we caused her. She beat my brother with the belt. Worse than usual — with the buckle. Lucky for him it was plastic that time, so there weren't any stitches, only the scrapes. But I'll always remember the two good weeks."

"Your Mom writes here to the house. Two new letters this month."

She attacked her knotted yellow hair with a brush. "I should never have let her know where I was. Burn the letters. Burn 'em all."

He wouldn't though. They piled up in the desk.

"I don't blame my daddy. I left too, as soon as my brother graduated high school. At least I didn't have to die like Daddy to escape."

But hooking must be a little death. He offered, "I had trouble with my parents too."

"Really? I thought they were perfect, the way you keep quiet about them." She did know how to tweak him.

He said, "My Dad kept a string of neighborhood women jumping in and out of bed. It had to be our neighbors of course, so my ma and I'd both know. And my ma and me, we didn't have a lot in common. We were polite, but... "

"You took care of her, that last year."

The old-world apologetic voice, the withered flesh, the mutual shame. "Yes, I was there."

Molly patted his hand. "You be there for me."

He couldn't endure this — like a portent. "The car's already packed."

She slipped on her five inch heels, the blue ones with the white silhouette of a naked woman on the toe cap. "Come on, shake a leg. You can drive me to my apartment to drop everything off. Then to work."

Work meant a particular block in East L.A. She conducted transactions at the Grenadier Hotel, one of the most ludicrous names he'd ever heard. He gathered her makeup and tucked it in the bag. He had to ask. "How about staying here this Sunday?"

She frowned at him like he was the village idiot. "Horny, huh? Frankie, I've told you many times, I don't do it on Sunday mornings. It's a sin." Even now she loved her dead daddy the preacher. She didn't attend church or anything, but she lived by this rule.

"We don't have to make love. You can just hang around here. Enjoy your day off."

"Naah. I told my roommate I'd dye her hair."

He hated that roommate. "You don't have to work at all. You could live here, live safe."

"Poor Frankie. You think there's anywhere in the world that's safe?"

He knew by the third time he met her — Little Wheezy beat her periodically to keep her in line. Wheezy's fists and boot had once provided the Moth an extra Sunday. His good luck smelled more like guilt.

It began with one of the best Saturdays they had spent together. Molly rolled in off the street full of energy, with no desire to go to bed and sleep the day away. She whipped up mustard potato salad and sent him out to the twenty-four-hour grocery for ham and rolls.

1981 – Molly Comes To Stay

According to her, they would act like normal people. They spent the morning at the L.A. Arboretum and gazed at things green "rather than that Christ-forsaken concrete boulevard." They picnicked and lay on the scratchy Arboretum grass in the pale fall sunshine.

Saturday night into Sunday she slept for eighteen hours. But come the evening, she hiked back into the meat farm.

The Moth's shuttle service whisked her to her place, and then back down into the avenues and boulevards. A half-hour before dusk, he dropped her as she insisted the half block away, back from the corner and the sidewalk she inhabited. The peeling paint on the buildings, graffiti scrawled across the walls, even a boarded-up window — but she brought style to it all the way up the block. He knew later, under the light at the corner, she'd stand out like a painting by that Hopper guy. As she strutted her stuff all the way to the corner, he watched her tush in those hot pants, swinging above long legs and high-heeled shoes, the blonde hair sailing out to the side. He experienced the slash of anguish and a sad variation on lust.

Sunday evenings tormented him and this one turned out no different. He listened to his radio in the kitchen, tuned up and down the bands. He spent a moment with an evangelist, caught ten minutes of a ball game, listened to a debate on municipal water in San Diego. No music, just talk. By ten, he twitched with his own desperation. He shuffled into old clothes and worked at framing out a closet in the second bedroom — for her clothes, if she'd allow any of them in the house.

At two, he leapt out of bed to answer the phone. His heart thudded. He had no friends — no one had any reason to call him. It had to be bad. "Can I help you?" Absurd words — the joke on him.

"Yes." Molly's voice — a hesitation, a catch in a drawl that tried to hide the pleading. "I'm at the motel. Room Sixteen. Please, come and pick me up." It scared him stiff.

The Moth

The Gremlin slid around corners, bulleted through stop signs without qualms. He reached the Grenadier in fifteen minutes. At the only parking spot available, the tires slammed into the concrete bumper. He thudded past five doors, lurched around two whores and their customers. Sixteen waited with the door ajar.

She lay curled on the bed. He touched her shoulder. "Molly?"

She rolled her head up to search his face.

He chronicled the damage. A bloody nose. An eye already darkening. A split lip.

"Help me sit."

Bad, but not awful. He eased her up, his hands on her upper arms. She curled around the pain that boiled off her. He'd been wrong. Worse than he had hoped. "What is it? What did Little Wheezy do?"

"Kicked me. I broke a rib."

Tears salted the corners of his eyes — he strangled a sob. "No. *He* broke your rib."

"Drive me to your house, Frankie. I can't work like this."

"You shouldn't have to work anyway. I'll kill him!" That little knife had waited in his pocket for three years.

"Frankie, you're sooo sweet. But you could no more kill Wheezy than you could kill the President."

In the house that he had robbed for, bought, fixed up, provided for her when she deigned to visit, he taped her ribs. Long white skeins of tape bound her to him.

Out on the boulevard, Little Wheezy worked his other women. The Moth could wait for his chance. *The hyena will get his.*

1981 – Molly Comes To Stay

Their lives, Molly and Frank, intersected across Saturdays and Sundays, but it all fell apart late on Wednesday, Hump Day, though most days were hump day. The Moth slept, dived deep, dreamed about a room with a black door that man after man tramped through. The door opened and closed like a metronome, shutting him out. A ringing phone — maybe trouble, maybe Molly. Stunned by sleep in that dark bedroom, he answered like some store or business. "Frank here. What can we do for you?"

Little Wheezy's horror of a voice crawled up the wire into his ear. "I found your number in her book. She told me about you, how handy you are. If you're ever going to help her, get over here now. The Grenadier, Sixteen."

The door presented a black, scarred face to the world. The Moth's legs wobbled as he rapped on it. The door creaked open, revealed the pimp, the lamplit wall, someone on the bed — concealed behind the fat man's bulk. Little Wheezy said, "Get in here." He jerked the Moth forward into the room and locked the door.

Someone had tied his Molly to the posts of the cheap headboard. She lay naked except for her panties. Her hands hung loose, the rope knotted around her wrists. Her head lolled on her chest. The shape of crucifixion. Her legs stretched out in front of her, her knees splayed apart, showed the crotch of her underwear. Black tape walled up her mouth and her eyes hid in the shadow of her hair.

Leaning hard into the Moth's shoulder, Little Wheezy coughed. "She's dead."

The Moth's feet steered him to the bed. His shuffle over lasted an eternity. Burns ran down her arms and across her breasts. On a table by the bed, an ashtray full of butts. The Moth stared at her, shook like a tree in a windstorm. He reached for her wrist and tried to summon a pulse, but his hand quivered. Her skin flowed with warmth, not the hot fever she sometimes threw off, but not yet the clamminess approaching.

A bullet had dug right into the center of her chest, with an entry wound no thicker than the Moth's little finger. He stared at the purple bruise around the blackish, gore-clotted hole. No blood in front, but the sheets bunched behind her splashed red, crimson. The Moth choked out, "Did you do this?"

"No, man! It wasn't my fault."

"You bastard. One way or another you killed her."

"No, no! She didn't come back to the corner — I thought she was screwing off, so I hustled over to check on her. The john sat right here, burning her nipple. I whipped out my gun. He charged me. Hit me hard and cold-cocked me against the door jamb. The bullet hit her, not him. When I came to, he was long gone."

Wheezy's words were muffled, strained through the cotton wool in the Moth's head. It could be a lie. Or not. But Wheezy had killed her. The Moth's heart hammered in his chest. He eased himself onto the bed, beside her. His knee touched her hip. Little Wheezy's words rumbled on, but the Moth didn't grasp anything. He reached to her face and peeled the tape away, a gentle tugging. The Moth reached into her mouth and fished out a rag, sodden with saliva. With his thumb he rubbed away the grubby adhesive left behind by the tape. The Moth lifted her face by the chin and stared into her fixed eyes. He thumbed her eyelids shut, caressing them.

Little Wheezy shifted across the room behind him, restless. He jiggled the Moth's shoulder. The Moth shrugged him off.

Frank allowed her face to droop, touched his lips to her forehead. He untied her wrists, the left, the right. Left her hands palms up and open in her lap. But he didn't cry. "Did the customer have a name?"

"The john? A pervert named Estevan Faro."

Time hung like a dirty cloud in the room. "Why am I here?"

"Two reasons. One, you're going to help me kill the sick bastard. Two, I shot one of my own girls. I can't let the cops know. We got to move her. Hide her."

The Moth slumped on the edge of the bed. *Hide her. The shit wants to hide her. Hide Molly.* He groped in his pocket for his knife — he had left it at home.

Wheezy grabbed him by the arm. "Come on, man. Get it together. We got to dump the broad."

The broad. The Moth stared into his face. "Okay. You're right. First, give me the gun. I'll ditch it."

"That's more like it." Little Wheezy passed him the revolver.

The gun hung heavy in his hand, smooth and cold. The Moth stared into his face. Little Wheezy's dark jowls. His black eyes. The scowl that could back down a pit bull.

Wheezy turned away, to Molly. "Your car parked close? Drive it up to the door."

The Moth rose, slow. The shakes had died. He picked up a pillow. Held it in front of the muzzle. He shot Little Wheezy in the back of the head from four inches away. A quick snap, another, another.

Now he had to dump Wheezy. The pimp defiled Molly as he sprawled by the bedside. They might search the Moth's house. But his neighbor had driven home to Texas for a couple of weeks. First he moved his car, just like Wheezy had suggested. He wrapped Wheezy's bloody mess of a head in a threadbare pillow case and dragged the hulk of the body out to his car. The Moth threw in the shower curtain, rolled the pimp into the Gremlin's back and slammed the hatch. The weight didn't trouble him — he could have picked up a truck. Maybe someone noticed him, maybe not. But — nobody had made the call after the first shot.

Once he had driven Wheezy to his street and leaned him up in the neighbor's lawnmower shed, he changed clothes, scrubbed his hands raw, and returned to the motel. For three hours he sat vigil. Then the call to the police.

"Okay, dude, let's go over it one more time." One uniformed cop fit the big-white-policeman stereotype, military-cut hair above pink scraped jowls. Another policeman appeared Chinese but sounded like a California high-schooler. The third cop — a blond woman, Ray-Ban sunglasses propped up in the middle of her forehead — leaned against the wall. She watched her two compatriots play big men. They didn't arrest him, even though he was the only live one there.

Why didn't they spot the evidence all over the room? The Moth had wiped her face and body, but the bed, the headboard were spattered by Wheezy's death. "She phones when she finishes work. She didn't call, so I drove down here to check. Her pimp sometimes beats her."

The white cop yawned. "When did you arrive here?"

"Maybe three." *Tell as much of the truth as you can.*

The Chinese cop leaned against the scarred bureau. "So, Kemo Sabe, why didn't you call until morning." It wasn't even a question, merely a narration.

"I wanted to sit with her." *Tell as much of the truth as you can.*

The jowled cop pointed his pencil at the Moth. "How do we know you didn't kill her in a jealous rage?"

"I was her friend. Nothing more." *I prayed for more.*

The cop ripped out a belly laugh, an ugly sound. "Why the hell should I believe that?"

1981 – Molly Comes To Stay

"Because I'm a homosexual."

"You know we can check that out."

The Moth knew they wouldn't bother, not over a hooker — unless they linked him in deeper. "It had to be the pimp. His name is Little Wheezy. He beat her."

The Asian cop snickered. "So where is this pimp? You shoot him, stash the body?"

The Moth hunkered over, his hands in his lap, said nothing.

The white cop slapped the Moth on the top of the head. "Let's take this down to the precinct. You may be clean — you may be the killer. Either way the Suits will wanna talk to you."

The policewoman flicked herself off the wall that had supported her all this time. She sauntered for the door, stopped as she crossed opposite him. Leaning down she whispered, "Liar."

He cocked an eye at her name tag. Granovich.

She strolled out the door.

Weeks before, in his backyard, the Moth had cleared away the trash and the brush piles. He had laid out the forms for a patio, her patio, for her to sunbathe, to mute that white whore color.

The Moth buried Wheezy and the gun in the middle, two feet under. He chopped up all the soil between the two-by-six forms, disturbed all the dirt, not just the grave.

The Moth called for the cement truck and the helpers. They sealed Molly's agony away. The cement guys couldn't guess the real reason for the slab. The Moth contacted a realtor and listed his house. *Molly's house.*

When the morgue signed off on their cursory autopsy, the Moth had Molly's body transferred to a funeral home and cremated. The morticians threw in a small service for free, with a bored preacher-by-the-hour presiding. The Moth hunched over in the front pew and two working girls settled further back. He asked their names and didn't hear the answers.

He conveyed the urn to the house, cradled in the Gremlin's passenger seat, surrounded by his coat. When he opened the urn, he discovered the gray ashes he expected and also bone chips and a tooth, sifted to the top by the Gremlin's bad suspension. He hunted out a silver box he had bought Molly and dumped out its potpourri. Using a soup spoon, he ladled a portion of Molly in and sealed the lid shut with Magic Tape.

He had General Motors Finance to handle; call in sick to work. He sprawled alone on the couch in a somnolent house for a week. Light scratched its way in past the blinds to stripe the ivory walls — he stared at it as it tracked across the wall. On Saturday, the second already without Molly, he tucked the urn into a box with some packing peanuts. He addressed it to Molly's mother, with a note on top. "Here is your daughter come home. I know you're to blame, and you do too."

1983 — Bong, Bong

The Moth had owned his L.A. pawnshop a year and struggled in the financial climate. Reaganomics passed his neighborhood by, and unemployment reached four-out-of-ten. He resorted to selling false IDs. He accepted goods he knew beyond any squeamish doubt had been ripped off and hocked. After all, it was the neighborhood — everyone scrabbled for some small advantage.

News of the government's urban renewal plans sifted down to him late in the game: early days for him in this end of the world, before he would tap a spiderweb of gossips to keep him up to date.

He polished the glass counter. Below the glass, his selection of wrist watches. Two purported to be Rolexes, but he had scrubbed off a patina of green from the back of their cases. *Nothing easy. Paid maybe thirty percent too much for this place to Big Daddy Albornoz.* The pawnshop struck him as a touch squalid, with its moldy carpet and a bubbly gray sunfilm glued to the front window, but he sneaked as many pennies into improvements as he could. *Smart old bastard. Retired and out in the burbs.* Robberies turned out frightening. *Robbed at gunpoint twice. So far. Took my cash and my third-rate guns. Why not crap stereos instead?* The loan ground his bones into dust. *Need two grand by the first of the month.* He polished

The Moth

the same spot of glass over and over, till his stomach grumbled. Lunch.

He had discovered a taco stand a block or two away that could provide a welcome relief from his mac-and-cheese. An ex-Marine named Ramón owned the food truck and prepared the best chicharrónes in town, extraordinary pulled pork, plus a burrito that could feed a family. Without fail, the Moth ordered the chicken tacos, which he considered kind-of-dry.

Ramon owned four picnic tables with ruined umbrellas, squatting nearby in the vacant lot, and even though he scrubbed them each morning, they were spattered in hot sauce and picante by the time the Moth arrived. The Moth liked his seat to face towards the street. Just not at the back table. There the old men played Lotería among themselves or checkers with their grandchildren. The Moth ate off by himself and ignored any gaze. But they knew him.

Today, a gnarled-up pygmy named Fidel Naranjo showed. He plunked himself across from the Moth with a word of greeting and ate as fast as he could. Fidel weighed in at ninety pounds. Thus far, he had consumed half of a breakfast burrito and now gnawed on pulled pork in tortillas. He had an unfortunate tendency to chew with his mouth open and belch. He chugged up another fruity tribute to stomach gas. "Pardón."

"No es nada grave." The Moth took pride in his smattering of Spanglish.

The old man rolled another tortilla. "They buy your house?"

"What?" The Moth had leased an apartment an inconvenient distance away.

"You gonna sell your house to the Government?"

"No, I rent."

"Too bad. The Feds plan to buy three blocks somewhere west of here, tear everything down, and build casas de pisos. Subsidized rent." Fidel ran a fingernail between his front teeth, in an attempt to loosen a strand of pork.

The Moth didn't know what a piso might be. He considered. People in the neighborhood might find some money. *Good news.* They might not need to pawn things as frequently. *Bad news.*

"Of course, that's two years away. If a man wan' the pesos today, Mickey Barat will buy it from him."

"Who's Mickey Barat?"

"You joking? You don't know Mickey the Russian?" The Moth could tell he disappointed Fidel — the shriveled man joggled his head over this idiocy.

"No. I've never met him."

Fidel picked at a fleck of pork tattooed on his lower lip. "Pray you don't. Mickey got so much money and so many politicians, he's our local mayor. Only unofficial, see?"

"Influential?"

Fidel plastered on a grin from ear lobe to ear lobe, showed a missing incisor and a front buck tooth. "He got soldados who see he's influential." Fidel pointed his index finger and chanted, "Bong, bong! Bong, bong!"

"Bong?"

"No, not bong. Bong like she's a gun. Mickey's a crook and a murderer, even if he's a first class crook."

High class murderer. The Moth asked, "Are you going to sell your house?"

"Sure, why not? My daughter will let me live with her. I take Mickey's money. I know enough to thank him for it."

In the coming months, the more he heard the more the Moth wished he owned a house to sell to the Feds and the County. He could have applied the money to the pawnshop and he might have snagged a subsidized apartment. It sounded magical to him, to live in a concrete tower high above East L.A., with real views, like the Wilshire rich. He wondered if the west-facing apartments would see the ocean. *With L.A.'s brown air, probably not.*

Mickey liked the Towers too. The Moth picked it up from a customer who dropped in to pawn a child's bicycle. The customer answered to Chi Chi Infierno, a most unfortunate name, since Infierno translated as Hell and his nickname meant "breasts" in Tijuana slang. The Moth didn't worry much that the bike was stolen — Chi Chi shared two kids with his wife and had sprinkled another three across the neighborhood. Most likely Chi Chi had paid for this bike, maybe in more ways than one.

Each Chi Chi pawn transaction lasted a half hour minimum. Chi Chi practiced only one social outlet besides rendering women pregnant — he hocked things.

Chi Chi held up the front of the bike and spun the tire. "White sidewalls, see?" They both watched the spokes flick by. "That Mickey Barat, he's a bandido ruso." Chi Chi scratched his goatee, displaced a smatter of dandruff.

"What do you mean, Chi Chi?" the Moth said, as he leaned away from Chi Chi's morning breath,

"He's locked up the excavation contract for the new projects, you know, the Towers. And he's gonna buy up all the property." Chi Chi's single eyebrow waggled like a crow that arrowed in for a landing.

"How could he do that? It's three square blocks. People want the full price — they'll wait years."

"Not when Mickey's people drop by. They make an example of a neighbor, everybody fall in line, real quick like. This bike got tassels hung from the handlebars and she's all pink. Sure, that's worth more."

"Maybe. What do you mean, Mickey's people?"

"Mickey owns misioneros, missionaries. For the Spanish part

of the neighborhood, they're Latino. For the black part, they're the big mofos. And for the whites and everybody else, it's Russians he brought with him from New York City."

"Missionaries. You mean thugs."

"Muscle, misioneros, it's all the same. They make the money for Mickey. Mickey needs giant money to pay for all that giant muscle. Don't you like this chrome bell? Sweet." Chi Chi jabbed the bike's bell, filled the shop with sharp ringing.

The Moth decided to pay more if Chi Chi stopped. "I'll give you twenty-four dollars."

"Man! I promised Bernice I'd bring home more than that. Can't you bump it up a bit?"

"Twenty-four is the right price, Chi Chi. So why doesn't the neighborhood do something about these missionaries, as you call them?"

"Like what, stand up and get all dead? But, I hear there is maybe an Association or could be one."

"An Association? Like the Chamber of Commerce?"

Chi Chi hooted. "More a Chamber of Broke Bones. We see, we see. How about thirty-five."

"Look, Chi Chi. I'm the lender, you're the borrower. Twenty-six and not a cent more."

"That's a problem. I got commitments to meet."

"Who runs this Association? I'll give you twenty-nine."

"Father Dominic and Romero Archuleta. But they got their eyes peeled for a white and a black to help. They want Dye-veeer-sit-eee. You give me thirty-four, I don't tell them you want to join."

"Thirty, final offer."

"Okay, but the Father gonna hear how you want to sign up for his cause."

1983 — The Church Deals a Hand

The Father did visit, with a neighborhood map. Father Dominic turned out to be a short round man, a Chicano with a pencil mustache and a full head of hair. Leaning over, the Father pointed out the houses involved and his own church. "They've agreed to leave Our Lady right where she is and even provide some parking. But all these other houses have to go."

The Moth believed it odd — a priest in his pawnshop poised over the glass countertop. *What next, nuns?* "You think that's a bad thing?"

The Father wagged his hands, like he warned off a small dog. "No, it might work out for the best. This whole area by Interstate 710 is run-down — I haven't seen anything this bad since the Montana Reservation where I began my ministry. Most of these people live in tumble-downs. They'll be happy to have new kitchens and toilets that aren't cracked."

"I can guess what the "white," "black," and "Sp" mean written by each house."

"Hmm, yes. It doesn't sound very Christian to identify the flock like that, but it's handy."

Some of the Father's hand-drawn houses were colored with a green pencil. "What's the green mean?"

"Willing to join the Association or already joined. The black shading means they already sold out to Mr. Barat." A third of the neighborhood showed black.

"Mickey is doing well."

The priest cocked his head. Like an admission squeezed out of him, he said, "Really well. He swung a contract to tear down his own houses for the Projects. The neighborhood already looks like a smashed mouth with missing teeth."

"Listen, Father, this is all very interesting, but...."

"But?"

"I'm blocks away. I'm a business — not a house owner. I'm a newcomer."

"You practiced those answers, didn't you?" When the priest smiled, the whole room lit up. The man could convince an astronomer the earth was shaped like a flat disc.

The Moth promised himself to stay strong. "I cannot tell a lie. I also can't say yes."

The priest set his face into serious-but-sincere mode. "Here's the thing. The Association should be larger than the three blocks. We'll need businesses too. And you're white."

"I am? Boy, Mom and Da are going to be surprised."

The priest said, "No need for sarcasm." He chuckled, a pleasant sound that forced the Moth to grin.

Don't get carried away. "Why me?"

Father Dominic raised his eyebrows. "For a pawnbroker, you're not poorly thought of. I say this with no intent to offend. And also, four white families live in the three blocks. We need someone respected who can speak to them."

So they'd slated the Moth as the token white. "No, I'm sorry. Defying muscle isn't my idea of a good time."

The priest gestured with a finger, like he believed the Moth's point reasonable. "Tell me, my son. Are you a Catholic?"

The Moth

"No, I'm a pawnbroker."

"One doesn't preclude the other. I bet your mother and father are Catholic."

"She was Catholic. He was an adulterer."

"There you are!"

"Just because my mother was Catholic doesn't mean I'm joining."

Father Dominic folded his hand-made map with care. "We meet Wednesday night at Our Lady, at seven. Let me write it down for you." He dragged the pawn ticket pad towards him, filled it out in detail. "I'll see you there."

The Moth carried a box of his possessions, a box he had lugged on and off the bus and down his alley to his back door. From a half block away, he could pick out a figure on his step, a large man. As he approached, he picked out a twenty-inch neck, a strong wiry beard. Deep set eyes. Pockmarks scattered across the face. White teeth — either a grin or an ursine grimace. The man rose, collected the box from him.

It shocked the Moth. A giant, with a barrel chest, but he stood only as tall as the Moth. *Shaped like a gun safe*.

The voice delivered the second shock. Tenor, so high it hung above the rooftops. "You're locked up in front, so I waited back here. My name is Romero Archuleta. Father Dominic sent me to drag you to the meeting."

"Frank. Glad to meet you."

Romero laughed like a chihuahua barking. "I don't think so, but we'll see if you change your mind. So what's in the box?"

"I'm moving into the back of the store."

"A box at a time?"

"I gave up cars."

The Church Deals a Hand

Romero flared his eyes into shiny quarters. He probably didn't know anyone else in L.A. without a car. "My friend Eduardo drives a truck. We'll pack and unpack you Sunday, but you come to the meeting, no?"

"No." The Moth hated dumping his apartment, but he also owned the space in the back of the pawnshop and it could save him rent money.

"C'mon man. What's the harm, Frank?"

The Moth thought about it. "The harm is death by murder, courtesy of the Russian mafia."

Romero shrugged. "That's what I'm here for, Frank. I watch your back. I watch everybody's back."

"How good are you?"

"Two tours in Nam, man. And I work as a bouncer. Keeps me in shape."

The Moth knew guns didn't care if you were in shape or not, but he could use some help with the move. And the meeting didn't obligate him.

The Moth scanned the people in the pews. Bring me your sick, your tired and desperate. These people needed the government money and the housing.

Father Dominic said, "All you have to do is to say to these men that the Association and Father Dominic represent you. Then close the door."

A brown-black woman with shining white hair, her rheumy eyes aimed somewhat towards the church altar, said, "What if they insist on coming back?"

Father Dominic said, "Arrange the meeting. Either I or Romero will be there with you."

A young, overweight Latino in a wheelchair said, "What if they try to force their way in?"

"Tomás, I'd suggest you block the door. I don't think they'll wiggle around you into the house."

Laughter swept the room. Some of it for real, some cracked by tension.

Tomás said, "No, serious. What do we do? They shoved their way into Fernanda's house, scared her half to death."

"Do whatever they tell you. After they leave, call me and call the Sheriff."

A brown woman in the back, a grandmotherly icon in a flowered dress and a huge hat, humphed. "Like *they* care what happens down here."

Father Dominic strode back and forth, gazed out over the small collection of people. "I'm sure they do care. But they don't have many resources. I'll see if we can arrange better coverage."

The woman with the white hair and the blindness said, "Why shouldn't we take Mickey Barat's money? Get what we can, get out before they hurt us."

Romero turned around in the front pew. "More money later. Soon, in fact. And as one of the original neighborhood owners, you get on the priority list for an apartment in the tower. That's why we hold on and say no to Mr. Barat."

"You can't be there all the time, Romero."

Father Dominic said, "But the rest of us can. We see them coming, we call, let the neighborhood know they're here. We'll get stronger and we'll support each other."

Contemplating the mixed bag of locals, the Moth thought they might get stronger, but so would Barat's men. *Escalation.* At best, these homeowners could only act as witnesses to each other's intimidation.

Springing up and holding his hand out to the Moth, Romero paced towards the pawnbroker. For one ghastly moment, the Moth believed Romero would yank him to his feet. "And as we sign on more members, we become stronger. Frank, here, he's joining us and he's volunteering not because he lives here on the block, but because he cares about the neighborhood."

Father Dominic said, "And Frank will be one of our Board, one of the leadership you place your faith in."

The Moth whipped his gaze from Romero to Father Dominic to protest. The sunniness in the man's face slowed him down. *That belief.*

The Moth's head swiveled to stare at the crowd. They appeared so weak. He couldn't do this.

Not only dangerous but ridiculous. Conned like this. They'd played the Moth for a patsy. He faced the crowd, raised his hand in greeting, tried to grin.

1983 — The Hammering

A tremendous banging on his back door. The Moth struggled out of his single bed — one he had accepted in pawn — staggered towards the steel windowless barrier to the outside world. He unlocked the door and snapped into realization. He poised there in plaid boxer shorts and a T-shirt full of holes, barefoot, clueless. He registered his own helplessness — he was about to die.

But not at the hands of Romero. The cinderblock-wall of a man shuffled his feet in the alley dust. "Mr. Frank. Haul your pants on. It's time to drive around on security patrol."

Hustled into a tawdry-orange Chevy Nova by this Latino force-of-a-Catholic-God, the Moth started to wake up, cheer up. There, a whisper of belief they could accomplish something. They cruised back and forth through the three-block area, stopped twice to use a pay phone.

In all the sweeps through the streets, Romero told the Moth of his time in Nam, how tough it had been to return home to a country that hated him for serving. "They told us not to wear our uniforms when we traveled, or we'd get spit on." The Moth counted his knuckles like a rosary while Romero talked him through the details of his suicide attempt — pills, not a gun. "I know rifles. If I had picked up a rifle, you'd be riding around alone." Girlfriends filled in a couple of

1983 – The Hammering

years, a patch of solitude and more despair. "And two years ago I came back to the Church. Sounds like a soap opera, I know, but it's what saved me."

Four times Romero hovered two car-lengths back of vehicles by the curb with their engines running. All four times they discovered the cars entertained drug sales rather than thuggish intimidation — though the dealers could also have been the Russian's employees. Back and forth, until the third time Romero checked by phone, he received the message — house intrusion. "It's Old Lady de Valles. She's the granny you met at Our Lady — the blind one. She calls about threatening noises four or five times a week."

Romero wheeled over to the curb, pointed left at a shabby stucco with a yard full of dead plants. "That's her place." He bounded out and set off across the street.

Maybe it would turn out a false alarm — the Moth hoped so. He tagged along towards the chain-link gate, but not as briskly as Romero.

Two cars pinned the Moth and Romero on the sidewalk. Both screeched out of the street, into the fence.

Four men clambered out. Three too many. The Army had trained Romero well, but as a soldier, not a street fighter. An ogre of a man sailed into them with a lead pipe. The first blow crashed into the side of Romero's knee. As Romero fell to the ground, he grunted like a pig as he choked back his screams. Two of them turned to the Moth.

They soon rendered the Moth into paste, throwing him against the car and beating his belly and chest. His rib splintered. His vision turned gray around the edges. He slid into an unclear place where space and time didn't work — only pain — all of him drowned in a morass of agony.

Time blinked. The concrete lay against his face, or maybe his face on it. He could smell the blood in his nostrils. He could just focus on

Romero as he crawled towards the Moth, his face dark in blood. *Is the fool trying to help?*

When the ogre-like man kicked the Moth, he sensed his hip shift, like a friend who skitters away, distanced from him and separated from his body. Disappearing into a chalky white world, he caught his mother's voice droning along, "A being at once corporeal and spiritual." The damn catechism, in a sing-song Lithuanian accent.

The Moth supposed L.A. hospitals shaped out the same as any in a major US city. Catholic — he lay under a cross above his bed and under air conditioning that strove to freeze him to death. Jesus' feet were caked in blood, but from his angle, the Moth couldn't decide if Christ displayed pain or only sorrow. The Moth's legs stretched under a tented sheet, and he knew the tent concealed a cast that wrapped him from his waist all the way down to his left knee. The morphine helped with the pain, but they wouldn't give him near enough.

Father Dominic waited by the bed. "I dropped by to visit you a couple of days ago, but you were pretty out of it."

The Moth formed words with his bruised lips. "How's Romero?"

"The knee will never be the same, but maybe he turned out lucky compared to you."

"He was smart. He fell down sooner."

The priest strolled over to the window, nudged up one of the Venetian blinds. He didn't tell the Moth what he viewed. "My son, I promise you God must be planning some sad, guilt-filled epiphany for the end of Mickey Barat's life."

Ironic — a promise Mickey would feel bad. "But we mustn't pray for the end of his life, must we, Father?"

1983 – The Hammering

"Even the Jesuits would have trouble with that, and I'm of St. Dom's Order. My namesake. Does it hurt much?"

"Only when I laugh. Or cry. Or shit." He had said "shit" to a priest.

Even in his compassionate mode, that aura of concern, the Father leaked an involuntary grin, a twitch in the corner of his mouth. "Ah, the body corporeal."

"Funny. Someone was talking to me about that the other day."

The priest patted his hand. "What happens next for you?"

"They say I'm trapped here for another three weeks. I return to the pawnshop in a wheelchair. I graduate to a walker like an old person, and after a while, I receive these letters from the hospital that demand payment. And what happens next for you? What happened to the Association?"

A nurse's aide sped into the room, bobbed to the priest, whipped up the sheet at the edge of the bed. The Moth glanced over the rail edge. The bag hung there with an inch of dark yellow lurking. The transparent hose snaked upward and disappeared into the sheets. He didn't want to think about where it connected to him.

She said, "Now, Frankie, you're not drinking enough fluids." He wiggled his eyebrows. She gave a disgusted "tchaa," and her shoes squeaked their way out the door.

The Moth stared at the priest — his head hung down as if he inspected the linoleum. "Father? The Association?"

"Hmm...."

"Sore point?"

The priest tipped his head. "The Association finished off D.O.A. Our members caved one by one, in the four days after the gangsters attacked you and Romero. Mr. Barat owns most everything."

"All for nothing."

"We can't measure God's grace, my son, or His intentions."

The Moth

"We can measure results, though."

"Now, now." The priest gestured with his hands, as if trying to shush a kindergarten class.

"It's okay, Father. I just need some time to get over it."

Not time, but revenge. Payback, no matter how trivial, how petty, how anonymous. Anonymous would be good. He needed that cop, Detective Chelsea Granovich — and he needed a man named Clancy. But instead, fate delivered a neighborhood woman.

Marie, wife of Ramón's Taco Stand, perched in a chair by the bedside. He hadn't expected the visit, but he sniffed an opportunity to beg a favor.

Marie would have been the perfect mother but for her childlessness. She had been in the room five minutes and already she had palmed his forehead, straightened his sheets, and criticized the stitch-work that reattached his left earlobe. The Moth couldn't figure out how Ramón bore it. He said, "I wish you'd stick that Band-Aid back on."

With great certainty, Marie said, "Wounds need to breathe. If they fix that tape back on, you sneak it off."

"Very kind of you to visit me, Marie." Especially since they had barely met.

"Es nada. Ramón wanted me to and it's a breather away from the food wagon. You know, I can't bear the smell of pork? Ramón, he smells like it all the time. I force him to scrub himself hard in the shower."

Trouble in paradise. "Marie, you know Clancy?"

"That good-for-nothing negrito? Always wants the papas con chile?"

This sounded like Clancy. Clancy — maybe the guy's first name or maybe his last. He had a rep in the neighborhood for pyromania. If

1983 – The Hammering

you had a trash pile in your back yard, you'd invite Clancy over. He'd burn it for you and watch it to the last glowing ember. But he also worked on commission. "Could you ask him to drop by, the next time he stops at the food truck?"

Detective Chelsea, the statuesque embodiment of departmental ambition, lounged in the chair Marie had used the day before. She crossed her legs, magnificent legs with muscular calves. Mirrored Ray-Ban sunglasses that perched above her forehead held back her blonde hair. Her sports coat fell back from her right hip, showed off her gun. "If you don't mind me saying, you look like shit."

"That's weird. Everybody here keeps talking about how much better I look. I'm glad you remembered me, and paid a visit."

"You called me. But you — you've got an unusual story. A fairy whose best friend got murdered in a no-tell-mo-tel two years ago on account of being a hooker. And it turns out you're not queer and it turns out the pimp wasn't hid out — he disappeared from L.A. *And* it turns out you're a person of interest around Mickey Barat, some kind of sideliner to the Russians. You're a fascinating person."

Detective Chelsea had been Deputy Chelsea when they had first met, back in Room 16 of the Grenadier. After her promotion, she'd been by the pawnshop once to twist his arm about some info he didn't know and wouldn't have given her anyway. Her rep? She solved cases, even if the wrong person ended up in County lockup.

She didn't recognize scruples. He appreciated that, at least for this circumstance. "I don't know how to start." He lifted the book in his lap, a beat-up American Heritage Dictionary, and eased it onto the bedside table. *Not much of a plot, but lots of action.*

"Spill your guts, Frank. I'm on the clock here."

The Moth

"Mickey Barat must be a thorn in your side. Well, not your side, but the Department's."

She didn't say a word. She leaned forward, her elbows on her knees. A half-grin that toyed at the corner of her mouth.

He stared at the sheet as if its coarse weave told him something, ran his forefinger around it in a circle. "Maybe I could help you out, at least for a while."

She slapped her thigh. "You'd snitch? Sweet! Whatcha got?"

"First, I'd like some assurances."

"Assurances? Like what?"

"Like nobody ever knows. Like Barat won't kill me." *This is a bad idea. There's no such things as secrets, not in L.A.*

She leaned further forward, a forearm on her knee. Such eagerness. "Screw all that, Frank. Once you make the offer, you're mine."

"No, I'm not."

"You clam up now, I'll build the pressure on you till you think that broke leg is nothing. You're my confidential informant from here on."

He'd stepped into quicksand. Back out now. "Hip."

"What?"

"Hip, not leg. I've changed my mind. Go away."

"Look, bubby. You called me."

"Maybe that was a mistake. I don't think we can work together."

She leaned back in the chair, her face blank except for needle eyes. "I have a friend in Burglary. We'll secure a warrant and we'll compare every item in your chickenshit pawnshop to the stolen property logs. And we'll enjoy ourselves."

Fenced bicycles. Mag wheels. Skill saws. And those fake I.D.s for the undocumenteds, in a folder in the back of the cabinet.

Chelsea grinned at him like the headlights of a car flipped up to high beam. "That got you. Something behind that forehead bone isn't right. And you know, I think I could reopen the case on that murdered hooker and her pimp. What was his name?"

He stared at her. His face tingled, burned up, and he knew his eyes bugged out from jacked-up blood pressure. "Little Wheezy. That's all I ever knew."

"A murder investigation. Sure you don't want to be my CI? A weekly pointer or two. Or a life of misery, your choice."

She had him on the ground kicking him, like Mickey Barat's thugs. He had handed himself over to a predator. "Hey, I intended to give you something for free. I didn't even ask for money."

"I can live with that deal. No money, free information? You're like the public library."

She had hooked him and the longer he wiggled, the deeper the barb. He picked at the sheet with his fingernails. "Okay. Mickey's operations. I heard about a book, upstairs over a dive bar at Alma and Whittier."

"That's it? I drive all the way down there to throw a bookie in the slam?"

He'd have to give her something else. "A chop shop on South Western and Florence, clean out of our neighborhood. They boost high-end cars in places like Venice, because the parts are worth so much. You might rope in a few foreign auto repair places when you check the buyer list."

"See, that wasn't so hard. Listen, you keep my number of arrests and convictions high, you win a Stay-Out-Of-Jail card."

At least Mickey would lose out.

Clancy slid by to speak to the Moth after the hospital closed for visitors. He popped up by the bed in generic blue scrubs.

"Jesus, you startled me." The Moth glanced down, picked out the white shoes. He flicked his eyes up and read the name tag. Clancy liked authenticity, but the name said Mabel.

"Heard you had a job."

The Moth said, "I wanted to see you. That doesn't mean a job."

Clancy's skin ran to dark amber, with a dusting of large dark freckles. Brown soulful eyes. "Right. Cause I'm your best friend."

The Moth leaned over and opened the drawer of his metal bedside table, extracted his slip of paper. "This building." The building harbored Barat's stolen goods, and had been known to house Russian emigrants, the type that received a handgun the moment they arrived on US soil.

Clancy flicked his eyes across the address. "What about it?"

"I suspect it's a firetrap."

Clancy snorted through nostrils like a double tailpipe. "So?"

"So what would it take for you to confirm that risk?"

Clancy shrugged. "As a firetrap? I could do that for seven-fifty."

"I want it to be obvious someone torched it. Is that cheaper?"

"Four-fifty, since I don't have to jump through hoops on the accelerant."

The Moth cocked his chin in agreement.

"Cash up front."

"Then we have to wait until I get out of here."

Clancy shuffled his feet. "It sounds like fun, so I'll front you the fire. But remember, if you don't pay.... I hear the pawnshop is a fire trap too."

But... always a but. Mickey Barat had sold his chop shop to a fellow named Arthur Sandoval — too much work for Barat's people to drive across L.A. into Crip country to check the operation. Detective Chelsea enjoyed the bust though, and she told the Moth, "You and me, baby. Gonna make music together." Rather than mess with the bookmaking firm herself, she farmed it out to Vice to earn some favors. Vice leaked like a cheap swimming pool and the bookmaking firm slipped through the holes long before the raid. The Detective admitted it herself, "Bunch of crooked jerk-offs. I shouldn't have trusted a single one."

Clancy reported great success and collected his fee, but later the Moth learned Mickey's kassir, his money man, had over-insured the building for their own intended fire. Mickey paid the inspector to overlook the obvious arson and to rule it a wiring short.

To avoid an ambulance charge, the Moth asked Ramón to fetch him home in his pickup. Marie, shining in approval, parked half in Ramón's lap to avoid injuring the Moth further. He hugged the door, inhaled her old-fashioned jasmine. His wheelchair rode behind, in the bed.

The turd floating downstream on this squalid river of events appeared the week after the Moth arrived home.

At the pawnshop he slumped in his wheelchair outside in the sunshine, to shake off some of the refrigerated chill infused from near-four weeks in the hospital. The dark windows, the white stucco, the three-foot mansard of red barrel tiles backed him up, or framed him on a stage.

A brute of a man, someone who should have played pro ball, waddled up the sidewalk. His huge thighs had trouble edging one past the other. He grunted down into one of the Moth's folding chairs, drooped over both sides. The brute owned a cauliflower ear, a beady eye, and the pits of ancient acne strewn across his cheek.

The Moth did what he did. He waited.

The bullethead never turned, gazed only out into the street. "My name is Yevgeny. I work for Mr. Barat."

"I've heard the name."

"You look better than the last time I saw you, few weeks back. When we left you on the ground, I didn't think you'd get up, much less buy a smooth ride like that wheelchair."

The Moth said, "Rent — not buy. It's comfortable enough."

"Better you than me." Yevgeny's shoulders jerked up and down, an over-muscled version of a horse laugh.

"I assume you didn't come here to pawn something."

"Got a message. Mr. B — he knows you sell false I.D. Now you know he knows."

"Hmm. So everybody knows. So?"

"Here's the deal. He forgive your rudeness for fifty percent. Maybe he prefer you pay an annual fee. He'll let you know."

1984 — Apprenticeship

Ylsa Perez drove the Moth up in her taxi, glad to snag a long fare. Glad, she said, not to be headed to the VA clinic or the Hospital or the Employment Development Department. But in truth, this destination didn't clock out to be any more glamorous. California State Prison at Lancaster sprawled there in all its razor-wire glory. The Moth trekked up here on a regular basis to visit Julio. And Julio's friends. Some could be suppliers, once they squeezed out the gate. Or customers. They all *knew things.*

In the harsh sun, giant towers that could have worked at a local airport anchored the fence, spiked into the corners. Ylsa drove past the entrance, a three-story box of chain link and mechanized gates. Here, incoming and outgoing vehicles received the inspection that included a mirror on a cart that whizzed around underneath.

She wheeled through the parking lot to the Friends Outside, a charity where he could leave his possessions locked up. "You call me when you're done. I can't park here — I park up the road a half-mile, get a coffee."

The room where the prison's outside and inside brushed against each other didn't resemble what TV audiences viewed on cop shows. The room held no booths with bulletproof glass and telephones. Instead, it sprawled out maybe fifty feet by forty, full of bolted-down tables and rickety metal chairs. The Moth said to Julio, "Parole Board meeting in six months? That's faster than expected — how'd you swing that?"

"My brother-in-law works as a clerk in the main office. He kind of erased the fight I got in." Julio wore California Orange. He appeared older, tired. Only burned up eleven months of the stretch.

"That's great." *What else can I say?*

Julio cocked one shoulder, a half-hearted shrug. "I'm never the one who starts it. Easy to have trouble fall on you in here."

The Moth asked, "What do you want to do, you know, when you're out?" He had the shakes — prison cramped his shoulders, left him on edge.

"I been cooking, working the line in Food Services."

"Hmm." The Moth glanced over his shoulder — the visitor door in the wall behind him. *Locked.*

"I'd like to find a job in a restaurant. Cooking, not washing dishes. You know anyone?"

"Sorry, Julio. The only restaurant I know is a one-man food truck." The Moth stared at Julio's hands flat on the table. One knuckle was swollen to twice life-size.

"Shit. Ask around. Meantime, the con you meet today, he's named Leroy like I said. He's a güero, a white, but he's okay. He cracks safes and that's what you asked for."

The Moth hunched over the scarred table top, an eternal wait for Leroy. He shot glances around, lining out the prisoners and their families. The prisoners appeared somber: some miserable, some trying to assert their fatherhood. The families — they rowed up in all colors on the other side of the table. Prison, the great integrator.

Mostly fat women, an occasional man who might be a father or brother. Children, quiet, but used to it all. They stared at Daddy, not saying much, even when prompted.

The Moth stared down at his interlaced hands, trembling. The ceiling hovered, hung there at seven feet, not any decent height. This apprenticeship, could it be the eventual slide into this room? *Only with me in the jumpsuit, hunkered down on the other side of this table. But there's no one to visit me.*

He snapped his eyes up as his ears picked up the sound of clanging steel, the prisoner door slamming shut. A guy his size, hair plastered flat on one side, stuck out the other. Buggy eyes, a mouth that chattered shut, open, shut. Of course this would be his safecracker, a real peterman stoned on some vile prison drug.

Leroy didn't so much rest on the bench opposite the Moth — he twitched, winced, blinked like a sandstorm that rocketed around the room. He said, "Pleased-ta-meet-cha. We got a half hour." He didn't thrust his hand out for a shake — the System banned human touch. Guards watched, their backs to the walls around the room.

The Moth drew four pieces of folded paper out of his shirt pocket, ferreted out a three-inch pencil. "So tell me how you tackle the door and what type of equipment you use."

1985 — Sweet But Empty

Makarov fabricated a semi-automatic pistol, a weapon with a rare caliber and ammo that had to be imported, somehow, from the Soviet block. The Moth's Makarov showed up as pawn, but it was smeared in gunk. He laid out a raggedy towel on his glass countertop, set out a bottle of nail polish remover. He dabbed at the grip. Black changed to dark red on his rag, spread out through the fabric like pollution off a whale ship. *Blood. Of course.*

The Moth's hands flinched back, as from a fire, and stopped dabbing at the pistol. He leaned back from the counter, hovered on his stool. Something. He remembered something.

On the police scanner, about a month ago. A surprising attempted robbery. Two hoods in hoodies and masks had hit a check-cashing store, wounded two and killed one. The Moth remembered the radio traffic because protocol had disintegrated. The language had turned human — unusual bullet casings at the scene. The police sounded bubbly and euphoric — a shooting freighted with something besides mundanity.

He had to be careful. With a couple of weeks of cadging around, he located Estevan Faro, living long-term in a motel in the next neighborhood towards Downtown. Four years ago, Estevan had held a cigarette to the breasts of a woman the Moth loved. The Moth had many times thought of Estevan, out there alive and free.

At the motel, a wonderful coincidence. The maintenance man had popped into the Moth's pawn, brought in goods the Moth now understood to be pilfered trinkets from the guests. Under the burden of a veiled threat, the handyman loaned the Moth a master key. The Moth had an acquaintance who cut keys, no matter what was stamped on them.

The Moth wouldn't employ anyone from his neighborhood for surveillance — he wanted no connections of his scheme and its execution to anything or anyone. Though it wounded him, the Moth closed shop for two days. December cold enveloped the town, so he could wear a hooded jacket, a baseball cap, brown base makeup from Thrifty Drug. He carried a plastic bag full of hats and changed them out every hour. The Moth drank coffee in a donut shop with a window that faced the motel. He wandered the street with a thrifty-shopper newspaper. He bought pinto beans at a local tienda de comida. All the while, he watched.

Estevan spent those two days behind his locked door, his shabby drapes. At night he journeyed out — the Moth didn't care where, just how long. Estevan wandered home by midnight each time.

As the streetlights flickered on — those that hadn't been knocked out — the Moth slipped up the stairs to Estevan's door, shoved in the key. He didn't check left or right, or glance behind him, just scrunched in his neck, hunched his shoulders, and sidled in. A quick scan. He tugged the chair to the dresser, crawled up beside the TV. The two screws to the vent at the top of the wall yielded to his screwdriver and he manhandled the dusty louvers down. Set to plant his evidence.

Surprise. Estevan concealed a bag in the duct. The Moth dragged it out, tucked it under his arm. He eased the Makarov in its rag back into the ductwork, then fished in the bag. The bag smelled like semen. Inside, five hundred dollars and a set of photos from Hell. He pocketed the money, leafed through the twenty or so photos. Three women, all tortured. One dead. The photos shook in his hands, and two fell. He kicked them off the back of the dresser to slide down the wall. He clambered down onto the chair. His stomach nearly betrayed him. It wouldn't do to leave any forensics at the scene beyond the planted gun, but he could taste the vomit in the back of his mouth.

The Moth trudged six blocks to a bus stop rather than use the one in front of the Mexican grocery. When he reached the Pawnshop, he called Detective Chelsea.

Even then, the System let the Moth down. After the search, the arrest, the six weeks while Estevan sat in County, his public defender counseled him into a lesser plea of one count of murder. In return, Estevan rolled on his sister's boyfriend. *L.A. is really something, isn't it?*

1992 — Famine Beats The Moth

The Moth didn't consider Sunday morning much different than any other day of the week, just as 1992 held the same worries as '82 when he had bought the pawnshop. The Moth kept the pawnshop open for two types of customers. He served the ones who discovered the need to pawn something because the week had gulped down all the food money. He served the ones in search of his extralegal products. At nine he carried out his empty 2% milk carton to the dumpster. Someone had parked a light blue Chevy Chevelle in the alley ten feet from his door, jammed against the chainlink fence on the other side of the lane. Bobbing heads behind tinted glass.

The Moth sprinted for the back door of his apartment, as much as he could sprint with his hip. He slammed the door and locked it tight. He stood tiptoe on his kitchen chair and peered down through the transom above. Through the chicken wire in the glass, the dirt, and the bars in the casement, he could stare through the windshield. The Chevy bore its weariness like a shroud — white splotches covered the hood like a salt lake. A gang wouldn't have owned this ugly a Chevelle. And it wasn't detective issue. Ludicrously small heads jounced around inside.

He eased open the door, slipped along the back of the building, sneaked towards the open window obliquely. He approached the car like he'd creep towards a rattlesnake coiled around his wallet.

A round face popped up over the windowsill. A pale face with scraggy hair, a snub nose, and missing front lower teeth. He had cornered a child.

The mouth opened and lisped out, "Hello."

The Moth stopped three feet away. Who knew what dire contagion grew in that decaying mouth? "Hi."

The child scrubbed a grubby cheek with a fist, and he or she snickered. "You look funny."

"I get that a lot."

"My name's Declan. What's yours?" It sounded more like Decwan, but the Moth could translate.

"Mine is Frank. Pleased to meet you."

The boy extended a slobbery hand to the Moth. "Pleased to meet you."

The Moth surveyed the hand, more than a bit glistening with saliva and probably snot. "What'cha doin', Declan?"

The kid was aged, what — four? Seven? "Sleeping. This is our car *and* our motel. We're sleeping."

"That's nice, Declan. How many of you are there?"

A second face popped up behind Declan. A little girl? Two scrunchies gathered her short hair into pigtails. She had a wall of dirt for a forehead and a smear across her chin. Declan said, "Me and my sister and my daddy. He just got home from work."

"Work?"

"Daddy goes to school. They pay him to go. He cleans the gym. But only on weekends."

The girl behind Declan said, "I wanna go to school."

"Where is your daddy?"

"Asleep back there." Declan flopped his arm over the front seat. "He's too tall for the front seat."

"I'd like to talk to your daddy. Do you think you could wake him up for me?"

Declan's grin spread across his whole face. "Sure." His voice soared in pitch and strength as he stared straight at the Moth. "Daddy. Daddy. A man wants to talk to you."

The face that jolted up into the side window — painted with surprise, apprehension, maybe fear. The Moth peered into the openmouth face of a man awakened from a deep sleep.

The Moth peered through the smeared glass at Daddy's rawboned face, with a beak of a nose that had been broken a couple of times. His hair, reddish even in the backseat shadow, stuck out on one side and flattened on the other. His eyebrows hung only two inches below his hairline.

The Moth fell back on politeness. "Good morning, sir."

Daddy glanced at the two children in the front seat, cranked the window down four inches. He brought his chin to the top of the glass, the top of his head hidden somewhere in the headliner. He said, "Sorry. You scared me." His breath drifted across the divide between them, corrupted the alley's fragrance.

The Moth inclined his head in a gesture he thought king-like. Or pompous. "My name is Frank."

"I'm Quinn."

"Quinn, it seems to me you should shift your car to some other spot. Parking behind a pawn shop can't be the safest for your children."

Quinn's face screwed up in a pucker. The Moth wondered if he was about to cry. When Quinn opened his mouth to speak, the Moth catalogued a gray, dead incisor. "Ah, Mister. Do we have to move right now?"

The Moth stepped back, glanced up and down the alley. It wasn't exactly a hellhole, but it was neglected. *What's the harm?* "No, I guess not. Get your sleep and then you can search out something better."

When the Moth closed, he checked out the alley. The Chevelle had migrated fifty feet, had lit behind another store. He limped down the alley, avoided a black, sheen-streaked puddle where someone had changed their oil. Leaning down and peering in the passenger window, he discovered the two children playing some game with three empty plastic bottles. "Where's your father?"

Declan said, "Working. He runs Pepe's. It's a restaurant."

Right. Homeless guy runs a restaurant.

The girl chimed in. "Pepe's. In the kitchen."

I've made this mistake before. "I'll be back before you know it," the Moth told the boy, He limped the block and a half to Ramón's Taco Stand and purchased his three chicken tacos, tortilla chips, and salsa. With his acid reflux, he knew he should drop the salsa. At the picnic table, he craned his head sideways, ate his way in from the end. He tried to avoid the taco's eventual shattering and the shower of tomato and meat onto the paper sack. Unsuccessful. He gazed off into the late afternoon sunshine.

With a sigh, he bought another two orders of tacos. He had Ramón leave out the salsa and double up on the chips. Ramón handed him the two bags. "What's up Frank? Are you off on a trip and packing lunch?"

Ramón was as close to a friend as the Moth had. The Moth opened his mouth, and closed it. He gazed up into the man's face, collected the bags, and limped off down the street.

The Chevelle baked in the late day sun. The Moth handed the bags in the window as he avoided the boy's grubby hands. "Wait a minute." He stumped into his apartment and fetched two bottles of water. The Moth drank only bottled water, convinced the city wanted to poison everyone in East L.A.

He handed Declan the water. "Tell your daddy he has to move his car. Again."

When the Moth stuck his head into the alley the next morning, the car had shifted a hundred feet down the alley the other way and squatted closer to Ramón's. He stuck his head in the window to discover only the two children — no Quinn. *These kids spend all day and most of the night alone in the car.* They huddled up asleep under a soiled blanket, one to the left and one to the right. A quick inspection revealed a floorboard full of wrappings from Ramón's, but no other food. With a sigh, he turned and stumped off to the Korean grocery at the end of the block. *Yeah, I've been here before.*

The Moth and the Korean owner had a hate / hate relationship. For years, the grocer had supplied the neighborhood with questionable produce and processed foodstuffs, and the children with cigarettes. The lack of quality and legality didn't bother the Moth. Rather, his animosity sprang from personality differences.

In the second aisle, near a row of dusty jarred kimchi, the Moth spotted Pop-Tarts. He toted the box up to the register and dropped it on the mat, along with the proper change. His nemesis elbowed aside an employee so he could ring up the sale himself.

To the Moth, the store owner parodied a bronze, sweating Chinese lion, with the wide-set shining eyes and the pug nose that displayed its contents. The owner grinned. "I know you come back, sooner or later."

"Yes, I couldn't stay away. Now, can you please take the money and give me the food?"

Another limp back to the car. He handed the box in, along with more of his precious water. Declan was overjoyed, the little girl nearly hysterical as she bounced up and down.

"I take it you don't often get Pop-Tarts."

Declan, his mouth smeared towards his ear with grape byproducts, chanted, "Pop-Tarts Pop-Tarts Pop-Tarts!"

The Moth waited until Declan had wolfed his and ripped open a wrapper for the girl pawing at his shoulder. "What's your sister's name?"

"Missy."

Safer not to know. Don't ask. The Moth grinned his fake smile. "What's your last name?"

Declan grinned right back. "The same as Daddy's. Clayhorn. Missy's name is Clayhorn too."

"When do you think your father will get back?"

"Soon. He stays here all night tonight."

"That's nice. Does that happen often?"

The grin again, pure happiness. "No. All night is special." Good vocabulary, for such a rotten lisp.

The Moth tugged at his lip, considered a bit. The children shredded their way into second Pop-Tarts; the foil packets cascaded to the floorboards. "Ask your father to knock on my back door when he gets home. It's the one right down there, painted gray. Okay?"

"Okay."

Not convinced the boy would even remember, the Moth asked, "Promise?"

Declan chewed most of the way through a strawberry pastry. "Promise."

Quinn stood to attention in the alley, his hands wrapped around a baseball hat. He appeared clean and he had slicked his hair back, though the inside collar of his shirt showed gray-brown stains. "The boy said you wanted to see me."

1992 – Famine Beats The Moth

The Moth stepped across the threshold, locked his door, and slipped the key in his pants. He waved a hand at the concrete step and said, "Have a seat."

The two mirrored the same posture — forearms on knees, hands loose, spines curved in the disappointment of life. They directed their gaze across the alley — they both pretended to watch the dumpster. The Moth opened first. "Can't help but notice you've settled into the alley."

"Gonna make us leave?"

The Moth shrugged. "Too late for that, I guess. Why this alley?"

"It's better than most. Close to the restaurant."

"Declan said you had two or three jobs."

Quinn stared at him.

"It's okay. I'm not a cop or anything. I've been feeding your kids, so you kind of owe me."

"Maybe I do."

"So you're working three jobs?"

Quinn shrugged. "It's what it takes. The restaurant is regular — I'm on the payroll, but I can't work more than thirty hours a week. That way they don't got to give me benefits. The other jobs, they're what you call irregular. You know, off the books."

"Even the school?"

"Schools can be crooked too. It's one of those private schools."

Hot on the step, in the sun. The Moth endured the concrete that burned his buttocks. "I take it it's hard to find the right job?"

"In 1992, in the middle of a depression? With unemployment what it is?"

The Moth objected. "That's only in certain sectors. And the crash was in '83." He knew all this from his compact radio, late at night.

"Sector? Talk like that is what gets me depressed. And the crash ain't over. It's never over."

The Moth

The Moth measured Quinn up. He looked so low, his tongue might fall down his throat. "You merely need the right job."

"What is the right job, nowadays? My real job is coal mining, but that don't work out too good."

The Moth bowed his head. His pawnshop had filled up with the things people abandoned to weather the recession. If Quinn had been brown and owned anything, he could have been one of Moth's customers.

"We come out west to avoid freezing to death. Winter was on the way and I lost the trailer to the loan company. Hadn't seen no work for a year, except for odd jobs and some helper stuff for a farmer."

"Where is your wife, the mother of your children?" The Moth realized she might be two different women.

"Darn, you want to know everything. She left us back in the good times. She likes honky-tonks, and dancing, and men with flash."

"So you been raising your kids by yourself for... what? Three years?"

"At first my wife's mother helped us out, but she vanished into the old folks home. Declan is a real good boy, real responsible. He's only six, but he takes care of his sister." This guy leaked out his soul, drip by drip.

"And you all live in the car."

"They can't take that from us."

"How do you clean up?"

"Why, a water bib sticks out of the back of the grocery store down there. I fill up three gallon jugs and we take turns in the back seat."

"And the bathroom?"

Quinn flinched. "That part's more embarrassing. When the timing is right we use the john in the mall. Otherwise, anyone from Kentucky knows how to go in the woods. Alleys aren't that much different."

1992 – Famine Beats The Moth

The Moth had witnessed a lot in life, but this amounted to bare-naked last ditch. Quinn couldn't inch much closer to the edge. The Moth did what he did, he waited until the other person spoke.

"I know it looks bad. I can't make enough to afford a motel, and apartments are a no-go. They want two months in advance and a security deposit. And with my work schedule I can't get Declan into school neither."

The Moth rose, groaned as his hip talked to him. "Wait here."

Maybe Quinn expected a handout, but the Moth had something illegal in mind. He returned with a pick set. "Now we take a short walk."

The Moth limped down the alley as the younger man trailed along behind. Beside the grocery store he stopped at a battered steel door. He drew out his lock picks and fiddled with the dead bolt. "I don't do this for a living, so I'm not good at it." Time crawled, but he suborned both locks and stepped inside.

Quinn said, "Why are we here?"

"You have to move off the street. If they scoop up the kids while you're gone off to work, they'll take your children."

"Homeless ain't a crime."

"Even if I'm wrong, aren't you tired of the car?"

"Man, *are* we tired of that car!"

"This used to be a loan company. You know, money for the title, eighty percent interest. You're going to live here."

Quinn gaped at the room, stunned. *How bright is this guy, anyway?*

The Moth rummaged a key off a nail by the back door. "See, you'll use only the back offices — no noise, no movement out in the front of the place. Keep this door shut — you'll use the two rooms here. And here's a john. No shower, but you know how to get around that.

"We do, for sure."

The Moth

The Moth said, "The big problem would be utilities, but I know a fix for gas, water, and electric." The Moth lead Quinn to a utility closet in the back corner. He pointed at two gnawed holes in the wall, one that sprouted PVC pipe and one with an armored metal hose that snaked out. He waved his hand at some raw wiring that dangled down the wall. "You'll hook this copper up here where there's a jumper to the plugs on this wall. Don't electrocute yourself."

"I done lots of wiring. But what is all this?"

"The people that ran this place were no better and no worse than most of the neighborhood. They stole utilities from the grocery store. I think the Korean next door will undergo a kick-up in his bills again." He turned the tap that routed water back into the building. "When you get a match, turn on the gas and light the hot water heater."

Quinn shuffled his feet. "Stealing don't seem right."

"You're already carrying off his water from the outside tap."

Quinn twitched his head. "We do what we got to. What about light? There aren't no windows back here. And cooking?"

The Moth sighed and reached into his back pocket. "No windows is a good thing. I'll get you two lamps out of pawn. Here's a twenty for lightbulbs. You find a junk store and buy a hotplate somewhere and feed the kids right."

Quinn ducked his head, cleared his throat. "Thanks. This is the best thing to happen to us in months."

The Tuesday after, Quinn had no job running, so they carried the Moth's new fake documentation down and registered the family on federal welfare. A week later, the Moth coached him through daily child care with the Department of Education; they worked the system in a mere five hours. The week after, they burned a whole day to sign up for food stamps at Agriculture. With three part-time jobs, it might all add up to a bare-bones living for three people. Declan might be able to attend school. Assuming the day care for Missy wasn't staffed with freaks and pedophiles.

The Moth, not a fan of other people's children, believed he could step back and let Quinn run his own life. Quinn, in his vague, not-so-quick way, laid out grateful noises. The Moth thought Declan had figured it all out faster than his father — "This is as good as our old trailer!"

The sirens yanked the Moth out of his uneasy sleep, brought him out of his fortified apartment into his shop. At first, he thought the fire blazed *at the pawnshop*, but once his fluttering heart slowed, he experienced worse, a welling fear like drowning. The flashing lights dragged him down the street towards the grocery — he discovered the loan company on fire, a blaze of spiteful, malevolent glee. He rushed the door — a fireman and the Moth's own common sense stopped him. The firemen charged in with hoses, but they didn't come out. Black as hell inside, nearly as dark out in the street.

He watched all through the hour the firefighters used to wrestle the flame down on its knees, where it couldn't torch the grocery or, importantly, threaten the pawnshop. But the fire guys lingered in the yawning charred maw of the shop, huddled up and talking. The chief, or assistant chief, or whatever rank he held called it in on a mobile. Soon a white van with the County Sheriff logo on the side wailed up. Two clambered out, donned white paper suits with hoods, carried in large briefcases and cameras. The Moth could see the flash firing off inside. A second, larger van eased over the curb, crunched over cinders, idled near the collapsed storefront.

The Moth hovered on the sidewalk, watched Fire confer with

Forensics, stared at the engines as they slid away from the curb. He lingered long after the rest of the neighborhood had faded back to their lives. He was rooted to the pavement when they brought out the first small body bag and placed it on the morgue's gurney.

1997 — DETECTIVE CHELSEA WITH THE SQUEEZE

Even before he morphed into a *real* paranoiac, the Moth preferred to meet his handler some place neutral. Anywhere in the neighborhood smelled too dangerous, since he was a snitch — one of the lower forms of life. Meeting at the station was far too depressing. And marching into the Department also assumed every cop was clean and nothing would leak. Safety lay in museums — even more in museum coffee shops. He was infatuated with the turnover of middle-class nobodies. The players were so easily identified, among the suburban moms.

Today he gave it a 25/75 chance Detective Chelsea would finally arrest him for murder. This after he had to travel across town to his favorite, the L.A. County Museum.

He viewed the buses as grand. Most people in his neighborhood — relegated by insolvency to bus travel — hated them, but not the Moth. Once he swung up the steps and spotted a seat midway back — he was picky about seat location — he sank into anonymity as deep as he had ever waded in during his long life. He could rest among the detritus, the used-up, the struggling of Los Angeles and he *looked* like them. He *was* them. He was a pair of glasses thick enough to look like fish eyes. He was a tattered button-up sweater with snags and rents and a fair-sized hole on the left collar bone. A sweater, in the gross

August heat of L.A. The air conditioning on the buses gave him colds.

The ride ran clear across Downtown and further west into civilization. It gifted him with ninety minutes to prepare for the Detective, and time to reflect on his life. If the contemplation of where he had ended up became too painful, he could distract himself with the panorama of sun-soaked life outside the window. The bus proceeded down Whittier Boulevard towards twenty rich acres of concealment and sanctuary.

At Fairfax he climbed off the bus and limped the remaining half block to the massive L.A. County Museum. Showing his annual museum pass — he prided himself on his thriftiness — he proceeded inside and chose a backless, wooden-slatted bench beneath the gold-foiled frames of the Grand Tour. The bench created a sharp needle of pain in his hip. Detective Chelsea Granovich arrived a half hour late, with her new partner in tow. Sweeping into the room, she spotted the Moth. Over her shoulder she said, "Okay, beat it. I got this."

The other detective, one of those two-for-the-price-of-one suits, appeared startled, chastened. His burr haircut and his scrawny Adam's apple caused his stare to be particularly poignant. The Moth was filled with sympathy for the cop — a displacement of the Moth's own self-pity.

Detective Chelsea churned toward him, and he watched her eat up the marble floor. She sparked like a dynamo — six feet tall in slapping flats, blonde hair cut in a flip and held back behind her ears with her sunglasses. Shoulders like an ax handle, tough long legs with bicycler-knotted calves. A slash of red lipstick. The gold badge under the coat, hung on the waistband of her skirt. The Moth had even been attracted to her, for a bare moment, before he learned how to spot a natural disaster.

She slid herself onto the bench beside him. "Hey, little mouse. Before we begin, do you have anything free for me?"

"Free?"

1997 – Detective Chelsea with the Squeeze

"You know, something I don't have to ask for. You use it to curry favor and to pay down your debt."

They had this conversation recurrently. He waggled his head. "Most CIs get paid by the police department. Why am I different?"

"Vive le différance. I keep you safe, I keep you warm, I keep that dead case file closed." She dropped her hand comfortingly on his thigh, squeezed him hard. His forty-five-year-old quad muscle yowled.

As usual, he stared at the mole on her upper lip, and failed to meet her eyes. "No, nothing today."

"Not very useful, that. Okay, let's get down to it. The Grandpoint job? The hackers broke in and destroyed the loan records for one of our big banks?"

"Detective, that's not crime, that's vandalism. The banks keep backups."

"Plenty of people are upset. Including my Sheriff. Do you know a name?"

He let out a sigh. "I don't know computer guys. You know that."

"Moving on, what can you tell me about the Kento job?"

She had played him — this is what she wanted. He blew out his breath in a sigh. "That's the jewelry store one? What do you want to know?" The Moth stalled. She could sense it. *Better get it together quick.*

She had handed him a two-fold problem here. Number one, Detective Chelsea knew him, read him like a book. Number two, Robert Zlata had cleaned out the jewelry store.

Back in May, Robert Zlata had dropped by on a shopping trip. From his counter, the Moth spied a short man with long, blue-black hair poised outside his window. He knew by the shape of the shoulders (big, packing the top of the jacket like stuffing), the arms akimbo (relaxed), the slow scan of the head (probably stoned again) that Robert had arrived. The Moth's invisible half-grin prickled at him — his own amusement constantly surprised the Moth.

The sleigh bells on the door rang out. The visitor stepped in, closed the door firmly, and checked out the window again. He turned — the Moth got his first glimpse of the man's face.

Definitely Zlata. Burned darker than his usual Eastern-Euro duskiness: Latino-looking in fact. Zlata frequented the night hours — *Why had he been out in the sun that much?* Zlata glided forward, like some ferret. "Nice store."

Arm's length. "Thanks. Poke around, check it out. I stock some nice tools."

"I'm always on the lookout for the right tools. Have we met?"

Involuntary nerves twitched at his mouth — he needed to control that smile, needed the poker face. "I think so."

Robert stuck his hand out "Tom Foley. Pawnshops are a bit of a hobby for me."

The Moth hesitated, accepted Robert's hand, allowed the cool, firm handshake. He pumped a hand disinfectant into his palm, rubbing vigorously. "Frank Pachuco."

"Maybe we haven't met. I'd remember a name like that."

"Let me reassure you — Tom — we're alone. There's no one listening. I swept for bugs yesterday."

Zlata bobbed his chin once, a short jerk. Delving in a pocket, he produced a sheet of paper, unfolded it from thirds into a shopping list. "Good. These are the tools I'm interested in today."

The Moth ran his eyes down the list. "It will take me a week to procure the plasma torch. There aren't many around except in factories. There's no problem finding the manuals for this alarm system. The comms I can hand you today and I have a selection to choose from.

1997 – Detective Chelsea with the Squeeze

"Will the torch be portable?"

"Kind of. About the same size as a regular oxy rig. I can find one on wheels for you."

"How much?"

"Rent or buy?" The Moth liked "buy," since sometimes the police ended up in possession.

Zlata spread his hands. "I may not be able to return it. So buy, but with an option to sell back."

"Okay, forty, but the rental would be ten for a week. Let's check what else is on the list." The Moth finger traced the list and his busy brain totaled the take as he cruised down the page. Curiosity tickled at him, but he never, never asked about the score.

Detective Chelsea ground her fingers into his thigh again. "You're thinking too much, little one. Out with it. Do you have a name?"

In spite of himself, the Moth liked Robert Zlata. He appreciated the shopping trip every three or four years. "Tell me about the job."

"Somebody knew the alarm systems, knew to cut the telephone and how to disarm the master console. The walk-in safe in the back had the door cut off at the hinges and the bolts sliced right through. They had to be in there for hours."

Stalling, he asked, "How did they break in?"

She raised an eyebrow. "You don't know? Really? It was on the news. They cracked in through the skylight and opened everything up. They used the back door, wandered in and out as easy as kiss-your-hand."

The Moth lay between the hammer and the anvil. "Could be Howell Cobb. He admires jewelry stores and he's a safe man, not a smash-and-grabber."

She leaned forward and breathed in his ear. "Frank, Frank, don't put me off. You know as well as I do Howie is in Calipatria doing his dime. Come across, bubelah, or we'll be visiting your old house."

He did indeed know Howell had gone up for the count. After all, he had financed twenty percent of the job, and never recovered a penny. He would need to burn Zlata, or someone like him. "Okay, maybe Willie Bankhead's team." He coughed, a giveaway. *How did I end up a snitch? If I could do it all over again.*

She leaned in close, way too close. "Look at me, little one." He *was* looking at her — how could he not, she'd slid in so tight. He could discern that sixteenth-of-an-inch blood spot in the white of her eye, the pores in her nose that weren't filled in by makeup. She had her hand on his thigh again. He tensed, glanced at the iron fingers.

Her voice sifted velvet across his face, her breath sweet. "Don't screw me around. You know Willie does liquor stores and boosts cars in between. You're not giving me shit. There's a house and yard I can tear up that will rip open your life."

"But what you don't know is Willie's team has two new guys. His brother and a friend came out from Mobile. Brother is called Alabama Bankhead. Friend is named Brock."

She was cuddled up right on him. From a distance they must have formed a one-act vignette. A young well-dressed woman sharing a confidence with an old, worn-out lover.

She breathed out the question. "And I should care because.... "

"Alabama is a box man. He likes it quiet and organized, and he's attracted to big hauls, not banging cash registers in liquor stores."

"Interesting. Where is Willie these days?"

"Not far. Up in Highland Park. He hangs in his favorite bar, the Xavier."

She had what she wanted. "Later, little one. I'll call." She tossed

1997 – Detective Chelsea with the Squeeze

him back into the waters of L.A. and finned away, smelling out L.A. blood to guide her.

Alabama Bankhead *had* made a living out of locks and safes, before someone had smashed his right hand in prison. But the Moth had to give up someone, and Willie owed him two big for license plates for about a half year. Maybe the Moth's lie would slide by. Maybe Willie would resist arrest.

Alabama slouched at the Moth's counter, humming softly to himself. In front of him lay the shattered remains of the glass top, rained down into the merchandise. He awkwardly waggled a gun in his hand, but pointed at the Moth nonetheless.

The Moth hung motionless. The pistol muzzle wavered as if in a faint breeze. His eyes flicked from the gun to the action behind Alabama. Willie had picked up a pipe wrench, and now danced back and forth in the pawnshop. At each item capable of quick ruin, he jerked to a stop and swung away with the wrench. First, the sound of Alabama humming, then the shocking racket of a TV cracking, a set of dishes exploding, a stereo caving in.

Alabama threw a question over his shoulder to his brother. "About done, Willie?"

Willie stopped in the aisle, breathed hard. "Goddam right. This is real work."

Alabama tipped his head in recognition of Willie's hard work. "What now? We gonna bust him up?"

"Naa. It's worth more to shake some money out of him every month. Gotta have him on his feet to *make* that money."

151

The Moth

The Moth watched Alabama use his good hand to turn the cash register around, open the drawer. His heart was as bruised as it could be — the Moth had just received payment for a small job he had funded. The money hadn't been shifted yet to his stash in the floor.

Alabama's pasty face burnt up brick-red. "Willie, there must be a thousand here!"

With a bound, Willie arrived at the open drawer. "Woo wee!" He stuffed money into a plastic bag. "Shit, our lucky day! Alibis for that jewelry job, and now we're on the gravy train. Our little snitch will pay."

So the Bankheads switch over from smash-and-grab to blackmail. Detective Chelsea could frame them up for something, but then I'd be her slave forever.

1999 — Lock Up Your Daughters

The Arpías crept into the Moth's life as a static-filled call on the police scanner. Seven o'clock on a hot summer evening — he had closed his pawnshop, with the day's incoming goods a complete set of melamine dishes, four mag wheels, and a wedding ring. He had returned a stereo and a set of socket wrenches for the requisite fee. He had also sold a set of bump keys to Rocky Sanchez and his brother. He limped past the steel door that isolated the pawnshop from his apartment and locked himself in. The kettle in his diminutive kitchen served up hot water for tea and for a dried packet of French onion soup. He perched on the side of his bed and listened to L.A. County's law enforcement proceed about their business, a copy of *Jonathan Livingston Seagull* in his lap.

He picked up on a call-in, four women battering a man. "Reported Four One Five F at the corner of East Hubbard and Clela, male being assaulted by four perpetrators. Perps are women, reported to be armed with clubs." In a few minutes, the Moth caught the call to scramble an ambulance (Nine Oh One N) and the announcement the perps had fled before the police arrived.

Nadine Lobato would know.

The Moth lugged his pitiful laundry down the street the next night, brought his quarters and his box of soap. While his meager linens circulated in a top-loader, he plunked heavily into a chair by Nadine. "Nice night."

Nadine's spindly shanks hung out of tangerine cargo shorts.. A wife-beater over a purple bra. "It sucks. The one cool September night and I'm stuck in here at a constant eighty-five."

"It's not that cool outside. The city is always hotter than the country."

"Are you trying to cheer me up? Forget it, asshole."

Even for Nadine, this was extraordinary abuse. He rotated his head to stare at her. His neck vertebrae popped as he twisted around, brutally loud in his ears.

She perched in the plastic bucket of a seat, a thin woman whose dyed-blonde hair looked like it had been cut by a five-year-old with kindergarten scissors. Vertical lines of sour disapproval cut past her mouth to the jawline, and her eyes had a squint of suspicion and distrust. Nadine had once, long ago, been the hottest Latina girl in the neighborhood, before childbirth, smoking, and vodka. He asked, "What's eating you?"

"Hey! I like you coming in every week with your gray shorts and your gray sheets and your dingy gray towels. You're a good customer. But don't you get in my business."

The Moth did what he did. He waited.

She dropped her chin. "Sorry."

More waiting.

"I shouldn't have took it out on you. My boy got hurt."

The Moth knew Nadine's son from a cautious distance. She thought the sun shone out of his butt. Everyone else thought he was a real piece of work. "I'm sorry to hear that. Car wreck?"

"No, not a car wreck. It's an unbelievable story, just unbelievable. He got beat up by four women."

Bingo. The Moth couldn't help it. He snickered.

"Don't laugh, asshole. It's pretty serious. He was in the hospital

1999 – Lock Up Your Daughters

all night. I didn't get him home until this afternoon. His arm is gonna require surgery. Some kinda pins."

"Four girls did all that?"

"Luis says they had broomsticks."

The Moth inclined his head, now all solicitous. "Sounds serious."

"They were out to get him. Luis says they were dressed all in black and had those terrorist masks on and wore those lace-up boots."

This startled the Moth. He let out a "Huh."

"Beat the hell out of him. Got my baby down on the ground and kicked him half-to-death. He's got a broke nose and his kidneys are all bruised. Pissing blood."

These women *were* out to get Luis. Disguised, armed after a fashion, and angry. "Does the Sheriff's Department have any leads?"

"Of course not. This is East L.A." She stared fixedly at the dingy wall of machines. "I don't know where I'll find the money for an operation. Maybe a loan shark."

Tags appeared around town on graffiti walls — what the Moth called the "bulletin boards." They were painted carefully, over a layer of white to block the noise of previous messages. The graffiti showed testicles and a penis, with a large knife descending. They had a tag that showed a bird with breasts in a crop top. The Moth thought it amusing till someone painted the bird four times across his store, on the posts between the windows. They'd brought a step ladder and painted them high, just under the orange mission tiles.

He painted slowly, methodically over the tags. First two coats of KILZ primer. A cheaper primer for the entire store front. He had begun the first coat of white top-paint when Jeeter stopped by to visit, or more likely, to cadge money.

Jeeter was eighteen. At least he said eighteen. Could have been fifteen. Jeeter had a thatch of black hair that had been in severe conflict with a windstorm. The scrawny build of someone who never had enough to eat. "Watcha doin'?"

The Moth eased down the ladder, his left leg a silent complaint. Today he wore a broad-brimmed hat that contained his frizzy cloud of gray hair. In the reflection of his own glass front, he glimpsed a used-up old man. "I could be solving the problems of the universe. I could be nailing up going-out-of-business signs."

Jeeter was one of the throw-away kids. Maybe Arab, maybe Central American, but definitely no family. "Naah. You're painting over the graff the Arpías are smearing up everywhere." The shrimp of a teenager oozed confidence; his white teeth gleamed out of a brown face.

"Why didn't anybody see them tagging my storefront?"

Jeeter snickered. "Plenty must a-seen them. It's doing something about it — never happen."

"What does Arpías mean?"

"Your Spanish sucks, man."

"Beats your English."

"Arpía is Spanish for harpy, whatever the shit that is."

"Hmm. Mythological woman. Has a woman's face and body, but with claws and wings."

"No shit? Anyway, the spray paint is going up everywhere. The Arpías got it in for any dude strutting his stuff. It's more than these tags. Word is they caught Ernesto Gonzalez right by his car, bloodied him good and knocked him out, smashed all the windows in the car. And Cesear "the Grope" Piño got his hand broke real bad, on-purpose like."

"What's behind all this?"

"Revenge chicks dressed all in black. Like they're enforcers, or cops even."

"That's called vigilantes. Taking the law into their own hands. Are they Latina?"

"Beats my shit. Probably. Maybe. Nobody sees their faces or hair."

A week after Jeeter's revelations, Thursday night rolled back around. The Moth watched his dryer rotate and drop clothes in an S shaped cataract, rumble away for a dollar fifty. Nadine folded clothes nearby. She held up a thong in brilliant yellow, a size XXX. "Look at this. Can you believe this? The only thing worse than the fact I have to handle this is the picture it has left in my mind. Skanky bitch."

"Intimidating."

"How come you got to talk like that? You never even finished high school."

That stung. "I got my GED. Besides, I read."

"High school has changed a lot since I went. Usta be all broke out by which nation your mama come from. Still is some, I guess. But now it's Gang." She threw a bra the size of two grocery sacks onto the pile.

"That's on racial lines mostly."

Her mouth cut in a slash of disagreement. "Not as much, according to Luis."

He bet Luis would know all about that. "Got an example?"

"That girl gang, the Arpías. Nobody knows who they are, but a lot of the high school girls, for sure the sluts, are dressing like 'em. Doc Martens laced to the knees. Black scarves around their necks. Brown girls, black girls, white girls."

"I hate that gang. They painted the front of my shop."

"I saw that. It was an improvement. You shouldn't have fixed it."

"Thanks."

Nadine held up a pair of men's boxers, shot through with holes. With a quick flip, she folded and stacked them. "You're welcome. Stupid bitches. Gonna get themselves hurt."

"And that means?"

She jerked a rolling cart over to her hip, stacked folded clothes into it. "The boys aren't going to stand for these beatings. Those women touch a gang member, they're dead meat."

Bitter Nadine did foresee the future, at least in the broad sense. Six Arpías descended on a Sureño named Hot Rocks Torribios as he sauntered across the parking lot of a liquor store. Because of his popularity, he lay bleeding in plain sight for a half hour while customers skirted him. Eventually, the Asian who ran the store spotted Hot Rocks out there.

The Asian store clerk called a Sureño who drove over and peeled Hot Rocks off the asphalt and transported him home. Torribios suffered an additional delay in medical aid — that delay truly about killed him. The EMS wasn't summoned until hours later when the hoods in their gang house figured out Hot Rocks was filling up with loose blood.

The Moth expected the worst possible outcome. The world held no secrets — God knew his time as a police snitch had taught him that. The women in the tough gang of vigilantes couldn't keep their mouths shut. At least two of the leadership had already been outed.

The first, Cordelia "Cordy" Ambra, was smugly informed by high school security her Dodge Neon had been torched. It had set fire to the two cars beside it. She was the lucky one.

Crystal Estevez, though, her luck dried up entirely.

The Moth's police scanner had squawked out a message he didn't understand, so he called Jeeter. Jeeter wandered around a full day to scrounge up names and details. He reported back in and reminded the Moth that he had so far turned over two free pieces of intel. Jeeter's narration, once the Moth sorted through bad grammar, ran this way; Crystal Estevez had a white mother and a black Nicaraguan father. All of her life she had been the one who wouldn't take any crap from anyone — her ganged-up father, her brothers, the guys whom she condescended to date. She was the athlete and the gymnast. She studied at a Taekwondo academy where she learned how to break people's necks. And she was known as an okay-looking babe. All that didn't help her at all.

Crystal had a steady squeeze named Benito, who fell prey to fear and panic as often as not. A visit from the Sureños convinced him that he should ask Crystal to meet him in the parking lot of a burger stand. He should suggest she leave her girlfriends behind since they were all cows. Three Sureños caught her there, pinned her on the car hood. She broke the collar bone of one and busted open the cheekbone of another, but she delivered only a couple of kicks and punches before the Sureños' superior strength nailed her to the hood. They took turns on her.

No one charged out to help her and the Sureños were in no hurry. Once they finished and had their pants zipped back up, they shoved her against the bumper and hammered her face. They knocked out the majority of her front teeth and her nose ran off at an angle.

His grudge against the Arpías dissipated, the Moth hoped Crystal had passed out early. Bad for the girl, bad for the neighborhood.

To check out his best source, the Moth limped down the street to Ramón's Taco Stand. After paying for his three chicken tacos, he lingered at the counter. Ramón settled his elbows on the counter, leaned over the side of the roach coach, and asked, "What do you want to know?"

"The Arpías. What's going on with them?"

Ramón shrugged. "Getting worse, getting better. They're not stupid. They cut a deal with the Maras. They subcontract a small volume of drugs, transport guns around to where they need to be, that kind of thing."

"Why?"

"Cause they're under the wing of MS-13. Gets the Sureños off their backs."

"I heard they were out in the open." He cocked his head, prodding for more.

"Oh yeah. No more hiding and a lot more strutting. They may be girls, but they're a force."

"Kind of changing their goals aren't they?"

"They're still whacking the cojones off these boys, any man they find who beat up a woman. But they branched out. I'll be paying them protection before long."

The tacos, crunchy and mildly spicy, waltzed in his mouth, but the Moth took less pleasure in lunch than usual. The world had invented one more reason for him to check over his shoulder.

The Arpías didn't wait long to pay a visit. They traveled in a posse, or a fighting unit. He wondered if "posse" described a gathering of Arpías. Maybe "murder" was better, like a murder of crows. Four staked out territory in his pawnshop, two as sentries in the windows and two at the counter. They all dressed the same — the boots, the black pants, the jackets with red stripes, patterned after the Crips in South Central. The two close enough to hurt him showed as black Latina, one a sallow yellow and the other vibrantly dark.

1999 – Lock Up Your Daughters

The yellow one leaned forward on the counter, her hands clasped but drooped over his side of the glass — how he hated that. She angled her face up at him and said, "We understand you carry weapons of mass destruction."

He cleared his throat. "I've never heard it called that before."

She snickered. "No, really, we want to buy some guns off you. What you have in stock?"

"I'm assuming you are representing your organization?"

The beautiful dark one said, "Right. We the Neighborhood Nuns."

"It's like this. I'm kind of a specialty supplier, mostly military or burglary gear. I don't think I'd have what you want."

The skinny yellow one said, "Let us be the judge of that. Dig out the list of what you got on hand, then we'll talk about a special order."

"I haven't been in the business of supplying gangs. Mostly I sell to criminals."

"How criminal you want me to be, midget man?"

"What I meant was that I supply for commercial ventures."

The two young women swapped considering glances. The sallow one rolled up on one elbow, practically lay on the glass. "We going commercial."

"I don't think this is a good idea."

Two smiles flashed out like high beams in the shop. The dark one, her eyes luminous, said, "If you're not our supplier, there's no reason for you to be here. We wouldn't be surprised if you was burnt out."

The sallow one broke up, like it would be a party — or a fireworks display at the marina. "What a pity. Burned to the ground. And beat to the ground too."

He had lost this argument. "This's Eloy-the-Rent's turf. I pay him to protect the store."

"Eloy Poulter be my cousin."

He spread out both hands on the counter, like an inverted crucifix. His chin hung onto his chest, he squeezed his eyes shut. "If you obtain guns from me and fire up a war with the Sureños, it will all blow back on me."

"Naah, these purely for self-defense. Besides, we're not interested in your problems. You *are* selling to us. Show him, ladies." The two Latina women on guard at the windows unzipped their jackets and strode towards the counter, one up each aisle. They whipped out broomsticks that had been cut down to two-foot lengths and fitted with leather wrist loops. Grins split their faces and they wagged their heads back and forth, flashing their eyes, like they invited admiration. They strutted straight up to him, whacked the sticks into their palms, created threatening rifle reports that echoed around the shop.

The Moth gazed across the four implacable faces. "I can see that."

"We need personal protection for fifteen, something we can carry easy, and two shotguns."

The Moth tried one more attempt to keep some control. "Here's the deal. First, Eloy has to okay this transaction.

"You setting terms on this, midget man?"

He kept talking, because if they talked…. "Second, I can supply small frame nines, seven shot. For my side I need nine hundred apiece. That's standard pricing, three times gun store value. I guarantee they don't trace back to anything. Brand new, fresh out of the box, all identical. Delivery in ten days."

The dark beauty glanced around at her friends, decided to squash him one step further. "Here's our deal. We'll pay for five and you'll give us credit for the other ten. Maybe we do you a favor later, pay our debt that way."

Maybe he could talk to Eloy-the-Rent, ask him to intercede. *Right — like that will work.* "Shotguns are two thousand each. Or you can buy them cheap at Walmart and cut them down — after you fill out the forms."

The sallow woman flapped her hand like he was an unreasonable mosquito. "Naw, you procure the shotguns." She liked the word "procure" — she sniggered. "Then we talk about if one of those be fire insurance. Now, what's under the counter we can walk out with today?"

So he had turned gang supplier for the Arpías. *Doesn't change a thing.*

2002 — The Ax

Many of the Moth's extralegal customers frightened the public at one level or another. He knew a smash-and-grab man named Kevin — Kevin inclined to sudden rages that opened up possibilities, like he might kick you to death. He styled himself as the Wolf, but the neighborhood knew him as a homosexual. Behind his back the Latinos called him "Chachi Mariposo." But they left him the hell alone.

The MacDonald brothers could face down a Rottweiler and compel it to whimper. Eloy-the-Rent Poulter could extort cash out of any store owner in the neighborhood, even the ones who kept baseball bats or guns under the counter. Even the Arpías' head, Crystal Estevez, could give the Moth the shakes. She exhibited single-minded toughness while she ran the only independent girl gang in the 'hood, and she displayed facial scars and a broken nose she had picked up from three Sureños. Sureños she later shot before their management arranged a truce of mutual respect.

But none measured up to Bruno Gutierrez.

Bruno had arrived from Argentina in the 80s, speaking Spanish, German, and a smooth English. Bruno eliminated problems, as long as those problems equated to specific human beings. On the street, word about his implacable malevolence spiraled up like smoke — created by a smoldering fire beneath it.

2002 – The Ax

Too many stories were whispered around. A Burbank police captain left the world when he was knifed in his own station, in his own interrogation room. But more whispers traveled around. The CEO of a sporting goods conglomerate had his head divided in two by an ice-climbing ax — and the shadow community renamed Bruno "the Ax."

The Moth had supplied the Ax once with a crate of Claymore mines. He hadn't heard of their use yet and wondered where they waited for the right human problem to shamble into their killing field.

And Bruno didn't care about other outfits and their reputations — he'd do anybody. The Moth flashed on another history, maybe apocryphal. It concerned a Chicago member of organized crime who choked to death on a half-pound squid, beak and all, in his own seafood restaurant's kitchen.

Now Bruno Gutierrez blocked his pawnshop doorway — a wall as much as a man. The bottom plummeted out of the Moth's stomach and he experienced a moment of vertigo. He expected something new. Bruno didn't repeat himself.

Today Bruno dressed like a high school football coach out of the Valley. He paused in the doorway, checking the store. The Moth tabulated the khaki pants, the athletic shoes, the Pittsburgh Steelers jacket. Hair shorter than last time, a buzz cut on the sides. Sunglasses — Oakleys — masked the eyes. A ball cap that announced "Coaching Staff" screened his forehead.

Bruno edged into the pawnshop towards the Moth, like a bear saunters up to a loaded picnic table. He placed his hands gentle and slow on the glass. The Moth counted one-thousand-and-one, one-thousand-and-two, one-thousand-and-three.

Bruno's voice surprised clients, suppliers, victims — a high tenor, with perhaps a bit of a German accent. "You're older, Frank."

"Aren't we all?" The Moth was relieved — no shake to his voice.

"I'm serious, Frank. You should take better care of yourself."

The Moth flapped his hand. "Is there any chance you use the old name?"

Bruno smiled. A gentle, wry grin. "Sure. This trip."

The Moth blinked under that stare. "Bruno it'll be. Perhaps there's something of particular interest you're searching for?"

"Always helpful, Frank. First, I need three small tubes of the new mil-spec epoxy, the instant set kind. Here in California it's available only from Vandenberg."

Relief. He had a man there. "We can do that."

"Second, I'd like you to supply an armored vehicle and a driver. Discretion is of course something that would... interest me." Bruno gazed to the side, like some pawn item had caught his attention.

"Discretion. In the procurement or in the vehicle?"

"I depend on your confidentiality of course. But the vehicle shouldn't be something deployed to Desert Storm." The Ax leaned in — the Moth leaned back.

"Ahh. Difficult. An executive limo? Appropriately bulletproofed?"

The Ax shrugged. "Rather obvious, wouldn't you say? I'd prefer something more nimble."

The Moth gave a shudder — maybe he couldn't bring this one off. "For regular fire, or for armor piercing?"

"Regular. If they have anti-tank weapons, if they're that prep'd, we won't reach the car anyway."

"Do I have time to have it built?"

"Afraid not. I'll need to use it next week."

"Very difficult requirements. I have only one possibility and it would be expensive, so perhaps you should seek alternatives."

"I'll pay one hundred large."

The Moth gaped. Bruno had offered him one hundred thousand

dollars for a ride. The Moth needed that money — he'd recently lost a big chunk of his own savings backing a large-scale insurance con.

"And I expect you to deliver." The Ax tapped the counter with a finger the size of a pipe bomb.

Like a card player sneaking a glance at a hole card, Bruno noted, "Let's see, you're about a thirty-two short in a coat, right?"

What the shit does my size have to do with it? What's the Ax measuring me for? A box?

"Make it happen, Frank. I'll call later today."

Maybe it was an illusion, but the floor trembled with each step of the Ax as he left. Without thinking about it, the Moth reached in his pocket and tapped out a Zantac from his dispenser. Zantac wouldn't help.

The Moth thought of only one solution — Reckless Tommy. The mobile number the Moth had on hand sang him a message of abandonment. He suspected Tommy had switched over to burner phones.

Since the Moth refused to drive any more, he hired Ylsa Perez's cab for the day. They searched for Tommy and his armored car for four hours. His anxiety level rose like like the thermometers of L.A.

Ylsa had known the Moth for years and knew his ways. She allowed him to settle into the front seat, and only once argued with his directions. They cruised the various hangouts the Moth identified or she knew, but no Tommy. They checked several clubs, a distribution warehouse that sold glassine envelopes by the thousand, a favorite whorehouse. They checked a diner halfway to civilized L.A. and they checked Tommy's church.

Tommy seldom spent his time in East L.A. His clientele had more cash than East Angelenos. In desperation, the Moth had Ylsa cruise first Wilshire Boulevard and then detour up Rodeo Drive.

The Moth

When they stumbled on the Impala parked by the curb in a tow-away zone, he could have sung with relief. His voice was far too loud for the cab interior. "There! There! There!"

Ylsa said, "I see him. You think I'm frickin' blind?" She grumbled some more, but she whipped right over behind Reckless Tommy's car.

Reckless Tommy slid around town in this thirty-year-old Impala. He had acquired it from the girlfriend of Alphonse Llamas when Alphonse had passed away. Tommy ran the business for her for a year after.

As many enemies and irate customers as Alphonse had stockpiled over the years, the Moth never understood his death. How could the drug dealer have been cut down by cancer instead of someone with a gun? The Impala, though, had saved Alphonse's life numerous times. He had armored the doors and roof, welded steel underneath, and added bulletproof glass. He had employed it for deliveries of heroin — Mexican brown — and later on, flake. Now it protected Reckless Tommy.

The Moth eased out of the seat, his hip aching. No one in the garishly painted '74 Chevy. The Moth stumped into the glam-fab store in front of him. He couldn't have been more out of place in his ragged sports coat, his prehistoric glasses with large square frames. A young woman, intent on shooing this homeless person back out onto the Rodeo Drive sidewalk, bustled towards him.

Reckless Tommy sauntered out of the store's depths with an insanely beautiful white girl who appeared maybe fourteen. Compared to her, Tommy was bracingly non-standard. His genes had stamped him with a high-yellow skin, so much white his own black heritage revolted and insisted on a flat nose with ample nostrils, creased three times by cross folds before it reached his eyebrows. The nose gave his face a formidable, imposing power and it had established Reckless Tommy as the monarch he deserved to be. He said to the

2002 – The Ax

sales clerk, "It's okay, Trisha. I know him." Tommy grasped the Moth by the arm and steered him behind a dress rack. "What the hell are you doing here, man? You'll cut into my sales. That babe is a new starlet who called and asked to browse my inventory."

The Moth pinwheeled, to check for eavesdroppers. "It's something out of the ordinary. I need you for a job, a serious one."

Reckless Tommy snorted — practically a threat with his nose. A Benin Empire nose. "Not interested."

"Seventy-five K."

"We'll talk in the car."

Reckless Tommy marched out in his Rio Mercedes cowboy boots. The Moth limped out and eased himself into the passenger seat, heaved the armored door to. "I told you it was big."

"Too big to be true. What's the job?"

"A client wants to hire an armored vehicle for the evening, along with a driver."

"So you thought of my Impala." Tommy gazed out over the flame painted hood, considering. "Seventy-five implies a likelihood of dying. Better tell me the rest of it."

"The job's next week. It's for cash. That's all I know."

"Right. Tell me all of it."

The Moth turned his head, stared into Tommy's cynicism. "It's Bruno Gutierrez. He won't reveal details until he's in the car."

Reckless Tommy's eyes twitched like a mini-seizure. "The Ax! Why didn't you say that first?"

"Will you do it?"

"Christ! It had to be the Ax, didn't it?" Reckless Tommy tapped on the steering wheel with his fingers, a drumroll of thinking.

The Moth spoke towards the bullet-proof windshield. "Bruno doesn't appreciate no for an answer."

"Does he know my name?"

"Not yet."

Tommy's forehead wrinkled like a washboard road.

The Moth let Tommy work through it. Probably Tommy started with the fact Bruno never was apprehended. Then he would slide on to how the murders were solo gigs, how Bruno must be fabulously rich, how lethal he could be. Tommy's mouth twitched, like he was talking to himself. He grabbed his own chin and pinched hard. "And he could kill you with a plastic straw."

"You'd be working for the best." *Why am I trying to talk him into this?*

"Hell, my name is Reckless. Tell him yes. I'll overpaint the car black so she won't be so noticeable."

The rendezvous was scheduled behind the Moth's pawnshop on the next Thursday. The Moth and Reckless Tommy lingered in the steel car covered in temporary black paint. The Moth waited to be paid. Reckless Tommy waited to learn if this turned out a death sentence. Tommy twitched, his eyes and his hands. His knees drummed up and down.

The Moth asked, "What'll you do with the money?" The car was heating up — he cranked the window down.

Tommy grinned. "You wouldn't believe me if I told you."

"Try me."

"I'm going to buy my sister a house somewhere. Her son's autistic and she's never caught a break in her life."

The Moth coughed into his hand so the other man wouldn't catch his smile. "Tommy, you've gone soft."

"Fuck you."

Bruno shocked them when he appeared at their elbows. "Gentlemen. I hope you're ready."

2002 – The Ax

The Moth trickled a dribble of urine into his pants. Reckless Tommy dipped his head.

Bruno wore a tuxedo. "Here's the hundred." Bruno handed a paper grocery bag to the Moth, who started counting out seventy-five for Tommy. All in C notes, non-consecutive.

Tommy shoved the money back at the Moth. "You keep it for me. I don't want it on me, no matter what the outcome is. You know who gets it."

The Moth shook Reckless Tommy's hand, and, after a moment's consideration, offered his hand to Bruno. Bruno glanced at the pallid, limp digits and said, "No need. You're taking this ride too."

This news slapped the Moth's brain like electroshock therapy. He stuttered.

Bruno said, "The decision happened days ago. I don't know your man here, so if things cave in and he screws up.... "

The Moth stared into Bruno's face — Bruno projected only a great calm. He couldn't wriggle out of this one. "I need to stash the money in my shop."

Bruno's mouth curved up in one corner. "I'll allow that. If you're not back in three minutes, I'll break your friend's neck and drive myself."

So the men turned out second priority — it was about the car.

Bruno unzipped a bag slung over his shoulder and shoved a bundle of clothes in the Moth's arms. "Get naked while you're in the pawnshop. Slip into these. They're your party clothes."

The Moth turned through the pile of clothes. They smelled faintly of gun grease. Bruno had handed him a tux with a black shirt.

The Moth drummed his fingers on the Impala's bench seat — strapped in like the seatbelt could save him. Reckless Tommy piloted down out

The Moth

of the East L.A. night, his descent towards the coast. In the back seat Bruno, his hand heavy on the Moth's shoulder, clued them on where to go, where to turn.

Down into the Platinum Triangle past the Beverly Wilshire. Reckless Tommy, his eyes white like headlights, his teeth a flicker in the dash lights, decided to enjoy the whole thing. "Mr. Gutierrez..."

"Call me Bruno. We're all friends here."

"I was thinking. I know a lot about L.A. If you told me where we were going...."

Bruno hummed, a thrumming calm.

"I mean, I could be thinking about escape routes."

"It's an estate. One way in, one way out."

The Moth noticed the marsh under his arms, in his crotch. "Does this mean what I think it means?" *A hit, on a guarded estate.*

Bruno beamed, his teeth shining white in his brown face. "It clearly does. Here's a bolo to wear." He handed over a western tie studded in diamonds, or rhinestones.

Bruno directed Reckless Tommy on, deeper and deeper into the big money of Bel Air. They drew up to the gates of a mansion, but not before the Moth had popped an anxiety attack and calmed back down, a bit. A rent-a-cop with a clipboard leaned in Tommy's window. "Unusual vehicle, there. Gotta check you against the guest list, gents."

Bruno reached out an invitation from the backseat and in a broad Spanish accent said, "We're on the party list. Señors Hacha and Guerra."

The guard opened the card. "This is for two. There are three of you."

"Es posible our chófer will wait with the car?" Nothing would faze Bruno; he smiled calm as glass.

The guard stepped back, waved at the camera on the gate post, and motioned the car forward into the drive. Bruno instructed Reckless Tommy. "When we leave the party, we may be in a hurry.

Don't get blocked in, don't sleep, don't wander off to pee or smoke."

Tommy spat out the window, grim. "What if you don't come back?"

"There's a gun in the bag in the backseat."

The asphalt drive led to the brand of elegance only towering crags of money can buy, a Tudor pile that pretended to be English in Southern California. The lower story brown-brick-and-stone, the upper story timbered beam and fake wattle and daub. Three raw-boned black men at attention on the steps in their formal attire, hands crossed over their crotches. White coiled wires twisted out of their ears and disappeared down their collars. Their toughness was manifest; maybe they had been burned to sinew and muscle by a threatening sun.

The Moth lurched his way out of the front seat, held the seat forward so Bruno could exit. He waited for his employer to straighten his tux jacket; he caught a phrase or two from the guards as they talked French among themselves. As he and Bruno tramped up the steps he leaned into Bruno and hissed, "This is General Bolamba, isn't it? You've brought us to Bolamba's."

Bruno glanced at the Moth with an expression the Moth interpreted as pity. "Relax, Frank. His name is General Paul Ngandu Bolamba. As you know, a refugee from Zaire, or the DRC as it's been renamed."

The Moth ate two Zantac. "Are you after his money?"

"Spare change? I don't think so. I'm after the goat-sucking general. Not all my assignments are commercial in nature. Every once in a while, there's a termination that is somewhat moral."

"Why am I here?"

Bruno grinned, tipped his head affably at the Congolese guards. "Don't hiss at me, Frank. You're here for a civics lesson.."

Great — Bruno is showing off. The Moth shivered, a wave of revulsion. The last time he'd been involved in community work, he'd had his hip broken. "I don't like it. I'm not civic. I'm not supposed to be here."

"I, I, I. There's no "I" in Team, Frank."
Two more armed guards flanked the door. The Moth whispered again to Bruno. "You could never shoot our way out of here!"

"Relax, relax. I don't even have a gun on me. See, here's a metal detector — all the best mansions have them. Empty your pockets out into the bowl." They passed through into the inner sanctum.

For an interminable hour, Bruno and the Moth circulated through the crowd, dined on the hor d'oeuvres as waiters wafted them by, ignored the champagne.

Bolamba stacked up shorter than the Moth expected, much grayer than when he had fled in 1999, and as ebullient as only a genocidal maniac could be. Two times they edged close enough to hear his French-African accent leading his circle of sycophants in mutual admiration. The Moth was most surprised at the two beauties that flanked Bolamba, absolute stunners even in a town that had invented Hollywood. A Swedish blonde versus an Italian heartbreaker.

Bruno murmured, "Soon, I think. Bolamba is a well known sex addict, and he hasn't engaged in his obsession since we arrived for the party." In ten minutes, Bolamba gripped his two beauties by the elbows and escorted them towards the stairs.

Bruno dropped back, dragged the Moth with him. "Okay, no hurry. We'll meet him upstairs." They paraded through the kitchen, where the Latino staff froze and stared. Bruno held up his wallet, flipped it open. "It's okay, folks. California Bureau of Investigation, not Immigration." Up the servants' stairs, the Moth limping hard. The

2002 – The Ax

broad hall paneled in some dark wood, double doors into the bedrooms. Bruno counted his way. "Number four, and voilà. Don't worry, I've already scouted the place."

Bruno fiddled with his watch. "On the clock. Three minutes, in and out." He threw the doors open, strode in like it was his house. The Moth stumbled along behind. Bolamba knelt in bed with the two women, about to sink into the blanched Swedish flesh. The other woman braced his arm and helped his aim with her hand. Three shocked faces whipped around to Bruno. He jerked his thumb over his shoulder. "You women, grab your clothes and get out."

As the women scrambled for the door, Bruno intercepted Bolamba in his dive for the phone. He seized the Black by the wrist. The General howled in pain. Bruno grabbed the other wrist and Bolamba sobbed. The watch beeped. In a conversational tone, Bruno said, "Thirty seconds. Frank, I wonder if you'd grab my suitcase out from under the bed and open it. That's a good boy."

The Moth didn't know if "good boy" was directed towards him or Bolamba. The man crouched on the bed doing his best to keep his wrists from snapping. This meant Bruno could steer him backwards anywhere across the sheets he wanted, like conning a boat.

The suitcase held a rubber shawl like scuba gear, with chunks of hardware hung from it. At Bruno's insistence, the Moth wriggled the vest around Bolamba's torso, locked the sides tight with straps. All the while Bruno applied relentless pressure and the naked man moaned. "Ninety seconds."

"Now, you'll find your epoxy in the suitcase. Open one, and be careful not to squirt any on you. Good, good. Stick the nozzle in his armpit and squeeze. Another, and the other armpit. And the third, distribute on the back of the vest. Two minutes." The watch switched, beeped every ten seconds, counted it off. The Moth could catch the watch's ding underneath the General's moaning.

Bruno picked Bolamba up by loops on the vest shoulders and glued him to the headboard. "General, I thought of this ending when I read about you fastening women to trees with piano wire." He activated the vest. "This vest has both a timer and trembler switches. Jiggle and you die right away. If you don't get the world's best bomb expert here within the hour, you also die. Enjoy your time." Bruno's watch gave four sharp alarms. "Frank, time's up."

Bruno led the way through a dressing room door, into another bedroom, and out onto a terrace. They descended a spiral staircase and re-entered the house. The Moth protested. "Are you crazy? Back in? The women have the troops scrambling by now."

"A tiny ounce of faith please." Bruno bumped him down a service hallway, showed him a grenade in his hand, and opened a door. "Video security room, central comms. Guards are all upstairs with the boss. Grenade is phosphorus." He dropped it, closed the door, and they ambled back into the party. They left behind a small popping noise and a fizzling like water in a hot skillet.

Midway across the grand salon floor, they and everyone else in the room bounced a jig and a half-step. The champagne fountain and all its ranks of glasses sounded an alarm with tinkling sounds. Bottles on the bar rattled. The Moth grabbed Bruno by the shoulder. "Tremor! Bet you didn't think of that! It's California, Bruno. Our luck has failed!"

Bruno half-picked up the Moth and sprinted for the door. "The vest will explode in five seconds. Ceiling's about to collapse." The quake's major shock punched them and the floor rolled in a wave. As they staggered through the metal detector, the house behind them rammed them hard with a thunderous explosion. They plummeted down the steps, landed beside a knot of guards on the ground. They bolted for the car park. The breath of a bullet caressed the Moth before he heard

2002 – The Ax

the crack of the shot. A cacophony of shots. He doubled over and ran faster than he had since age thirty. His heart pained him; his lungs tried to burst. For once, the hip didn't hurt.

The limo he rushed by developed a strong case of blemishes and the windows starred up in spiderwebs. Guards' pistols had been replaced with automatic weapons. The entire parking area whipped around in a maelstrom. The Moth dived through the Impala's window into the back seat. Bullets hit the back of the car and shook it. Reckless Tommy waited the additional two seconds for Bruno to stuff himself into the front seat. He dropped the hammer. The Impala tore off the lot asphalt onto the lawn and slewed across the grass, narrowly missing a row of blue spruce. With a lurch they rocketed over a berm. Tommy spun the wheel and they cut around a fountain, spraying gravel everywhere. He jolted up onto the driveway. Ahead, the gates — he leveled them.

The Moth clawed his way up to the seat-back. "Goddamn you Bruno — I hope you're happy!" His heart hammered hard — his vision had narrowed to a dim circle.

Bruno turned around to stare the Moth down. "Great times, Frank. Your first murder?"

"*I* didn't kill anyone."

"You strapped the vest on, didn't you? Glued him in, didn't you? Pretty good for a civics lesson." He tapped Tommy on the arm. "LAX, if you don't mind."

2010 — Mickey Barat's Price

The Lincoln Continental slid up to the curb in front of the Moth's pawnshop, as misplaced as a Hollywood red carpet would have been rolled out from the Korean grocery store. He read it as a sign. *Something evil this way comes.*

Lately his coping mechanism was to rip a gray frizzy hair out of his sideburn, in order to concentrate on a problem at hand. Times troubled him enough that he possessed a small bald spot on his right cheekbone. He flicked the latest curly hair off his fingertips into his waste paper basket and turned back to the door.

Another shock; a woman swept in the door, not the mobster he had expected. He scrambled around in his memory as he took her in. She stood five eleven, crane-like, wore her hair in a bun and her glasses on her forehead. Shining dark skin. Cuban or Haitian he guessed — Junie Guillermo, that was her name. "Hello, Junie. I haven't run into you in a while."

She sniffed. "Different circles, I expect. I don't believe I've ever been in here."

Plenty from your church have. Silence, patience.

She said, "It's not as awful as I expected. In fact, it's quite clean."

"It's nice to see you too. Is there anything I can do for you?" He wished so hard she had sauntered in to pawn something — *fat chance*

— that a serious muscle in the back of his neck popped. The more he tried not to flinch every time it jerked, the more he understood epilepsy.

"Are you all right? You look twitchy."

"That's Mr. Barat's car outside, isn't it?"

Her smile lit up with middle-class smug. "I'm Mr. Barat's personal assistant. It's a brand new position and it comes with some benefits." She aimed her chin back towards the door. "Like a chauffeur for little errands."

"Congratulations. Ummh. Aren't you — ummh — the first black to work directly for Mickey?"

The frown reached clear into her hairline. "Mr. Barat — " she leaned on the name — "is an equal opportunity employer. He hires Asians, Latinos, and African Americans."

True. Mickey hired Latinos for the Moth's neighborhood. He'd invaded an Asian neighborhood with an Asian brigade. And Blacks hired on as shock troops. But he chose all his officers from the ranks of the white and Russian. "Sorry, sorry."

"Let's turn to the purpose for my visit. Mr. Barat has booked a time for you tomorrow morning at eight o'clock. I am sure that will be convenient?"

He dipped his head in assent. Whatever time Mickey wanted would be what everyone agreed to.

"We'll send the car for you."

Great. He wouldn't even have Ylsa or Tommy at the curb. Not that it mattered once he crossed the front-door sill.

No Junie the next morning. Rather, Yevgeny dragged him through the Altadena mansion, hand tucked under the Moth's arm. The driver or butler or lieutenant — whatever his title — leaned down to hiss into the Moth's scalp. "Speed it up, you. Mr. Barat doesn't like to be kept waiting."

He scurried along a wide hallway covered in stone flagging, half lifted into the air by his guide. They turned into the kitchen and discovered Mickey.

Mickey smoked alone at the kitchen table, a table for eight. He had read half-way through the *Times*, smoke from his gasper curling in the still air. The remains of a healthy breakfast had been swept aside. Mickey hadn't changed much. His hair shone a glossy black and fell into his face like a sickle. His nose reached out long and thin, with a knob where it had once been broken. Mickey weighed in as the most important man in the room at all times, but his head overshadowed his small body and his shoulders appeared boney underneath the tailored shirt.

Yevgeny jerked a Windsor chair out from the table — the legs clattered on the flags. He settled the Moth into the seat, as gently as he would pitch a hammer onto a workbench. "Here he is, Mr. Barat."

Mickey slid his eyes over at the Moth. He shook the newspaper and closed it, folded it in half, rolled it into a tight cylinder. "Here's a souvenir for you."

The Moth cradled the paper in his hands. He shot a glance at it, at Mickey, and back again.

"That section is three weeks old. My boy is in there, along with my name and his mother's. Page nineteen, I think. I kept it for you."

The Moth cleared his throat. "You called a while back, said we should talk."

"I been thinking for these three weeks. Some real consideration about what you would say, what I'd say. And how you'd react to what I did."

2010 – Mickey Barat's Price

"It was a great tragedy, what happened, Mr. Barat."

"Please, call me Mickey. We have a lot in common."

The Moth waited. Mickey had arranged this moment for a monologue.

"My son, point in fact."

Crap. Here it is. "I didn't know Butch well."

Mickey dropped his hands to the tabletop and shoved the oversized ashtray down the pinewood, as if he knocked away the Moth's words. "It isn't every day a father loses a son and a gun seller loses a customer. You knew him well enough for that." Mickey's eyes showed black as hell.

"He just walked in."

Mickey's fingernail picked at the table's raised woodgrain. "You know, sometimes crazy things happen in business. Me and Alexander's mother tried to keep the crazy things away from him. And now this."

The Moth dipped his head a bare half inch.

"You know why Butch came to you? Because no one here would have ever supplied him with a gun. He knew that, so he tracked you down, a fool with a fool's help." Mickey flopped his hand towards the goon at the Moth's shoulder. "If he had asked, I'd have sent Yevgeny with a couple of guys to snatch his car back."

The Moth said, "Maybe he wanted to show you he could handle it on his own. He lost it in a card game. Believed he had been cheated."

Mickey's face flushed. "You don't think I don't know that? You don't think I didn't get to those people, find out what was what?"

"No. I expect you know as much about it as anyone ever will."

Mickey stared at him. The house voiced small sounds into the pause between them — the pop of the wall as the sun heated it, the sibilance as the breeze brushed a Japanese maple against the window. The sound of his heart as it thumped in his ears.

The Moth

Mickey reached to the side for the cigarettes. "You own a giant set of balls. Not that they'll do you any good." Yevgeny brought the ashtray back up the table, settled it near at hand.

The Moth had been perspiring since he landed in the chair. His entire envelope of skin prickled with sweat. "Is there something I can tell you about that day, something you want to know?"

"Let's think about what I don't know. I saw the shotgun, or at least what was left of it. The stock melted in the fire. I saw one of the card players, dead and all burned up too. Alex died shooting back — he killed one of the little bitches."

The Moth's shoulders bound even tighter.

"Most of all, I saw my son, so charred I'd never have recognized him. Shot four times, they say. That was your gift to my family."

Stretch the conversation out. Live longer. The Moth offered, "Here's what you don't know. Butch told me you knew he came to visit me."

"You calling my boy a liar?"

Yes, but not to your face. "Not at all. It just shows how important it was to him. He wanted to handle it himself. Butch wanted an auto, something like a .9 millimeter. He kept saying 'they' so I figured he needed more of an equalizer. I rented him one of my best weapons. I thought he'd scare the shit out of them and collect his car and title. And I'd get my shotgun back."

"That doesn't change anything."

Where have I heard that before?

Mickey held the pack of cigarettes in his hand, tapped the filter end on the table top. He flipped them end for end, began to tap them again. "What am I going to do with you anyway?"

The Moth couldn't imagine a response to this. He knew Mickey had already determined the answer. His stomach lurched — he hoped it would be quick.

2010 – Mickey Barat's Price

"Here's the thing. You waded into my business without asking me. Alexander brought some of it on himself, but you gave him the gun and practically marched him up to the house to die. It was you who kicked the whole shoot-out into happening. You owe me, and I know the price."

So this is how it will end. Mickey's face had wiped blank. An empty set of eyes. The Moth searched them for the dark of the future. His stomach heaved, his esophagus choked down on the bile.

Mickey tapped his finger once, twice. He leaned on his elbows, so still, he didn't appear to breathe.

The Moth licked his lips. "The price?"

"Killing is too easy. We could pump a bullet in your head and it's done, and you don't even suffer. Hell, that's not payment. No, something better."

The Moth roosted in his hard wooden chair, inert, beaten down.

"This is the payment. Five card players robbed my boy that night. Some have paid, some will soon. Alexander killed one of them. That left another four I have to dispose of. You owe me four deaths. Anybody, anytime. I tell you I want someone dead, you do it. No questions, no screw ups."

Jesus suffering Christ!

"Now, you might ask how I know you can carry it off. It doesn't matter. You're smart in a stupid way. You'll figure it out, or.... "

Execute someone?

"It's perfect. It'll never ricochet back on me and I don't have to worry about how it gets done. I trade you four dead men for my boy. Tell me now. You take the deal, or you leave it."

The Moth stared at Mickey, his vision focused like he peered down a pipe. His mouth tasted like dust and his heart shivered in his chest. Four more dead. And Mickey might kill him anyway.

Mickey said, "Well?"

I'm just a thief. Not a murderer. A voice creaking out of his chest. It didn't sound like his voice. "I accept."

Mickey's eyes narrowed to a squint. "No handshake. I'd rather cut off my arm than shake your hand. Yevgeny here will run you home, make sure nothing happens to you on the way. You wait, however long it takes, for my call." Mickey flapped his hand, like he startled birds into flight.

The Moth lurched to his feet, desperate to leave the kitchen. Yevgeny seized him under the arm again and wheeled him towards the door.

Mickey delivered the final message as the Moth left the room. "And here's another thing to think about. You better hope it's not the L.A. Chief of Police."

Is this how relief is supposed to feel?

2012 — Starting with Reckless Tommy at the Taco Stand

The bricks that smashed onto the hood and crazy-cracked the windshield did more than anything to convince the Moth he had committed a horrible mistake. To even leave his pawnshop, much less embark on the thin bleeding line that led him to this folly. His sphincter quivered and whimpers escaped his lips. The two men on each side of him threw open their doors and dropped to the ground. The gunfire rang so loud in the small space, it punched him back and forth in the seat.

The Moth remembered from the beginning to this moment, from the everyday to the impossible. He had secured the door of his shop from the sidewalk, locked both the glass door and the steel grill that stood proud of the glass by three inches. The bars of the outer door held three brass-painted balls inset in the vertical grid, the historic sign of a pawnshop. Traditionalist ways comforted him.

He fished out his grubby white handkerchief, scrubbed dust off of the brass balls, blew his nose into the handkerchief, and stuffed it into his back pocket. The Moth paced down the street, limped a bit. Past his own shop, he crossed in front of the Washeteria — the one he used every Thursday night. On the other side of the street squatted the Korean grocery store — he didn't shop there because of a running feud, a grudge wrapped around electricity stolen off the Korean meter.

Halfway up the next block, in front of a vacant lot, Ramón's Taco Stand leaned against the curb. Ramón himself leaned on the counter, waited until the Moth had crossed the intersection. In an extended three-count, Ramón constructed three modest chicken tacos. As the Moth reached the counter, Ramón stuffed one cup of hot sauce, the tacos, a baggie of corn chips, and a plastic fork wrapped in a napkin into the bag. "Four dollars sixty-two."

The Moth glanced at his friend, a middle-aged Mexican with a hunched posture, a bit of chef's fat on him. "Thank you, Ramón." The Moth poured the exact change into Ramón's hand. He scooped up the paper bag with both hands and carried it like a chalice to the picnic table. With some small trouble, he wriggled his arthritic knees beneath the table and laid out his tacos on the paper bag.

The Moth ducked his mouth to the taco for his first bite, held the shell like a squirrel holds a nut. He gazed straight up the street to a '74 Chevy Impala two-door, a monster block of a car bereft of contours or charm. From his angle, he distinguished the swath of painted flames swirling down the car side. He could identify the new vinyl roof — gorgeous compared to the old one years ago with its ripped tufts of white and yellow padding. He squinted at the flashing sunlight that bounced off the chrome. He knew the car.

The Moth watched the driver door fly open, a leg in blue denim jam a cowboy boot out to keep the door from ricocheting back. The owner of the boot and leg heaved himself out of the car, achieved his full five-foot-two, adjusted his black drivers cap, and gazed about him like a king.

2012 – Starting with Reckless Tommy at the Taco Stand

Ignoring the sidewalk, Reckless Tommy strode down the street until he reached Ramón's. He checked out the Moth at his table with a searching stare, while he ordered an iced tea. The ten steps to bring it over. Giant-like for all his height, he plunked the tea down. "Mind if I sit here?"

The Moth inclined his head — civilly, he believed. "Afternoon, Tommy. Go right ahead."

Tommy maneuvered his cowboy boots under the plank top, thumping and knocking away. He drew hard on the straw that stood guard in the iced tea. "Thought I might find you here."

"Good assumption. I eat most lunches at Ramón's."

"You eat every lunch at the taco stand. And some dinners, too."

"Any special reason why you'd search me out?"

"I'm not looking for you. This is all coincidence. See, I needed something wet and this roach coach sells tea. You happened to be here."

The Moth dipped his head, approached his taco from the side, and bit off another mouthful. The entire time, he fixed his gaze on Tommy.

Tommy had bought more than the Impala from Alphonse's girlfriend. He bought the business. In return for the money, she supplied a list of names and numbers. Tommy changed the business and now dealt designer drugs, Ecstasy's children. Tommy preferred high end. No parking spot in an alley with lookouts posted, no desperate, shaking people to sneak by and swap a twenty for a glassine envelope.

Tommy delivered. From Bel Aire to Mulholland Drive, he'd wheel up the drive or park by the gates, and deliver the party, the redemption, the consolation prize — whatever the customer thought he or she was buying.

Reckless Tommy didn't work the Moth's neighborhood. He marked the cost up too high for local residents and he preferred the beautiful people. His first real words sneaked into the air. "I hear you in trouble with Eloy Poulter."

"Hmm."

"Got tired of the cost of protection, didn't you? Gave him a dirty gun and snitched him out."

The Moth flashed a peek around the taco stand's tables. "Could you keep your voice down?"

"I'd be nervous too. Coincidently, do you know Eloy Poulter's sister?"

"Ah, the lovely Eugénia." The Moth did indeed think of her as lovely, a milk-chocolate marvel. He wondered how Eugénia could spring from the same loins as Eloy-the-Rent did, popped out from her momma, Mercedes. Different fathers? Different races?

The memory in the Moth's brain scorched him. Eugénia naked in front of the tattered venetian blinds, her stunning backside more beautiful than anything he'd viewed since Molly. She edged the blinds apart, to check out who had driven up outside. Her shoulders were lustrous in the light, like bronze. That light even now hurt — his eyes stung.

Reckless Tommy slurped brown fluid up his straw. "Maybe not so pretty much longer, the way she's headed."

"Meaning?"

"She's hooked up with some cookers down off South Los Angeles Street, living in this warehouse and smoking like a chimney." Tommy didn't approve of crystal meth, but he didn't mind it much since it appealed to a more impoverished clientele. Didn't cut into *his* market.

"Not much life expectancy in meth."

"Word is you and her were a hot item, a while back."

"Not really. She worked as a bookkeeper next door, when she was twenty and I was fifty. I used to speak to her occasionally. Long time ago." But some things you don't get over.

2012 – Starting with Reckless Tommy at the Taco Stand

"Word is she had you twisted around her finger."

The Moth considered. He shredded off another bite of taco.

Tommy squeezed his paper cup until the lid sprang off and a fountain of tea escaped the cup, splashed both his hands. "Son of a bitch!"

The Moth offered his paper napkin.

Tommy, distracted by his liquid accident, forgot to edge up on the issue and jumped right to it. "So Eloy-the-Rent is plenty pissed at you and can't decide whether he's wants to pound you into a paste on the sidewalk, or double the insurance you pay him each week. But here's his sister, see, sliding off the cliff edge."

The Moth sensed a gnawing in his chest — something hidden nibbled away in there. "What's her problems got to do with me?"

"It's no skin off my nose, but I thought you might want to trade Eloy his sister for your shitty life. Earn his undying gratitude."

Only a 50/50 chance of success — Eloy was a terrible human being. "This is all about the Kevlar vest I sold you, right? The one you ruined four days after you bought it?"

Reckless Tommy fished out his wallet, pinched a yellow slip of paper. He placed it on the brown stained boards, poked it across to the Moth with a fat, immaculately manicured finger. "It was a nice vest. Here's the meth lab address."

The paper lay on the table between them. The Moth glanced at Tommy, but Tommy only stared at the yellow rectangle like it could sing and dance. The Moth sighed and reached out. The slip of paper twitched into his hand, disappeared.

A man had to know. The Moth couldn't form rational decisions if he didn't know the facts, the landscape. He needed recon, something he didn't do himself anymore. He leaned against the glass counter in his

The Moth

pawnshop and dialed Jeeter. "Hey there, guy. I hit on an errand I need you to run. It's worth fifty."

The phone yanged into his ear. "This is who?"

"C'mon. You know who it is."

"Don't know. Why won't you say?" The voice whined out of the earpiece, buzzed into his head.

"Why didn't I use your name? Think about it."

The voice on the other end considered it. "Someone listening."

"Could be. Drop by and visit."

Jeeter dropped his voice a half octave. He sounded like Mickey Mouse lampooning Darth Vader. "Sure. But I ask for at least fifty. My time valuable."

Jeeter slipped into the pawnshop like a fish flashing under a rock, and swam his way to the counter. He dragged a bar stool over from the furniture section, popped up onto it, and banged his fists across the glass. "Sup?"

The Moth slid the yellow paper over to the young man. "It says — "

"I know what it says. I can read." Jeeter stared at it, his head ticking and tocking as he acquired each number and word.

"Know this neighborhood?"

"Sure, and I know that address. South of Downtown. I wouldn't collect or drop off nothin' there. You find a stupid someone besides me to check into a meth cookhouse. Half a Benjamin. Hah!"

"I really don't know where you find these expressions. The fifty is to watch, and maybe evaluate a situation."

"Maybe."

"You heard of Eugénia Mondragón?"

"Oh yah. I'd like to do jimmy jam with her, you bet!"

2012 – Starting with Reckless Tommy at the Taco Stand

The Moth frowned. At least Jeeter used euphemisms. "You'd like to do that with practically anyone. Anyway, maybe she's in with the cookers. She may want to be there. Or not. She might be toked on meth, and on her way to the morgue. I'd like to know. And I'd like to know who owns the show."

Jeeter tipped his head and stared, like he had run into an exotic bird for the first time. "Why?"

"Just go see."

"Fifty now, fifty more before I tell."

The Moth opened the old cash register and handed over five ten dollar bills.

The Moth perched in back on the concrete step of his apartment, the phone in his lap. He waited for Jeeter, and didn't wait long. The young man, dressed in a scruffy T-shirt and baggy shorts, popped out from behind the dumpster and threw himself down beside the Moth. "You right."

"How exactly?"

"She in there. And it's the Arellano Cartel — I recognize Chu-Chu Cristobal. These guys cut your throat and jerk your tongue out the gash."

The Moth handed over the other fifty. *Great, a cartel, not a mere gang.*

"They chained her up in the back, to some pipe-rack shelves. At least I think it's her. I got a good look through the skylights. She ain't happy."

The Moth had hoped Eugénia lived there of her own free will. Now if he skittered away — could he deny her, like she had denied him? "Details?"

"She's smoking all right, but there nothin' else to do. She on a mattress and there's a pipe and a bag of crystal laying by her. You see she been crying and you see she share the mattress with somebody. Maybe more than one somebody."

The Moth gave a heavy sigh. "What's the layout like?"

"Two warehouse doors in front, locked. Guards. They got a bank in there — tables full of money I seen from the skylights. A rollup door in back on a dock. Skinny windows ten feet up on both the front and the back. No way in from the roof."

"Very thorough, Jeeter. Number of people?"

"They're in and out. Looks like maybe four shooters in there pretty much all the time, and some workers, cooking away in their underwear. That way they can't steal."

"Guns?"

Jeeter's head rocked up and down like it would fly off. "Way much."

Worse and worse. "Can you get a message to Eugénia? Bring one back?"

The young man inspected the Moth like the pawnbroker was a village idiot sitting on the curb. "Grate in the floor, way in the back. Drains out under the dock. Three hundred, I might be able. I get paid either way."

Jeeter returned at eight in the morning, when the pawnshop opened. As the Moth unlocked the door, he picked out a tapping, a scraping, and as he tried to twitch the blinds aside, the boy wriggled in. Goggle-eyed, the boy said, "Lock it back up. Wait till your ears catch what I tell!"

They perched opposite each other on stools, the glass counter between. Better that way, even though the glass case couldn't insulate him from what Jeeter had to say.

"Cooler than shit! I snuck in fine. The grate wasn't screwed down, just setting there loose. I crawl over to her and hide behind the shelves."

"How was she?"

"Real real bad. I wouldn't have placed her if I hadn't known it was her. She was crashing after a big drag-fest. Otherwise I think she woulda screeched or something when she first spotted me. But she could barely stay awake."

"What did she tell you?"

"Wants out. Been there two months in lock-down, even if she was there a couple more before. What true is she chained like a dog."

What the Moth didn't want to hear. "So she's a prisoner."

"Worse. A sex slave. And she three months knocked up. She say she gotta get out and get clean or kill herself, for the brat's sake."

The Moth would need an army. His reality had settled out clear, all the dross at the bottom. A traditionalist had to do stupid, honorable things.

The MacDonald brothers were conspicuous in a community principally Latino. They were as black as only men with Nigerian ancestry could be, a blue-black that radiated power, a dark light, and lots of perspiration. The Moth supposed their last name had derived from some Southern slave owner. Residents in their neighborhood — Central Alameda — knew them as Mac One and Mac Two, perhaps because of their penchant for automatic weapons. The Moth used their first names rather than One and Two. He inclined his head, solemn as the situation warranted. "Thanks, Lonnie, Germaine, for meeting with me."

Lonnie leaned over the kitchen table and picked up the bottle of Jaegermeister in front of the Moth. He poured a double shot into his coffee and offered the bottle to his brother. "What you come to say, old man?"

His brother filled up an empty coffee cup. "Now, Lonnie, don't be that way. Let's hear him out." Germaine resembled his brother except he wore glasses. This typed him as the intellectual one.

The Moth glanced around the dingy kitchen, cleared his throat. Judging by the grime levels and the sink stacked with plates and pots, the brothers Mac no longer had women in the house. "I have a pretty big score possible and I'm searching for two partners to go in with me. Hard men with a successful track record."

The two brothers' smiles erupted out of their midnight faces. The Moth didn't interpret these as happy or amused grins. He viewed them as the grimaces of predators, seconds before the snarl. Germaine waved his hand at his brother. "Lonnie, here, he pretty hard. I seen him skin a white man once."

Lonnie glanced at his brother, stared at the Moth. "I didn't do it for fun. He didn't pay up, at least not at first. And we dumped him at Emergency."

Not much to say about that. The Moth dropped his eyes to the tabletop, which had been used as a cutting board, deep slices scored across it. The Moth fingered a gouge.

Germaine rocked back in his chair. "Is this worth our while?"

The Moth forced himself to look up from the table, establish eye contact. "It's a meth lab."

"So? Have to be a lot of meth."

"There's a bank in there too." That much the Moth could confirm — the next he fabricated. "They're perched on three months worth of revenue. Between the drugs and the cash, it should be maybe two hundred thou." Completely invented number.

"We think we know which lab you talking about. South of Downtown, north of the Crips. They keep troops."

2012 – Starting with Reckless Tommy at the Taco Stand

The Moth shook his head. "We time it right, there will be only four. I'll supply the two guns you need. Full autos, AR15s."

Germaine leaned over to Lonnie. "I'm partial to the Moth's guns."

Lonnie inspected the inside of his coffee cup. "We get to keep them?"

The Moth wouldn't have touched the rifles after the job anyway. "They're yours, at cost. Say, ten grand for the two."

Germaine grunted. "I ain't gonna pay for the firepower up front."

The Moth hurried his words, "No, I meant out of the haul, after."

"What's your piece out of this?"

"I need forty, plus the cost of the guns, plus what I've spent so far. Anything beyond that is yours, free and clear."

Lonnie crowed. "Free, as long as we do the wet work. You gonna be there?"

Germaine chuckled, a horrible sound. "The Moth, he never there. He be hunkered in that pawnshop over in East L.A., bent over that police scanner."

The Moth cocked his head. "You're right. That's why my share is a flat rate."

Lonnie said, "How about you come along instead, so we watch you and know what you up to."

The Moth's tongue froze and all the spit dried up in his mouth.

Lonnie pointed at him. "Look, Germaine, his eyes popping out."

The Moth choked down a dry swallow. "Agreed. I'd propose my take as sixty plus guns and you get all the upside. One other thing. I get the woman who's in there."

Germaine drained his cup and banged it down. "They keep a meth whore? And you want her? I didn't think you had it in you."

"It's an old acquaintance. She's chained up in the back and she's pregnant. She wants out, and she wants to go clean for the baby."

Germaine refilled his cup. "They got a pregnant meth whore?"

"Yes."

"They still humping her?"

"Yes."

Lonnie jabbed his brother with his elbow. Their snorts brayed out into the kitchen. "That's pretty sick. These fucks deserve to die."

To plunder the meth lab cost the Moth four assault rifles, not two. The Moth didn't hole up in his pawnshop and listen to the scanner like any good coward should. He was trapped around the corner in a stolen trash truck, wedged in between Lonnie and Germaine. To distract himself, he thought of the woman chained up inside. That last afternoon, a short time together a long time ago, she had poised at the window while his eyes filled up with her. He wore a T-shirt and boxers — he glanced at his spindly shins, then back at her. She bent down one of the venetian blinds, gazed out with a secret look, an aloneness that closed her away from him. Eugénia shimmied into her underwear. She waited for a car. *And in the car....*

Across the street, Reckless Tommy whirled up in the Impala and Jeeter crawled out, jogged across. The Moth leaned over Lonnie to Jeeter perched on the running board. He handed Jeeter four hundred dollars. "Okay, here's four C's and you'll receive another six after. You remember your bolt cutters?" Jeeter held them up for inspection. "Good, good. We'll crash in the front door. Lonnie and Germaine's two strong-arms will blow the back door, charge in, and shoot anyone moving around. Germaine says they expect you around the back. Introduce yourself, race in behind them, and yank her out. Run her down the alley and stow her in Reckless Tommie's car."

Jeeter bobbed. "You bring the vest?"

2012 – Starting with Reckless Tommy at the Taco Stand

The Moth handed him a Kevlar vest, one with L.A. Swat Team badges. The boy shrugged into it, and faded off towards the alley.

Lonnie said, "Boy needs to eat something — he's too skinny. We wait, maybe four minutes." It stretched out long enough that the Moth became conscious of the perspiration that dripped down his ribs into the top of his pants. Lonnie punched buttons on his mobile, muttered into the slab of plastic, cocked his head at his brother.

Germaine turned the key and the diesel fired up. "You ready, Moth?"

The Mac brothers rumbled around the corner and up to the warehouse. They crashed into the garage door at a lumbering fifteen miles an hour, buried the beast of a truck in the building. Bricks fell into the street and onto the truck. The Macs leapt out with their rifles and ran into the cloud of dust. Across the hood, the Moth caught sight of a flophouse inside. Behind that, frames and plywood were draped in plastic. A warehouse inside a warehouse, a cookhouse for crystal. A flicker of motion — he picked up two Latinos, one against the right wall and one on the left, half visible in the gloom. Illuminated by a stuttering light, the muzzle flashes from the Macs' guns. The Moth stared at the Latinos as they attempted a jerky syncopated flight backwards, crashed into the plywood and plastic. They never squeezed off a shot.

A cataclysm roared through the warehouse — the pressure in his ears like a wallop. His eyes flooded with a yellow flash and then deepest black. The Macs' men had blown the back door.

Lonnie ran over to a half dozen card tables — cardboard boxes rested beside money counting machines, as new and shiny in the dim light as if they been delivered from the Federal Reserve. He unfurled a big trash bag and poured money from the boxes into it. Germaine burst straight through a plastic-sheathed door. His gun pounded out military-style bursts. Kak Kak Kak. An emaciated brown man, wearing only baggy white underwear, fell through the plastic wall. Collapsed on the concrete.

The Moth dropped to the cab floor, peered over the dash. Not the shit-your-pants option; instead the vomiting option. If he didn't die first. More gunfire. The harsh handclap of a grenade — *where the hell had that come from?*

Lonnie popped up in the truck window, his grin demonic and bright in the green dash lights. He threw a block of Saran-wrapped money into the seat. "Here, your take, more than you asked. Get your ass out now — our ride's coming and you got business elsewhere."

The Moth limped away from the warehouse as fast as his bad hip would allow, stumped along as he snapped glances over his shoulder. He staggered on the uneven sidewalk. Behind him, muzzle flashes flickered down the truck side out of the warehouse interior. The Macs continued to discover people to kill, maybe unarmed semi-naked men caught in the lab. He reached the car, wrenched himself into the front seat with trembling relief.

Reckless Tommy glanced at his watch — an expensive chronometer. "Four minutes thirty seconds." A white van careened up the block and burned to a halt behind the trash truck. The Moth counted twenty while nothing, nothing happened at all. A breath caught and not exhaled. *What is wrong?*

Lonnie and Germaine, the assault rifles slung behind their backs, bolted out with trash bags, hurled them into the back of the van. Twice they dashed back and forth. Their driver handed them four knapsacks.

Reckless Tommy said, "Five and a half minutes. Jeeter better be leggin' it out the back."

2012 – Starting with Reckless Tommy at the Taco Stand

Lonnie and Germaine pounded back into the warehouse. A moaning of a police siren, surprisingly close. More sirens. The Mac brothers pelted out again — sprinted. Flew into the van; its tires yowled as it bolted down the street. Reckless Tommy nodded and tapped the watch face. "Under six minutes."

The warehouse erupted up and out onto the street. The trash hauler shuddered backwards on fire, onto the pavement. Windows blew out up and down the street. A plume skyrocketed over the block, black against the night on top and on fire in its core. The Impala rocked from the shock wave.

The Moth whipped his eyes over to Tommy. "Jesus Christ Almighty!"

Reckless Tommy shrugged. "No evidence now." Calm as a grave.

Like a Jack-in-the-Box, Jeeter stuck his head in the car window, nearly knocked heads with the Moth.

The Moth thought his heart might pack it in from the shock.

"Here we go. I got her." Jeeter stepped back to reveal a hunched, sticklike figure wrapped in a blanket.

Reckless Tommy said, "Throw her in my side. Hurry, police on the way." He hopped out, they flung the wreck of a woman into the back. Sirens yelped. Jeeter dived in beside her. Tommy ripped backwards spinning the wheel — they skidded around. Thundered off the opposite way from the Mac brothers.

Four blocks later, snug against the curb, Tommy said, "Better check if she's dead. She smells dead." He flipped on the dome light.

With the engine switched off, they could hear her sobs grizzle out from the backseat. Jeeter had shrunk away to the window.

The Moth knelt on the seat and leaned over into the back. The woman he peered at did not look thirty, or even sixty. He couldn't recognize this human being as the Eugénia Mondragón he had known. Open sores adorned her face and her blackened front teeth roosted behind cracked lips. Skeletal — the flesh in her face sunk away from the bones. The stench of a long incarceration fogged the car. Reckless Tommy glanced at the Moth. "Goddamn. I knew we should have rented a car."

The Moth said, "Eugénia? Why are you crying?" She shook like a chihuahua.

"Thank you, thank you, thank you." Cathartic, heaving breaths flecked with tears and mucus.

The Moth added it up in his head. She better thank him — even if this worked to steer Eloy-the-Rent into a less murderous frame of mind, the Moth was down twenty thou in expense from the sixty he hoped to gross. And he was planted deep in a multiple homicide. "You're welcome, Eugénia. We did what we could."

Wrapped in that aromatic, wretched blanket, she shook her head. She hunched forward; her ravaged face swung close to his chest and peered into his face. "Yes, I thank you too. But I mean the Lord God."

A child, if Eugénia had not lied to Jeeter about the pregnancy. Hard to tell, because of the blanket. Maybe worth it, although the baby was bound to have problems. "Shall we take you home, Eugénia?" He steeled himself and patted her two hands as they gripped the seat back, claw-like. Actually touched her.

"I want my mama and my brother."

Reckless Tommy swooped away from the curb.

Circumstance forced the Moth to touch Eugénia again — maybe a long shower with harsh soap later. This moment in no way mirrored that afternoon, long ago, when she dressed by the door and swayed down the stairs, to ride off with the new boyfriend, the improbably-named

2012 – Starting with Reckless Tommy at the Taco Stand

Carlos Montevideo. *The job, the escape, the murders, was it all about the half-forgotten clack of the apartment door latch?*

The Moth wedged his shoulder under her arm and held on to her waist, toted her up the front walk. The two shuffled forward, alone in the dark. Jeeter and Tommy had decided this house was as dangerous as the meth lab. They waited in the car.

Eloy-the-Rent lived with his mother, Mercedes. Everybody knew this, and no one ragged him about it. The Moth supported Eugénia as she hobbled forward. He sang out as they reached the steps, "Don't shoot, Eloy. Show us a light." A bare bulb blazed forth on the porch and the front door banged back.

The house revealed itself as nice enough, spruced up and painted, modest in character and means. It appeared too small to hold the man framed behind the screen. Eloy stamped out, his mother right behind. She swept passed Eloy and shuffled Eugénia inside with halting steps. She crooned to her as she held Eugénia's elbow, "Yes, poor little one, you're home. It's gonna be all right, yes, my baby."

Eloy, motionless, black face like a mask, stared down on the Moth. Bigger than the skyscrapers in Century City.

The Moth reached into his coat pocket, brought out two bundles of bills he had liberated from the small bale in the car. "Here. There's maybe ten thousand in that. Use it to buy her detox and a tour in rehab. If there's any left, maybe a good pediatrician would be right." He stuffed the bundles into Eloy's hand.

Before he turned to stride back in his mamma's house, Eloy banged the nail in. "Doesn't change anything, anything at all. I guess we're even, but my expenses are skyrocketing, so yours are too. I'll see you next week, little man."

Eloy power-driving his way into the Moth's shop. *How can I get Eloy killed?*

2013 — Mickey Barat Orders Up A Death

The relationship between Mickey Barat and the Moth had grown as complex as any Shakespearean play and as toxic as most L.A. neighborhoods. From the Moth's perspective, Barat held an overwhelming balance of force and the Moth brought only persistence and stupidity to the liaison.

The Moth meddled here and there with Barat's operations. He on many occasions finked them out to Detective Chelsea Granovich — the only perk he received as a police informant. Through some misshapen calculus of revenge, Mickey persisted in believing the Moth owed him four deaths. The Moth handled this huge debt in the only way he could to save his sanity. He pretended the conversation had never happened. Until the Christmas payback.

Christmas itself twisted up the Moth, even after sixty years of life on earth. He attributed this disconnect to his Catholic Lithuanian mother, his Protestant Irish father, and a history that had taught him existence bordered on futility. Or at least comedy. Christmas was about to turn worse.

Miss Junie Guillermo trotted into the pawnshop on December 7th. The

Moth knew her as a quick, thin woman of Baptist tendencies, and to the Moth's amazement, Mickey Barat's handler. No doubt she handled the public Mickey, the philanthropist and general all-around good guy. The private Mickey carried on with the venal empire he had constructed in Altadena and East L.A.

With this visit, Junie Guillermo brought a mission. Behind her lurked the official Barat chauffeur, a block wall named Yevgeny. Yevgeny measured as six-and-a-half feet tall going-on-seven, had weighed in at two-hundred-eighty pounds of muscle before he had packed on twenty of fat. He dressed in cargo pants and a huge, loose, untucked shirt. Everyone knew the pants held extra clips and the shirt concealed a .45. Everyone but Junie.

Like visiting the sick in hospital, Junie sailed up to the counter, patted the glass, waved a hand at Yevgeny. "Frank, I'm delivering this gorgeous fruit basket from Mr. Barat."

Yevgeny, his face wrinkled in distress, carried said basket, a grotesquely-heaped container shrouded in plastic. His face announced how difficult he found it to participate in friendly activities. He marched forward — the wooden floor bounced with each footfall. He slid it onto the glass, stepped back, folded his hands past his big belly over his genitalia. Mission accomplished, he tried on a face-splitting smile.

The Moth jittered in place. *Hippos smile like that, just before they submerge. And bite your legs off.*

Junie fluffed the plastic wrap and rotated the basket, displayed all sides to the Moth. "Isn't this wonderful? Mr. Barat wandered in this morning and said, 'Junie, we have to do something nice for Frank. Let's buy him a fruit basket.' I had the best time picking it out and having it made up. Mr. Barat approved it himself."

The Moth rocked back from the counter. "Any idea why Mickey is thinking of me?"

"Mr. Barat —" she dropped particular emphasis on the Mister, "— says you provide an essential service to the community, and also to him. Although, I don't suppose he's ever been in your... shop."

He couldn't decide how to respond.

"I knew you'd be pleased."

"Please tell Mr. Barat I gratefully receive the gift in the spirit that it was given."

"Isn't that grand! I'll tell him just that, word for word."

"I'd appreciate it." *Mickey will catch the sarcasm.*

"Come, Yevgeny. We have more errands." Yevgeny dutifully bruised the floor on the way out, as he trailed after her energetic figure.

There would be a worm in the fruit. He opened a switchblade — only $15 — from his knife case and sliced away the plastic, discarded it and the yard of curly ribbon. He unearthed a small envelope with a card inside. The card read, "As per our agreement, I hereby redeem one obligation, due on or before December 25th. See the organic fruit label." His spirits sank like a torpedoed ship.

The Moth set each piece of fruit out on the glass, scrutinized the quarter-inch oval stickers. All white, but ... the fig wore a yellow sticker, and hand-written in red ink. "Juan Guillermo." Very bad.

Juan Guillermo happened to be Junie's brother. Juan had received his Bachelor's in religion from a small bible college out in the San Joaquin valley. He knew religion could be defined as half advertising and half guilt. And he believed true power was rooted in the women.

The women. At six feet, two-hundred fat-saturated pounds, and in a black suit with white shirt, he cut a swath up the aisle and to the pulpit. He cropped his gray curly hair. His bullet head and small mustache cried out dignity and the Lord's sanctification. He owned a pleasant tenor and he seduced from the pulpit. The Moth had seen him preach once years before, dragged there by Eugénia. "Come on,

2013 – Mickey Barat Orders Up A Death

Frankie. It won't hurt you to spend an hour in the Lord's house."

All the females loved Juan, from cute twelve-year-old Vidette May to the legendary antiquity, Widow Alterra Bodekie. Juan concealed one aberration, though — a flaw that rendered him human — or sub-human. The Moth had learned the flaw only in a round-about way. He had been in the right place at the right time for the wrong relationship — at Molly's motel, the Grenadier.

East L. A. exploited every niche of human weakness, but even the jaded working women were offended when a Vietnamese pimp trolled twelve and fourteen-year-olds on the mattresses at the Grenadier. Maybe because an *Asian* man shopped out pre-teen Latina girls.

June of 1981, the Moth had parked outside and shambled his way to Molly's room, Number Sixteen, as she ended work. On the sidewalk, a five-foot-tall yellow man hissed at him and tugged at his sleeve. Beside the man hovered a child, painted garishly like a grownup. Her pinched face appeared brutish and old. The door to room Four slapped back and another puny girl, smaller than the first, dashed out naked. The Moth's brain struggled, thrashed really, at the sight of Reverend Juan Guillermo, shirtless and in his bare feet. The pimp seized the girl in a talon-like grip and threw her into the preacher's arms. The Moth jerked his head into his shoulders and swallowed the sick in his mouth. He hurried on.

The Moth slipped into the preacher's office doorway, discovered Reverend Juan napping. He contemplated the man, contemplated his plan — the bluff. "Juan, wake up."

The preacher barked out a yip, leapt in his chair, his eyes as round as his face. "Oh, Frank, it's you."

"Dreaming of little girls?"

The Moth

Juan leaned back in his chair. His eyelids half closed, his caution apparent. "Hmm. I have no idea what you mean."

The Moth cleared his throat. All or nothing. "Room Four. Grenadier Hotel, 1981. She was twelve, fourteen at the most."

"Ah. I'm sure you are mistaken." He didn't even deny his understanding of the accusation.

"Other people saw you, Juan."

Juan's face drooped. "Unlikely. Not a neighborhood I or my parishioners know."

"How do you know what neighborhood the Grenadier is in?"

The Moth watched Juan's mouth twitch. Now Juan would try to turn the tables. "The Grenadier. An unseemly place. Are you telling me you visit there?"

"Juan, Juan. No one cares where a pawnbroker goes. We already live at the bottom of the food chain."

"But redeemable."

The Moth thought Juan might raise his hand and bless him. "Can preachers be redeemed? Hear that crashing sound? That's your reputation."

Juan's tone held no message. "What do you want?"

"I intend to spread this thing around, unless you disappear."

Juan burst out laughing, amused. He bent over his hands spraddled on the desktop, the belly-laugh rolling. "That's it? Give up my life here? Not hardly."

"I failed to mention something. Mickey Barat wants you dead. I think there must be an under-aged girl he knows and that you do also."

"Barat?" The voice cracked.

The Moth did what he did. He waited. He studied Juan's face.

Since Juan's guard had dropped, he read like an open book. He flickered through anger, that he was caught, that the Moth dared blackmail. That he could be dead. His eyes squinted up and he glared at the Moth. Anger, that's good. His mouth caved in, turned down. *Perhaps helplessness?* His eyebrows constricted together, his forehead wrinkled. *Maybe fear?* A gaze at the desk corner. *A sense of loss? Regret?*

The Moth rapped on the desk to grab Juan's attention. "I can make it easy for you. I'll help hide you from Barat. I'll spirit you away to a new town far away where you can start over. I'll have a story ready that will let your family continue. Even hold their heads up in the community."

"They hold their heads up now."

The Moth ignored the interruption. "Set your wife and two little girls free. Maybe they need you to leave."

Still the mask of authority on the preacher's face. "I don't want to leave... leave everything."

"Stay, and your reputation is dead. So are you."

That broke him. "It's not my fault. I... don't mean to."

"My best offer. I'll give you a day."

The Moth located their Lincoln Navigator parked in front of Paul Albireo's chicken restaurant; an eatery with a stainless steel front reminiscent of Airstream trailers — and enough neon to shove the night back half a block. In the front window, four girls — women really, in spite of their youth — gathered around a table, a bucket between them, straws in Cokes. Dancing attendance, two over-muscled jocks waited nearby; one faced the back of the restaurant, one watched the front. The bulls worked for the women.

The Moth had come to pay a formal call on the Arpías. The Arpías transported guns, ran extortion, and marketed weed to

The Moth

finance themselves. They also dabbled in nut-crushing — their charity work. The Moth approached the table much like he'd sidle up to a Rottweiler. He dropped his head, offered up the obeisance nod to the four women. "Miss Estevez, could I have a word?"

Crystal Estevez had once been beautiful. Her nose had been reset — but not quite right — and a tracery of scarring marred her lip and chin. The dental work had done her some good. She showed him a gaze not hostile or open, just cold. She twitched back and told the bull behind her, "Search him."

The Moth figured to run your own gang at age twenty required all precautions. He held his arms out and spread his feet. The guard must have wanted to show his diligence — the Moth might have bruises afterwards.

She gazed at him, folded her hands, prepared to listen. "What?"

"I have a disposal opportunity."

"Again, I ask. What?"

"You know disposing of a body is so difficult. If you only leave it laying around, you get blowback from friends and associates of the deceased."

"What makes you think I have a body?"

"No, I thought you might want to *create* a body. I need a cadaver, about six feet tall and two hundred plus pounds, preferably fat and Black or Spanish, with good teeth. I can disguise him as someone else."

Crystal leaned over to the woman on the right, whispered in her ear. The woman said, "Uh huh, him."

The Moth sensed hope, thought he might have a workable plan. "A candidate?"

Crystal said, "I think the person here who wants something is you. I find you a dead body, at great personal risk, by the way — what's in it for me?"

2013 – Mickey Barat Orders Up A Death

The field had tilted. "Umm. Last month you ordered ten handguns but haven't yet paid. What say this covers three of them?"

"Call it five."

Screwed. And he couldn't ask Mickey Barat for expenses. "Deal."

Crystal bared her new teeth — they flashed out shark-like.

"Maybe we can do the hand-over on Christmas Eve?"

Crystal held her hand up. "Work with Rona here. I don't need to know any more."

The Arpías not only delivered their client, but they volunteered to firebomb Juan's car once their guy was bundled behind the wheel. Rona said, "Sure, for free. On the house. I like your guns."

The new quasi-religious Buick roared skyward in a gorgeous flame in front of the Reverend's church, with the added attraction of an exploding gas tank. Police would stumble on a large charcoal briquet behind the wheel.

Two hours earlier, the Moth had settled the Preacher in Ylsa Perez's taxi. Juan carried only a small gym bag. The Moth suspected the bag held cash from this month's Sundays — the Moth would have done as much.

The Moth leaned in the driver's window to brief Ylsa. He counted off ten one-hundred dollar bills, and another three twenties. "It's eight hours to Reno and back, so here's the fee plus a bit for a motel room. If he jumps out of the car before Reno, you're entitled to shoot him." The Moth held out a .32 revolver.

"God bless you, Señor Moth, but I carry my .40."

"If you got to shoot him, plug him with the throwaway first and only the .40 if he stands back up. As a personal favor to me, kick him out of the cab in front of the Eldorado Casino." *Maybe he'll be broke in a week.*

The Moth

Yevgeny completed the mission on December 27th. He shoved another fruit basket onto the counter. "Mr. Pachuco, Mr. Barat's compliments."

It's working. He asked, "Where's Junie."

"She took some days off. Somebody snuffed her brother. Mr. Barat says 'Season's Greetings and Don't Get Too Comfortable.' "

The Moth had expected a signal of acknowledgment. And the fruit would be welcome. Reimbursement for all the cost would have been nicer. As soon as Yevgeny's back turned, he whipped out the switchblade and hacked away the plastic. The square envelope on top held a message. "Good. Now that you're practiced up on a simple one, the second shouldn't be so much of a challenge."

His shoulders slumped, his bile rose.

2014 — The Prostitute's Babysitter

The Moth had trapped himself, driven by fear of humanity — a collective mass he'd long distrusted. To avoid the beasts of L.A., he went to earth within the pawnshop itself — a battered white castle under its clay tile cap. But this staked him out like a lamb for anyone who chose to enter from the sun-crying street outside.

Eugénia Mondragón, brown, once stunning, and somehow stunted in that way of poor women, showed her face at his shop's door. Faded, a face seamed from drugs now kicked, Eugénia opened his door, flinched at the peal of the sleigh bells. She slid through the door and slipped left to conceal herself behind two stacked guitar speakers. She measured up the place, the risks, in no small way evaluated the Moth.

He sensed only the great harm she had done him in the past. Years ago she gazed out of his window as her new lover drove up and pounded the horn of his cheap-ass Chevy. The Moth hadn't caught up yet with whom she had become, the ten years she ignored him, the six months of drugs that burned through her like Drano, nor the child born on the back edge of her addiction. The child fetched through the horror house of addiction. The miracle of pediatrics that can keep any child alive.

The baby perched on her hip, cloaked in a blanket that denied L.A.'s blood heat. He had hidden from all this chaos for two years and didn't have any desire to bump into Eugénia now. He reached to the side and pumped Purell into the palm of his hand, twice, and rubbed the detoxicant over his chapped, age-spotted hands.

"Frank." She slid up the aisle, threatened the space before the counter. "Frank, I need a small favor. Just a small one." He snapped a peek at the baby — its face tragic, warped to the side with one eyebrow aloft, a statement of huge surprise to live this long. He wondered if the child would be able to speak when the time arrived. *Favor? Some form of parentage she'd try to inflict on me? Grandfather Frank, Uncle Moth.* He leaned away from the child, as Eugénia had once leaned away from him.

Eugénia said, "I need your help, for a friend."

The pawnshop breathed in at that moment, not in relief, but as a sign that one danger had missed him.

She said, "I need you to hide someone for me, for three days. For only three days."

He stared across the glass and replied. "No."

"Come on, Frank. You're a good person. This won't be hard."

The only shiny bit of pride Frank owned was wrapped up in his badness. At sixty-two, he had folded himself into a criminal life, financed jobs through the neighborhood and into Los Angeles for thirty-five percent, sold the tools of the trade to anyone who paid and who appeared smart enough to not link them back to him. He didn't want to be that good person she could con. He said it again, louder. "No."

"It's my babysitter. She needs some place out-of-the-way. It can't be my apartment. Her daddy knows my place. I'll keep my baby with me, so you just hide one, the babysitter. Three days."

"I won't. I can't. There's no place here."

"Sure there is." Eugénia paced back to the door, thrust it open against the hydraulic piston, shouted into the street. "Deemona, girl, get in here. The street ain't safe."

Deemona slipped in the door, a halfbreed of a child, maybe thirteen, maybe fifteen. She owned the black bushy hair of Mexican Indians. She pinned it on one side of her head with a twist but it erupted from the other side like a Mazatlan volcano. Her teeth, a wavering, gapped line across her face, showed white against a tawny face. He knew, before woman or girl spoke again, that he had been skewered, snared by the babysitter's utter ugliness.

Eugénia tugged the girl to the counter, seized her wrist, held the caramel paw out to him. "Frank, meet Deemona Suarez. Deemona... Frank." He stared at her hand like it was a rat in his alley, but compelled by convention, he grazed it. The girl snatched it back, as relieved as he that this forced intimacy ended. He inspected her arm. A welter of bruises — someone or something had wrung out her flesh like a wet rag. She could have been a poster child for Child Services, and she arrived in his store to ask for three days.

Eugénia handed the baby to Deemona — Deemona held the baby in the air, set it on the glass countertop and peered into its face. "It's like this," Eugénia said. "Her momma used to protect her but she's too sick now. Her daddy ties Deemona across a chair and does her like a dog, and beats the crap out of her when he's not doing that. Keep her safe for a while, till he's back out on the road. Till we got time to make arrangements."

The baby threw out a smell like sour milk. The Moth stared at the diaper, the glass counter beneath. *Another spot I'll scrub.* "On the road?" he asked. He watched Deemona, to decide if she objected to her unadorned story of frequent rape. Her face crinkled, like a stomped soda bottle, but no sign of tears.

Eugénia said, "He's a long-haul trucker. Off in a few days, handling a run to Chicago, Dallas, and back."

He didn't give a damn about these details. He didn't want this girl in his pawnshop. Especially while some bastard wandered the street, fondled his balls, and searched for his daughter. The Moth didn't want the contagion of L.A. here, in his oasis of neutrality. He asked, "Why not Child Services? Why not the cops and a rape kit?"

"Because they take my baby too. You know what I do for a living. They'll throw around words like 'unfit mother.'"

He spoke, an involuntary reflex "Yes. Three days and no more. Nobody to know. At all, ever." Had he literally said it?

Eugénia slapped her hands. "Deal done." She slipped a watch off her wrist. "I can't work for three days, since I got baby Mondragón to mind. No hooking, no money. You give me a hundred for this watch, hear? We're both in this."

Deemona toted a backpack. The Moth prayed to the Catholic god of his dead mother that it didn't have any drugs, or a phone, or feminine hygiene products. He opened the steel door in the back wall of the pawnshop to reveal his apartment, a reassuring three rooms of sharply managed space. "Here," he said. "You'll be in here." She cowered behind him; her shoes scuffed the flat carpet nap in the shop. She didn't venture into the space. "It's okay," he insisted.

Three steps, and she already bumped into his table. Behind that, a single bed with a mattress he had accepted in pawn and fumigated in the alley. A stack of books on the floor. A window inset in the wall above their heads, its glass run through with chicken wire, streaked with the shadow of outside bars. These had been storerooms and a restroom when he bought the place, painted white enamel.

Her eyes darted around. He inspected her, tried to figure out what she brought into this apartment, hoped it was nothing that couldn't be scrubbed out later. The back door, two deadbolts set into it, a transom above leaking in gray dirty light. He shuffled over to the door, picked up the baseball bat leaned on the cinderblock — he would lock it away from her in the pawnshop. Maybe he feared her as she might fear him.

"Nobody in or out," he said. "Keep it locked all the time. Here," he pointed. "This is the toilet. Don't mess it up. The shower is small, but so are you, so no complaining. The bed's mine. I'll make a pallet for you on the floor." He possessed one more blanket, two extra twin sheets, no pillow. They stacked it all by the back wall, preparatory for their evening of discomfort. He considered the pillow on the bed — flat and hard. He handed it to her.

He said, "It's nearly one. I close and go buy tacos at one. I'll bring you the same."

She rested mute at his table, after silence all afternoon. He had handed her one of his used books, the one on the top of the pile. Gibbon's *Decline and Fall* — fifty cents — lay open on the table all that long day. She perched quiet while he shot glances at her from the pawnshop through the open apartment door.

He shuffled in, locked the door. She jerked like he struck her. Like he'd strike her. Indicating the book, he asked, "Did you enjoy it?"

She darted a look at him. Her face apprehensive, like the answer mattered. She said, "I didn't understand the words."

"Which ones?"

"Most of them." She closed the book, held its bulk out towards him. A one-pound musty offering, suspended between them.

"You keep it," he said.

Reverential, she centered it on the table.

"Are you hungry?"

"Maybe. I don't want to be any trouble."

"I don't want you to be any trouble either. Something bothering you?"

She scanned around her, as if she checked for someone who watched or eavesdropped. Her shoulders sagged and she wrung her hands in her lap. "What if he shows up here?"

He knew she meant her father. He shook his head. "Eugénia will sneak you out of here in a day or two. Until then, he can't find you. Nobody would believe it anyway. That I'd allow someone in my apartment." He scrubbed his small counter, sprinkled flour over it.

Her eyes locked on his hands, the dance of food prep.

"I'll fix dumplings. When there's trouble, the Irish drink, like my old man — but I never took it up. Instead I'll cook dumplings — that's what my Lithuanian mother always did. Every problem can be solved with boiled dough and a hint of meat." He heard the echo of all his talk; he fell into dismayed silence.

He stirred the flour and water in a plastic tub that had once held lard. Poverty had become such a habit, even though he now had money. He formed thumb-sized balls on the white dusted countertop — used his thumb to dig in dimples. Meanwhile chicken broth melded with quarter-inch squares of hard sausage in a sauce pan. As he cooked he observed her, stole small snapshots. She hunkered over in her kitchen chair, stared at her hands in her lap. Damaged goods, cast out of a horrible childhood into a pubescent nightmare. She didn't even show any breasts yet, not much at least, but she knew the worst of sex. He said, "Not everybody's like your father."

Her answer held a hint of phlegm or a snarl. "I know. But it only takes one." Her voice sounded that little bit surly — something simmered away in there.

2014 – The Prostitute's Babysitter

He boiled his balls of dough. She needed something to do. He told her, "Grab two bowls out of the cupboard. And spoons. Paper towels, there, for napkins."

Frank lay awake in his narrow bed. He wondered about her father, his name. How to hurt him. He knew L.A., how people could be burned. What trust is and how it can be betrayed. For the first time in the long time since Molly, he thought about children, what it might be like to have a small, unformed human dependent on you, and you alone. *How did I get here, and how did I miss my chance?*

On the floor out of sight, her breathing hummed slow. Car lights out of the alley traced across the ceiling from the window. He reached for the gun he had smuggled in from the pawnshop. He hated to touch it.

A sharp breath from her. He said, "It's okay. They drove on by." All this time, she had lain still, faked sleep.

"Mr. Frank?" Her voice sounded as a broken bird chirp.

"Yes."

"You wouldn't hurt me, would you?"

Stupid question. If he was going to hurt her, he wouldn't admit to it. If he wasn't, she couldn't tell if it was the truth. "Shut up and go to sleep."

"Yes, sir."

Too harsh. Ugly words without any reason, except his own sense of frailty. Besides, she probably clutched the baseball bat with her on the pallet. He said, "We can be friends, after this is over. Long distance friends. Until it's over, we'll keep you hidden."

In the mid-morning, the Moth slid from his pawnshop into his apartment, threw both deadbolts. The sheets waited on the table folded, the blanket stacked on top. The pillow anchored his bed once again. But no girl. "Deemona?"

Nothing.

"Deemona?"

A sound from the bathroom. The door lock clicked. She peeked out, like an animal ready to bolt back underground. "You weren't here. I locked myself in."

He said, "Smart. How did you sleep?" Last night she had crawled under the table with her blanket, curled in among the chair legs. An illusion of safety. Earlier he'd thought he should tuck the blanket around her. But he knew she didn't want anyone to touch her.

Her mouth twitched, one of those broken smiles, like she hid a stomach ache. He figured out she wanted to please him. She saw him like the sleeping tiger. He saw her as the mouse that crept through the room.

"Okay, it'll be toast this morning and a banana. Here, I picked these up for you." He handed over old issues of *People Magazine* from the hair salon down the street. He said, "These should fix you up for today."

Already exhausted, the strain of another person a constant churn of nervous energy. This couldn't be easy for her either. Maybe he wouldn't open today. She'd stay in the back and he'd take inventory in the shop. Or something.

On day three, she toasted the bread. After breakfast, he closed the apartment door, a gray steel defense for both of them. Quiet, no sound from her side.

He knew a place, back in his boyhood, under the stairs. The plasterboard merely leaned on the studs. Once he eased it back, he could wriggle through into a crawlspace. For hours he could lie in the dark, wait for his father's anger to fizzle out, dissipate into a background disappointment in his son. He knew how to be quiet too, like Deemona.

She had developed a taste for the tacos from Ramón's, looked forward to them. But he brushed her hand as he handed her the crisp shell. She flinched as if burned by acid, and began to shake. Like a seizure. He couldn't bear to watch. Frightened, he backed away — retreated into his shop, eased the door shut between them. In an hour, she slipped into the pawnshop and tried to apologize. She didn't have any idea what was her fault and what wasn't.

He turned his back on her. "Okay," he said. He meant something else, but didn't know the words for it.

They settled at the table again, the place where he spent one quarter of his life. Deemona cubed yellow potatoes for a skillet fry-up, a pawnbroker's bachelor dinner. He had shown her a cook's rocking motion, and the chef's knife, a Farberware he had accepted in pawn, flashed fast and sure in her hand. She grunted — the cubes scattered off the cutting board onto the table. She boiled out anger at the potato, hissed at the cubes as she gathered them back. He had given a honed ten-inch knife to an angry, molested teenager. No idea why he didn't break into a sweat, why his heart didn't race.

He whipped eggs in a bowl, added salt and pepper. He popped into an idle dream, a dream he and Deemona had done this for years and would cook for each other until she grew up and left home. The dream infected him with its lies and illusions. He lurched, dizzy.

A car crunched in the alley, outside his door. They lifted their heads, like dogs that caught a threatening scent. "Not a word, not a move," he said. His eyes flicked to the counter — the baseball bat leaned against it.

Eugénia Mondragón's voice, muffled but recognizable, filtered through the steel. Time for Deemona to leave, to disappear where her father will never locate her. He threw the deadbolts and jerked the door towards him.

Eugénia staggered into the room, shoved by the man behind her. He grasped her by the scruff of the neck. She carried the baby in a sack, suspended below her breasts. The man screwed a gun into the side of her head. Deemona's father, his black-and-gray spade beard bristling, had taken over the room. A tall fleshy thug of a guy, with a baseball cap and a gut on him like a barrel. The shark in the water.

He waved the gun at Moth. "Sit down and shut the fuck up." The Moth should have screamed for help — or attacked. Instead he collapsed into a chair, hands spread on the Formica. The father slammed Eugénia back against the sink and leaned over the table into Deemona's face. "Aren't you going to say hello to your dear old papa?"

Her eyes shimmered, as wide as pie plates, Her lips sealed, the blood emptied out of her face. The Moth read her stricken expression as acceptance. Time hung static, like a hawk before it plummets down onto its prey.

The father had rooted out Eugénia and of course he threatened the baby. Eugénia led him here to the apartment.

Deemona would belong to her father again, like a piece of pounded-out round steak. The Moth and Eugénia would suffer, maybe die. The father laughed, like gravel sliding out of a bucket.

Eugénia seized the baseball bat, swung it. Like a lightning stroke, an instantaneous streak from the sky, Eugénia slashed the bat down onto the father's hand. The wood drove the hand and the gun into the table. He shrieked and cradled his hand — a brown lump like bread dough. With a howl, Deemona leapt up and flashed the kitchen knife across his throat. She ripped him from ear to ear. The blood exploded, spattered across Deemona. Across the enamel wall behind her. Sprayed onto the pawnshop door. The father's eyes stared. His mouth fell open. A gargling moan. Within seconds, he dropped to his knees. His head dropped onto the table. His heart pumped, a steady runnel. Blood ran across the table, saturated the yellow cubes of potato. Dripped onto the floor. The two women waited, patient as the ferryman on the black river.

Shock rolled over the Moth at how the crimson blood shone. How out of place on his table. Behold the vengeance wrought by the two women. His soul burned. *At last, something I understand how to do.* He'd call in a favor to dispose of the father. He'd clean the apartment, bleach away any DNA evidence.

Eugénia clasped Deemona by the hand, led her away from the body. The Moth handed over a roll of paper towels. The two women mopped the blood off the girl. Deemona passed the Moth a clutch of red soaked paper. Eugénia stared into his face and nodded, a contract.

He sank back into a chair. The women stopped in the alley door, peered back at the blood, the corpse, its arms drooped limp and its head cocked over on the table. They gawked at the Moth, astonished by joy. It had crashed past him so fast, changing everything. Or nothing. He said, "Go. Go now." His chest strained as if it could blow apart. This last chance for family slipped into the alley.

2015 — Binary Stars

To kill a man at random may be nothing in L.A. To kill a particular man on demand could be a big deal. The Moth realized he had locked into a silent, subtle orbit between two local warlords, Mickey Barat and Paulie Albireo. It balanced old money versus new, Russian melancholy versus Atlantic amiability. In a curve of elliptic flight, the Moth swung from the tremor of panic to the allure of easy money. A small and sad man, gray as fireplace ashes, the Moth already resembled a scorched comet.

The previous September, Paulie had ordered from the Moth chrome .45s with teak grips for four lieutenants, with the additional option of untraceability. "And I don't want any cheap Brazilian rubbish either. Kimbers, if you can." The profit margin induced a mood of ecstasy in the Moth.

In an obscene parallel, Mickey had demanded four wishes also.

Mickey had owned the neighborhood long enough that the locals thought he had been installed by God. Mickey's profligate rackets included the usual operations plus enough drugs to wash away the entire IQ of East L.A. He reported only in a loose fashion to the Russians in Brighton Beach.

2015 – Binary Stars

On the other side of this binary system, Albireo had become pivotal to the Moth's cash flow. An unpleasant shock when Mickey sent a terse six words to the Moth: "Payment Number Two, Albireo, June 4." Six weeks away.

The two stars were about to tear the neighborhood apart. The Moth already felt the gravitational tide.

The Moth perched mute, hunched up on a stool in his pawnshop. The polished glass counter reflected the fluorescent lights into his face. His own image in the glass — his eyes twitched like skittering pinballs — a manifestation of his thought process.

The two crime lords' approaches couldn't be more different. Albireo wanted to send a bit of illicit business the Moth's way — plunk him on the gravy train and co-opt him. Barat wanted the Moth to kill this mountain of cash and, because of Barat's dead son, suffer as he did it. The Moth wanted, most of all, to scheme his schemes, sell his tools, write pawn tickets — and die in bed. A searing pain raced out of his chest, cramped his neck muscles. He rooted a Zantac out of his pocket. *I've got some money in the Caymans. And ten pitiful percent of a casino in Elko. I could run.*

Hiding out in a casino might not be very bright.

Paulie Albireo had appeared in the neighborhood twenty years ago. He claimed "Albireo" as a Portuguese name and, with the level of literacy around, no one could challenge the assertion. Within five years, no one would, out of politeness. Albireo, a genial fat guy, spoke in an accent that came off more Spanish than Portuguese, whatever that sounded like. He had white eyebrows so bushy as to resemble bottle brushes, and silver hair swept straight back.

Paulie impressed everyone as an amiable man — but cross him and he had a volcanic black nature.

Paulie's operation laundered money — no one knew whose money. He had started small, with a take-out fried-chicken place. It displayed amazing cash flow even though the soggy chicken dripped grease — plenty of money to fix up the place. Soon the take-out morphed into a sit-down restaurant and better food. Albireo bought the next storefront and installed a real estate office, in a neighborhood where real estate had less value than Ford Pintos. The Realtors covered for a simple book-making operation in the back.

Albireo bought the next place down and dropped in a package liquor store that specialized in cheap sweet wine and Crown 7. This business rang true and legitimate, based on the foot traffic — it had paychecks scuttle in and scads of brown paper bags saunter out. Next door, Paulie invested in a bar, one that catered to his need for a place to hold court. Like an old-time Don, he had a booth in the back where he did business. This bar allowed Paulie to keep his bichon frisé, Toodie, on his table, right by his glass of aguardente. The bar charged six dollars for a beer — no one shuffled into the bar except to have a word with Albireo or to run errands. Maybe it was worth six bucks to join the king's court.

Like other locals, the Moth appreciated the river of money that washed through the Albireo organization — though his heart had thudded like a bass drum, alarmed over his first Albireo transaction. Albireo sent an emissary, one Big Peep, to negotiate. Big Peep, a key Albireo lieutenant, balanced the scales as white and outweighed the Moth two-to-one. Big Peep plastered on his disarming, crescent-moon smile. "Mr. Albireo would like to arrange a pleasant surprise for some foreign friends."

Albireo wished to purchase legitimate USA I.D.'s for five colleagues on their way from Central America. He wasn't fussy by half. He wanted each I.D. to have at least three years of legitimate records besides the usual birth certificate and Social Security card. The Moth said, "Yes. Tell Mr. Albireo I can do that, if he gives me four weeks." He set it up through an out-of-state acquaintance who specialized in the recently departed, and charged fifteen percent on top of the $50,000 each, for $37,500 clear for himself. These were numbers he would never forget.

Barat versus Albireo. The Moth couldn't imagine deeper trouble. Mickey Barat believed the Moth would kill this man for him. *By the fourth of June.*

The Moth didn't sleep for three days. *Probably. Definitely. Yes, I'll end up shot in the head in an alley.*

He had a giant bag of M&M's open on the table, spilled out as bright colored beads — the sugar buzz echoed inside his head. There had to be a way out that didn't invoke his death. He had a pad of yellow paper in front of him. Its narration read, "Ask Albireo for protection? Go to police? Buy contract on Paulie. Buy killing of Mickey. Take money and run away." Each except the last had been crossed out. One inhibitor. He had lost a big chunk of his money when he had invested in a dock hijacking that had gone bad. His armpits soggy, he reached into his shirt with paper towels and dabbed at himself.

In three days of purgatory, the dilemma bounced around in his brain. He developed a plan, weak and nebulous, but at least something he could attempt. *If it works, it's good for me and the neighborhood. If it doesn't — Mickey will kill me anyway.*

The whole scheme revolved around turning two Albireo lieutenants against each other. The Moth focused on Alcor Córdoba, a high-end drug merchant, and Big Peep, the overall consiglieri and the local prince of meth. His tools would be lies, deceit, and doctored photographs.

The Moth

The Moth queued Big Peep up first. Peep held court at night in a club called Jelly Rolls. The Moth didn't like being outside his apartment after 7 p.m. *But then, I don't like being dead on June 5th.*

Big Peep had his sleeves rolled up and his elbows on the bar — his bar after all. His forearms looked like hams, with a yellowish, coarse skin. Beside him perched Peep's number-one berserker, Peligro. If you were a white in East L.A., it helped to hire a Latino as your leg-breaker. Big Peep stared at the Moth, his mouth wrinkled up as if he sucked on pickle juice instead of Black Jack rocks. He lifted his hand and signaled the Moth forward. But they executed the obligatory search first.

A short man with the build of a buffalo kicked off the wall and stepped close. "And you be?"

The Moth wanted to say something smart, but his bowels quaked too much. Instead he said, "Frank Pachuco. You know me. You pawned those alloy wheels with me."

The buffalo said, "Stick out your arms." He patted the Moth down, ran his hands up each leg, clear into the Moth's personal space. He straightened and reached inside the Moth's battered old sports coat, fished out a flashlight. He scowled deep into the Moth's face. "What's this?"

"You think I could kill Big Peep with that?"

"I don't think you could kill anybody with anything." The buffalo handed him the flashlight, turned for the bar. "I tell him you be mucho armed and dangerous."

Big Peep picked at his lip, inspected a fleck of skin on his finger. "I'm not in the market for passports or guns right now. So if that's it, you may as well leave."

The Moth played it up, not that he had to fake the fear. He half turned,

turned back. He dithered. He leaned forward and dropped his voice. "It's like this. I think Alcor Córdoba is horning in on your business."

Big Peep straightened up. Córdoba was one of the Central Americans Albireo had brought in at great expense. Now a few years in business, Córdoba's franchise ran everything from pot to high-grade coke. "And how would you know this?"

"He's bought some specialized surveillance gear from me, foreign equipment."

"How does that connect with my trade?"

"I'll show you. Over here." The Moth limped around the bar. He shooed the bartender back, stuck his head under, behind the bar taps.

With a sigh, Big Peep unfolded from his seat. "Shit. You taking a stroll?"

"This is the place you primarily sit, right?"

Big Peep shrugged. "Sure. Everybody knows where to find me."

The Moth drew out his flashlight and grunted in effort as he illuminated the dimness. Hidden there — a four-inch tube. The Moth held his finger to his lips and escorted Big Peep down the bar. "That tiny jewel is German. It transmits digital on the same frequency as a garage door opener. You've been bugged for two weeks." Stretching it — two days, in fact. It had cost the Moth the price of a crooked locksmith to break him in and jump the alarm. The Moth did the install himself.

"Goddamn. I didn't think that peewee wetback had it in him. Wants to take my meth franchise, huh?"

The Moth inched back towards the door. It would be heaven to be outside on the sidewalk again. "I don't know him that well. But I don't see how he can take over unless your gang is out of the way."

"Shit. This a put-up. If you stuck that under my bar, you're going to be dead."

Death dominated all possibilities. The Moth held his hands out, palms up. "Why would I show you my own bug? And how would an old man like me break into your bar?"

"So it might be Córdoba. And he works for Albireo, like me."

The Moth flared his eyebrows. "Do you think Albireo sanctioned this?"

"He does like those Salvadorans."

Alcor Córdoba conducted daytime business in Mama Rosie's. Her place had a ten-by-twenty space with eight diminutive tables and a cold case that held chilled drinks. Behind that, her glass display cabinet glimmered, full of cakes, pies, fresh bread, and pastries. She had a cash register perched on top, where the drawer could rocket out and strike inattentive employees high in the chest. Rosie yielded only one concession to the Córdoba conglomerate — the addition of an espresso machine so Alcor could drink his tiny cups of Costa Rican coffee.

Córdoba set up shop at the table on the wall, near a pay phone. The thin man, elegant in linen trousers and a pressed white shirt, had a cell phone, a Bic pen, and a white legal pad on the table. A linen jacket hung over the chair back. His skin was light, blocked by black hair, long sideburns, a full mustache. He could have been Hollywood; instead he owned a piece of East L.A.

If anything, the Moth's fright mounted higher than in Peep's bar. He suffered the prickle of sweat, the hot flush, the sudden pressure on his bladder.

The Moth stuck his hand out. "Mr. Córdoba?" He could smell burnt sugar — his stomach flopped.

Córdoba flicked his gaze at the hand. "Take a seat, Frank."

The Moth let his hand drop and eased into the chair across. "Mr. Albireo said he'd call ahead. He said you might be interested in some merchandise I have."

"He *did* call. But he didn't say what merchandise." Alcor displayed flawless English, better than anyone born American in the neighborhood. The tinge of Central American accent bestowed a romance to grace the linen suit.

The Moth cast his eye around the bakery. He didn't spot any bodyguards. By way of respect, the three nearest tables remained empty and forever would. "I wondered if you had any interest in credit cards."

Córdoba twitched his mouth beneath the mustache. Maybe a grin, maybe not. "I don't use them myself."

Morning light shone through the front glass, painted an idyllic scene. "I was thinking more of commercial applications."

"Commercial as in bulk?" Like flicking a switch, things went from idyllic to shrouded. Córdoba had relaxed, loosened up. He had slumped in his chair. He must be interested.

The Moth pursed his mouth, eased out the lie. "I'm cadging around for a partnership. I can provide blanks, printers, and the read/write equipment for the magnetic strips. I can provide up to five hundred names and numbers a week."

"And what would your partner provide?"

"Not much. The distribution, usage, the ATM take."

Córdoba picked up his café spoon, rolled it through his fingers like a drummer working a drumstick. They stared at the flashing bit of aluminum, both as casual as cats that ignored mice in the room. "One could say the lion's share of the work is done by this partner."

The Moth coughed into his hand. "One could say the front-end is the critical part of the operation, and that the names and numbers constitute the greatest contribution."

"Point taken. What type of sharing arrangement did you have in mind for this fictitious partnership?"

This deal, had it been real, would be as if he lay down with a jungle viper. The deception beneath it, as if he rubbed the viper on its scaled belly. The Moth belched a fear-laced mouthful of bile. "Sixty-forty."

Córdoba gazed out the front window, swallowed a tiny sip of his coffee. He shaped his face into a tableau of sorrow.

The Moth placed his hands on the table as if he were about to rise. "I also visited with Big Peep. He seemed busy with a major expansion right now. But perhaps in a month or two." He knew he had talked too much, listened too little.

Córdoba straightened and leaned forward. "Ah, Frank, don't rush off. Tell me about my old friend, Señor Peep."

"Nothing much. He said there might be a war coming. When turf issues settle down, he might be interested in the cards."

"And you're telling me of his interest because?"

Because I want you to think about turf. Your turf. "Uh. I wanted you to know I had alternatives."

"Big Peep may not be a... comfortable... business associate."

Comfortable, like Córdoba? "Of course I'd prefer to start as soon as possible — time is money. And you know how things change. He might not be available later as a partner."

"Did Big Peep mention another neighborhood?"

The Moth deflected. "No. Why? Do you think he meant our own few blocks?"

Córdoba gazed out the window again, as calm as any man the Moth had ever encountered. "Anything is possible, I suppose."

The moment the Moth had angled for. "Wouldn't that require some kind of sanction from a certain gentleman we know? Mr. Albireo?"

Córdoba clicked the spoon on the tabletop. "I suppose someone could offer a higher percentage. That could cause a change in loyalties and ownership."

"But you'd know?"

"Not necessarily. There would be signs though."

"We seem to be talking about business that doesn't concern me. Perhaps we can return to my matter?"

Córdoba raised a hand, summoning a man from behind the pastry case. The Moth hadn't even picked him out. "Sorry, Frank. I'll have to turn you down at the present time. If you want to contemplate an outright sale of the equipment, and a fee for the numbers, I might be interested. Otherwise...."

The guard from across the room gripped the Moth by the arm and escorted him to the register. "Mr. Córdoba would appreciate it if you bought a pastry from Mama Rosie on your way out."

Not enough. The Moth had a lot more to accomplish in the remaining days before the deadline. So far, the Moth had two franchises of the Albireo machine who circled each other with knives.

The Moth chose Peligro as his wedge, a trusted employee who could be driven to betrayal. Peligro had a mother named Vega, whose forty years hung on her like only thirty — a beautiful black woman with Caribbean bloodlines. The best you could say about Peligro was that his face resembled a plank. *Must favor his daddy's side.*

Vega had been brow-beaten into a state of celibacy by her son — a celibacy that staged the Moth's opportunity. Big Peep was a white man, a güero. *Let's see how jealous we can make Peligro.*

The Moth loved the work of his acquaintance Elmore. Elmore worked for two national tabloids. Old school, he composited photographs with an X-Acto knife and a large digital copy camera, constructing embarrassing circumstances for celebrities.

The Moth

Jeeter, his black hair wilder than usual, jiggled up and down on the other side of the pawnshop counter. He had locked the front door as he entered, but also glanced back over his shoulder.

The Moth said, "You sure you know this Peligro?"

Jeeter's maybe-Arab face sneered. "Like my own butt. I run an errand or two for him. What do you want with Peligro? Why you interested in him?"

The Moth opened the folder on the countertop. "I'd like you to sell this photo to him. I figure he'll pay you a hundred, and there's a hundred from me." He flipped the photo around.

"That's Big Peep." The young man stared at the high quality, color print.

"Yes."

"And that's Peligro's mamma's house. She on the porch."

"I think the photo will interest Peligro. And I have another photo, this one for Big Peep." The Moth handed him a glossy color four-by-six.

Jeeter laughed, a delighted bird-like cackle. "That be Peligro drinking with Córdoba and Albireo!"

The photo did interest Peligro the Berserker.

The Moth listened for a few days, to sort out the truth from neighborhood myth. Peligro, a direct-action kind of guy, attempted the murder of Big Peep. Peligro tried first with a drive-by outside of a club named Jelly Rolls. Next he hazarded a pipe-bomb under Big Peep's favorite Cadillac. But at the moment of explosion the Caddy sat empty, and Peligro was observed close by, scoping out the result. Big Peep was a phlegmatic man — he had been betrayed, and he half-believed Peligro had thrown in with Córdoba. He rounded up a team and trapped Peligro at a table outside a taqueria, Judas at the last supper.

Sometimes Big Peep transported competitors clear out past Palm Springs to bury them in the desert. In this case, his boys looped a rope under Peligro's arms, opened a couple of veins in his thighs, and hung him off the base of a bridge strut on the Sixth Street Viaduct over the trains. He may not have been dead when he was hung out to drip-dry, but by morning his empty heart had stopped. A clear headline for Peep's organization. But now Big Peep wanted to suss out Paulie Albireo's and Alcor Córdoba's roles in the universe.

Elmore manufactured one more construct for the Moth. Alcor Córdoba had married a girl from the old country, and cranked out a daughter in the minimum time. Alcor named her Bianca and she was a swarthy thing; she had no charm or distinction beyond a puzzled expression and a semi-permanent case of weeping rage. No one could determine why she was such an angry three-year-old, or why Córdoba idolized her. Jeeter sold Córdoba a photo of his daughter on the playground. Beside her knelt her nanny, and behind her hovered Big Peep and Paulie Albireo, as out of place as virgins in high school.

Detective Chelsea, still a Deputy and not yet a Sargeant, longed to be Assistant Sheriff Chelsea. The Moth reckoned her results could fit Mickey Barat's purpose. He had a sit-down with his Detective in the park that bounded the La Brea tarpits. They had come to rest at a concrete picnic table under a scant tree.

Detective Chelsea ranked as the poster girl for "great-looking women cops in superlative shape." At this moment, he stared at bright red lipstick that reminded him of blood splatter.

She said, "Okay, little man. I drove all the way down here to satisfy your need for secrecy. What do you have for me?"

Jeeter's surveillance had cost him five C's — and he gave it away. "Here's a folder on stash points, a wholesale house, and the schedules for Alcor Córdoba's heroin business."

"Heroin? How old-fashioned." She snapped up the folder, churned through the paper. Included on the list — Big Peep's meth house.

He watched her eyes shine like a leopard's in firelight. Her pupils dilated, her breathing picked up. He said, "In four days the weekly shipment trucks in and fans out. You have to act quick." *Quick is good — less chance of police department leaking.*

She worked him. "Looks okay. Might pan out. I'll have to involve Narcotics. They'll suck up the credit."

"Too bad for you."

"I prefer an old-fashioned homicide. Keep it in mind for the future."

"Hmm. May have that soon for you. When you're promoted to Captain, will I retire from the confidential informant business?"

Her howl of laughter clattered like steel wheels on tracks. "You never fail to crack me up, Frankie. After I handled the Bankheads for you?"

2015 — Best Laid Plans

After the joint Federal and Sheriff Department raids, no one in the neighborhood could figure who had finked the big men out. Everyone *could* trace the battle's course. Córdoba showed himself a practical, methodical man. He drew his people back to protect his infrastructure. He marched up the block with four associates to talk to his boss Paulie Albireo about Big Peep and the trouble in Paradise.

Córdoba, genial as ever, lounged in the far corner of Albireo's booth in the glossy bar. The Moth, alerted by Jeeter that Córdoba was on the move, hunched over a table in the window with an untasted draft in front of him. He shivered like a naked man in a freezing pond. *What am I doing here?*

But he knew. Too important to handle long distance.

Córdoba slid the photo across to Albireo. The Moth couldn't catch anything said, but he could imagine the words. Córdoba would be calm and relentless.

The Moth believed it went down something like this — "I'd like you to know I will be eliminating Big Peep as a potential threat to my daughter. He also has something to do with the sudden attention DEA and the Sheriff pays me. As good faith I tell you this, and as a gesture that you aren't involved, I would expect you to step aside."

Paulie Albireo prodded the photo aside, pursed his full, wet lips.

He'd have said something like, "I don't think so. I made you, Alcor. Brought you in, set you up. I can't let you waste one of my assets on suspicion he's involved in some crime that is as yet uncommitted."

Córdoba nodded to his four men. He might have said, "Pity. Could you gentlemen escort Mr. Albireo out to the auto in back?" As a bodyguard jerked Albireo out of the booth, the front door banged open. The Moth nearly wet himself in the next few seconds. He crawled under the table.

Big Peep believed in quick and big. He invaded the bar front and back. This contributed so much forensic evidence the Sheriff's labbies later spent ten man-days at the crime scene. Local TV journalists were tickled to appear on national news and billed the shoot-out as "better than the St. Valentine's Day Massacre."

From what the Moth could discern, spread out on the carpet between chairs, Córdoba himself shot Big Peep, but succumbed to multiple head and body perforations. His remaining bodyguard dispatched a Big Peep soldier and destroyed a large quantity of bar stock — noise that somewhat buried the Moth's shrieking. This bodyguard sustained a bullet in his shoulder, but survived the encounter to later work for Mickey Barat as a bag man.

The three Córdoba men who escorted Albireo through the kitchen lost track of their charge when two Big Peep hitters opened up on them. The five men expended a substantial lethal effort on each other in the kitchen. This the Moth heard, but couldn't separate from the general haze of gunshots and his personal panic.

Paulie Albireo crawled under the sink and hugged the grease trap — he emerged untouched but rather grimy when the police arrived. Three soldiers in the kitchen also survived. All three were committed to their mayhem, and suffered wounds from the police. They survived on the whole because no one is as good a shot as in the movies. Big Peep, unsurprisingly, walked away lightly injured and began consolidating Córdoba's organization into his own.

Amore Dolce Florists delivered a wreath the next day to the Moth's pawnshop. The delivery guy hovered in the door, gazed around at the pawn. The poor fellow carried a huge spray of lilies well-suited to a funeral service. He sidled forward and asked the Moth to confirm the address. He opened the tripod that held the lilies aloft.

The Moth plucked the diminutive white envelope out of the foliage, removed the card. It read, "Nice try. Go again in six months?"

Would it never stop? *400 K is gone, lost in the dock job. But I've still got 50 K in the Caymans. They speak English. Starting over — that could be good.*

About the Author

Scott Archer Jones is currently living and working on his sixth and seventh novels in northern New Mexico, after stints in the Netherlands, Scotland and Norway plus less exotic locations. He's worked for a power company, grocers, a lumberyard, an energy company (for a very long time), and a winery. He has launched four books: *Jupiter and Gilgamesh, a Novel of Sumeria and Texas*; *The Big Wheel*; *a rising tide of people swept away*; and *And Throw Away the Skins*.

Fomite

Write a review...

Writing a review on social media sites for readers will help the progress of independent publishing. To submit a review, go to the book page on any of the sites and follow the links for reviews. Books from independent presses rely on reader-to-reader communications.

For more information or to order any of our books, visit fomitepress.com

More novels from Fomite...

Joshua Amses
  During This, Our Nadir
  Ghats
  Raven or Crow
  The Moment Before an Injury
Raymond Barfield
  Dreams of a Spirit Seer

Charles Bell
  The Married Land
  The Half Gods

Jaysinh Birjepatel
  Nothing Beside Remains
  The Good Muslim of Jackson Heights

David Borofka
  The End of Good Intnetions

David Brizer
  Cacademonomania
  The Secret Doctrine of V. H. Rand
  Victor Rand

L. M Brown
  Hinterland

Paula Closson Buck
  Summer on the Cold War Planet

Ann Abelson/L.enny Cavallaro
  Paganini Agitato

Fomite

Dan Chodorkoff
Loisaida
Sugaring Down

David Adams Cleveland
Time's Betrayal

Paul Cody
Sphyxia

Jaimee Wriston Colbert
Vanishing Acts

Roger Coleman
Skywreck Afternoons

Stephen Downes
The Hands of Pianists

Marc Estrin
Et Resurrexit
Hyde
Kafka's Roach
Proceedings of the Hebrew Free Burial Society
Speckled Vanities
The Annotated Nose
The Penseés of Alan Krieger

Zdravka Evtimova
Asylum for Men and Dogs
In the Town of Joy and Peace
Sinfonia Bulgarica
You Can Smile on Wednesdays

John Michael Flynn
Answer Only

Daniel Forbes
Derail This Train Wreck

Peter Fortunato
Carnevale

Greg Guma
Dons of Time

Fomite

Ramsey Hanhan
  Fugitive Dreams

Richard Hawley
  The Three Lives of Jonathan Force

Lamar Herrin
  Father Figure

Michael Horner
  Damage Control

Ron Jacobs
  All the Sinners Saints
  Short Order Frame Up
  The Co-conspirator's Tale

Scott Archer Jones
  A Rising Tide of People Swept Away
  And Throw Away the Skins
  The Moth

Julie Justicz
  Conch Pearl
  Degrees of Difficulty

Maggie Kast
  A Free Unsullied Land

Darrell Kastin
  Shadowboxing with Bukowski

Coleen Kearon
  #triggerwarning
  Feminist on Fire

Jan English Leary
  Thicker Than Blood
  Town and Gown

Diane Lefer
  Confessions of a Carnivore
  Out of Place

Rob Lenihan
  Born Speaking Lies

Cynthia Newberry Martin
The Art of Her Life

Colin McGinnis
Roadman

Douglas W. Milliken
Our Shadows' Voice

Ilan Mochari
Zinsky the Obscure

Peter Nash
Ghost Story
In the Place Where We Thought We Stood
Parsimony
The Least of It
The Perfection of Things

Michael Okulitch
Toward Him Still

George Ovitt
Stillpoint
Tribunal

Gregory Papadoyiannis
The Baby Jazz

Pelham
The Walking Poor

Christopher S. Peterson
Butter, or the Dairy of a Madman: Book One and Book Two

Andy Potok
My Father's Keeper

Frederick Ramey
Comes A Time

Howard Rappaport
Arnold and Igor

Joseph Rathgeber
Mixedbloods

Kathryn Roberts
Companion Plants

Robert Rosenberg
Isles of the Blind

Fred Russell
Rafi's World

Ron Savage
Voyeur in Tangier

David Schein
The Adoption Rana Shubair
And No Net Ensnares Me

Charles Simpson
Uncertain Harvest

Lynn Sloan
Midstream
Principles of Navigation

L.E. Smith
The Consequence of Gesture
Travers' Inferno
Untimely RIPped

Robert Sommer
A Great Fullness

Caitlin Hamilton Summie
Geographies of the Heart

Tom Walker
A Day in the Life

Susan V. Weiss
My God, What Have We Done?

Peter M. Wheelwright
As It Is on Earth
The Door-Man

Suzie Wizowaty
The Return of Jason Green

www.ingramcontent.com/pod-product-compliance
Lightning Source LLC
LaVergne TN
LVHW040045080526
838202LV00045B/3494